Rachel was intrigued.

"Preserving the business for Livvie was desperately important to my wife. It also connects Livvie to her mother. I have to keep Liv'ing Creations going for my daughter's sake."

It was a motivation that Rachel understood.

She didn't know much about Simon, though one of the Carthage residents had mentioned he was a successful businessman. But wanting to save the design house for his daughter—when it would be easier to sell or close the operation down—must mean he had a good heart.

"I admire your goal," she said, "but I'm not sure what I could do to help. Are you trying to find models who might turn things around?"

Simon leaned forward in his chair. "Actually, I realize this isn't what your agency generally deals with, but I have a special proposal for you..."

Dear Reader,

I'm sometimes asked how I come up with characters or book plots. When it comes to the Emerald City Stories, it began with Nicole George, the sister of Emily, who was the heroine of *At Wild Rose Cottage*, a Harlequin Superromance story. I wondered what Nicole's life might be like. What if she wanted to stop being a supermodel and try something new? At that point, her friends Adam, Rachel and Logan seemed to stand up and introduce themselves.

Nicole's story was told in *Moonlight Over Seattle*. And I was pleased to continue the series with Adam Wilding in *A Father for the Twins*. Now it's Rachel Clarion's turn. She's a woman whose beauty seems almost otherworldly to widower Simon Kessler. But underneath it all, he discovers a strong woman who might be the key to not only saving the design business his wife left to their young daughter, but to redesigning a new happy family.

I always love hearing from readers and can be contacted on my Facebook page at Facebook.com/callie.endicott.author.

Best wishes,

Callie

HEARTWARMING

Family by Design

Callie Endicott

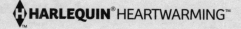

Recycling programs
for this product may
not exist in your area.

ISBN-13: 978-1-335-63392-7

Family by Design

Copyright © 2018 by Callie Endicott

Printed in U.S.A.

www.Harlequin.com

As a kid, **Callie Endicott** had her nose stuck in a book so often it frequently got her in trouble. The trouble hasn't stopped—she keeps having to buy new bookshelves. Luckily ebooks don't take up much space. Writing has been another help, since she's usually on the computer creating stories instead of buying them. Callie loves bringing characters to life and never knows what will prompt an idea. So she still travels, hikes, explores and pursues her other passions, knowing a novel may be just around the corner.

Books by Callie Endicott

Harlequin Superromance

Emerald City Stories

A Father for the Twins
Moonlight Over Seattle

Montana Skies

The Rancher's Prospect
At Wild Rose Cottage
Kayla's Cowboy

That Summer at the Shore
Until She Met Daniel

Visit the Author Profile page
at Harlequin.com for more titles.

To Mom

PROLOGUE

RACHEL CLARION STARED at the check she held… It was intended to compensate for the loss of a successful modeling career, but all she wanted to do was tear it into a thousand pieces.

Weeks ago, her agent, Kevin McClaskey, had made inquiries to see if anyone was interested in hiring her. The answer was no. He'd been given excuses about her being out of the public eye for too long, and that regardless, people might think more about the accident than the product being sold.

Rachel thought there was more to it.

She glanced at the check she held, then touched the faint marks on her jaw; she'd come to terms with what had happened, but the insurance company had boiled it down to dollars and cents. The money was supposed to pay for negligence, pain and lost earnings. But what could compensate for a year and a half of surgeries, self-doubt and the endless gossip and speculation of the paparazzi and mainstream press?

The slip of paper drifted to the floor.

All right, she was still *trying* to come to terms with what had happened. It shouldn't be this difficult—her modeling career hadn't been a childhood dream. She'd become a model by chance when she was fourteen. Her parents were down-to-earth people who ran a popular catering company. One day she'd been helping them cater a spring clothing photo shoot in Seattle, Washington, and the next day she was in front of the camera because one of the models had come down with the flu.

The doorbell rang and Rachel hurried to answer it, finding her close friend Nicole George had arrived early for the evening gathering.

"Hey, Nicole."

Nicole looked at her closely. "What's the matter?"

"Nothing, really." Rachel closed the door and retrieved the check from the floor. Managed right, the settlement would ensure she'd stay financially independent. "I got the money today. It's making me think about stuff."

She put the check away and settled on the couch with Nicole at the other end. Soon they'd be joined by Logan Kensington and Adam Wilding. Adam and Nicole were two of the hottest supermodels in the business, and Logan was a photographer whose services were always in demand. Rachel couldn't help wondering if it would make a difference to their friendship now that she was no longer modeling herself.

She chided herself for even thinking the question. Her friends weren't shallow, even if her ex-husband might be. Rachel wasn't sure about Hayden any longer. It felt as if he'd left because of her scars, yet he'd stuck around for several months after the accident. Ultimately the endless round of doctors and surgeries and meetings with lawyers had chipped away at their marriage until they'd both questioned what was left.

It was also possible that since Hayden was regarded as one of the best-looking men in the business, he couldn't handle being married to a woman who was now pitied and facing the end of her career. Still, they'd had a myriad of problems, so her appearance could only be part of why he'd left.

"Earth to Rachel," Nicole intoned.

"Sorry."

Nicole's eyes were sympathetic. "I can only imagine what that check represents to you. Some people would be dancing in triumph, but life isn't just about money."

"Yeah. It's like a final judgment saying my career is over, my marriage is finished and money is the only thing left." Rachel made a face. "Sorry, I hate it when I whine."

"Whine all you like. You deserve it."

"But feeling sorry for yourself doesn't help."

"True," Nicole acknowledged, "it just keeps you stuck in the same place."

"And that isn't good enough, so I'll have to build a new life and look forward to the process."

"You can do it. You're one of the smartest and bravest people I've ever known."

Rachel grinned. "You're just saying that because I'm feeding you dinner."

"You got me. I'm a sucker for your chicken lo mein."

The doorbell rang again and Rachel let Adam and Logan into the apartment.

"Hi, guys," Nicole greeted them. They fetched bottles of mineral water from the fridge and relaxed in the comfortable chairs across from the couch.

Furniture was another thing Rachel and Hayden had disagreed about; he'd wanted everything modern and fashionable, while she'd preferred comfort. *Compromise* wasn't in his lexicon. She'd let him have every piece of furniture in the divorce, and then purchased what she'd wanted in the first place.

"Before I finish making dinner, I have to decide what to do with my life," Rachel said. "Any ideas?"

"Wow, a new life plan in the next twenty minutes," Adam marveled. "Is this the latest Olympic event?"

Rachel laughed, feeling more normal. The four of them had known each other for years and no one could have been more faithful visiting her at the hospital and then at home, phoning and using Skype when they were out of town on jobs. Maybe friendship was better than romance. It certainly seemed more reliable.

"I thought you had two operations to go before making a decision," Logan said.

"The benefits would be marginal at best, so I told the surgeon that enough is enough. Besides, Kevin made inquiries and nobody wants to hire me. They say it's been too long and there was too much press about the accident—that my injuries are all consumers will think about. *If* they even remember me."

Adam scowled. "Advertisers are remarkably shortsighted. But I'm glad you've decided not to have more surgery. We've hated seeing how much it drags you down."

Rachel squared her shoulders. "Well, now I can rebuild myself and move on."

"What about buying into your parents' business in the Seattle area? You're a great cook."

She shook her head. "That isn't the answer. For one, my little sister hopes to eventually take over Clarion Catering, and my being there would be a complication. Not to mention it would be like going back to childhood."

Nicole shuddered. "What an awful thought."

Both Logan and Adam groaned in a chorus of agreement.

Ironically, of the four of them, Rachel had experienced the most normal life growing up, but she still didn't want to go backward. Anyhow, each time her parents visited, they wanted to coddle and protect her…and deny the reality of what a huge, ancient lighting boom could do to the human body if it wasn't properly secured. She loved them, but she needed to reclaim her life. It was what her trauma counselor kept saying, but that didn't make it less true.

Logan leaned forward. "Is there anything you're especially interested in doing?"

"Not really. I've enjoyed the travel connected to modeling, but I can't see becoming a flight attendant."

"How about doing makeup for photo shoots?" he suggested. "You've helped out several times when the professional artist couldn't get the look I wanted. And there was that one shoot where the entire makeup staff got food poisoning from sushi and you did it for everybody."

Makeup artist was an interesting idea. She had the insurance payout, so she didn't have to worry if the work wasn't regular. And she'd be in the same field as her friends.

"Would it be hard to work in a setting similar to where the accident happened?" Nicole asked, looking concerned.

"Maybe, but I'm getting counseling for

post-traumatic stress and I doubt that running away is the answer."

Rachel almost felt guilty for talking about PTSD. After all, she'd been posing for a picture when something heavy fell on her, not saving lives like the two firefighters she'd met in the hospital. They ran into burning buildings when everyone else was running out of them. But when she'd tried dismissing her own experience, they'd said to stop, that trauma was trauma, no matter what had caused it.

Rachel struggled to smile. Right now she needed to concentrate on getting through each day, one step at a time.

"What do you know?" she announced in a determinedly cheerful voice. "You've managed to help me plan a new life in less than ten minutes. I'm impressed."

CHAPTER ONE

Eight years later

RACHEL ATE BREAKFAST on the balcony of her new condo overlooking Lake Washington, relishing the crisp, cool air of early fall. The view was partly why she'd bought this place. At night, the sparkle of electric lights ringed the dark lake, and in the daytime the vista was ever changing, depending on the weather and which boats were out.

It was funny... She'd grown up in a small town near Seattle and had resisted returning after the accident, yet here she was, less than thirty miles from where her parents lived. Maybe Washington would always be home, or maybe she was just happy that the goal she and her friends had set three years earlier—buying a talent agency—had finally been reached.

Actually, they'd owned Moonlight Ventures for a year, but Nicole had run it alone at first, and then Adam had joined her. Now Rachel was here, and Logan would be joining them soon, as well. Becoming a talent agent was a challenge, the same as when Rachel had built her reputation as a model, and then as a makeup artist.

She decided to go for a walk and automatically checked her appearance in a mirror by the front door. It was Saturday and she didn't have any appointments, but makeup was a habit that made her more confident. She kept it as light as possible, using the barest amount necessary to cover the lingering scars from her old injuries.

Rather than taking the elevator, she ran down the stairs. Since her accident and being bandaged like a mummy so often after surgeries, she'd become slightly claustrophobic.

"Hi," said a childish voice as Rachel walked through the building lobby. A little girl gazed up at her. She was cute as could be, with brown eyes, reddish hair and an inquisitive expression.

"Hello. Who are you?"

"My name is Livvie. I'm seven."

"I'm Rachel. Do you live in the Carthage?" The Carthage was the name of the building, supposedly chosen to evoke images of strength and engineering excellence.

The youngster vigorously bobbed her head. "We used to live in Seattle before Daddy went to work in New York, but I asked if we could come back because this is the place I like best. It's…" She chewed on her lip. "It's where I remember Mama best."

Livvie seemed remarkably articulate and self-possessed for a child her age, though Rachel was hardly an expert on kids. "It was nice of your daddy to do that."

"Uh-huh."

"Ready for our walk, Livvie?" a young woman asked, coming up to them. She looked at Rachel. "Hello, I'm Gemma."

"Gemma is my nanny, 'cept I'm too old for a nanny, so she just takes care of me," Livvie volunteered.

"Hi, Gemma. I'm Rachel Clarion. I live on the second floor." Rachel deliberately provided the information, figuring a nanny worth her salt would want to know exactly *who* had been talking with her charge.

"Daddy's girlfriend was awful mad when we moved home," Livvie said blithely, "but Gemma was happy because she grew up here and wants to go back to college."

"Sweetie, you shouldn't talk about your father that way to a stranger," Gemma cautioned. She had a clear, melodic voice that probably appealed to a child.

"Why not?"

"Because it... It's because some things are private."

"Everybody knows. I heard Daddy say on the phone that Sandra whined to the newspaper people about us leaving."

Rachel suspected that explaining privacy to a seven-year-old was like trying to bail water with a sieve. It would be even harder if Livvie's father was well-known. As for his "whined to the newspaper" comment? The word evoked an image of a man who was impatient with women, maybe even scornful of them.

"Gemma, how long have you been a nanny?" she asked as a distraction.

"Since Livvie was a baby. When did you move to the Carthage?"

"A few weeks ago. I grew up in Washington, but lived in Los Angeles for a number of years. It's nice to be back."

"I know how you feel."

Livvie tugged on Rachel's arm. "Do you

want to go with us? I'm putting my new boat in the water. It has a motor and everything!"

As Livvie held up the toy, there was a vibration under their feet. Someone across the lobby called, "Earthquake," and Gemma let out a gasp.

"I'm sure we're okay," Rachel said quickly, "but let's get over by that column." She knew that the Carthage had been reinforced to withstand earthquakes and the central columns were part of the structural support.

"May-maybe we should go outside," Gemma protested.

"The column," Rachel repeated firmly, shepherding the other woman and Livvie close to the column. The possibility of flowerpots falling from the balconies above bothered her more than any chance the ceiling might come down in such a minor quake.

In less than ten seconds the shaking stopped. Her face ashen, Gemma had pulled Livvie close.

"Hey, it's okay," Rachel assured quietly. "We're fine. That probably wasn't even a 3.0."

"I know. It's just that when I was a kid I fell down a flight of stairs during the Nisqually quake and broke my leg."

"That was a strong one." Rachel remembered the Nisqually quake—it was hard *not* to remember being in such a powerful earthquake. "But this one mostly felt like a great big truck driving by, making the ground rumble a little. Right, Livvie?" she asked in an encouraging tone.

"Yup." Livvie didn't seem afraid, more excited. "Is there going to be a tidal wave?"

"I don't think so."

"Then can we sail my boat now?"

Gemma laughed, visibly regaining her composure. She seemed nice, if unsure of herself. "I guess that puts things in perspective. Let's go."

When they reached the lake, Livvie focused on putting her small remote-controlled motorboat into the water.

"What is your college major?" Rachel asked as they kept a careful watch on the little girl.

"Childhood development. That's why getting a job as a nanny seemed a good way to work my way through school."

"There's nothing like practical experience," Rachel agreed.

"Right, but I didn't want to leave my job when Simon… Mr. Kessler decided to go back East. When we got there he decided on homeschooling for Livvie and hired a teacher. Even so, it… Um, it didn't seem practical to attend college in New York, but I'm starting classes again here in January," she added awkwardly.

Rachel wondered how Gemma felt about her boss. The way she'd said his name had an odd tone and Rachel couldn't decide whether it was affection or wariness. Well, good luck to her, and to anyone who had dreams of a romantic happily-ever-after.

Simon Kessler was frustrated by the unusually heavy Saturday traffic. He'd expected to stay at the office later, but even though Gemma had called and assured him that Livvie wasn't upset by the small earthquake, he'd decided to come home and spend the afternoon with her.

At length he drove his Volvo into the building's underground garage and got into the elevator. It was used by all the Carthage residents, but the top floor could only be accessed by a special key.

The elevator opened into an entrance foyer. He unlocked the front door and the first thing he heard was his daughter chattering happily away. Livvie was the most important part of his life, the best thing he and Olivia had ever done together. But now his complex, brilliant, wonderful wife was gone, and he was a widower and single father. He still missed Olivia so much that at times he thought he'd choke on the pain.

"Where's my Livi-kin-kinnie?" he said, walking into the living room.

He stopped. A stranger was there, a woman who looked vaguely familiar but was still a stranger. She sat on the floor by the coffee table, while Livvie fussed over the tiny bone china tea set that had been one of her birthday presents when she turned seven. Quickly he glanced around and was relieved to see Gemma seated in the corner with a book. He would have been upset if he'd found Livvie alone with someone they didn't know.

"Daddy," Livvie exclaimed, jumping to her feet. "Have tea with us. Pleeeeze? Gemma has to study and it's a much better party with more people."

He couldn't resist her big brown eyes pleading with him.

"You talked me into it." Simon chose the opposite side of the coffee table, preferring not to sit close to the woman. The spot was awkward since the huge redwood burl table was low and he had to arrange his legs around the bulky base.

"Who is your other guest?" he asked.

"This is Rachel C-Clarion. Rachel, this is my daddy."

The woman smiled and nodded as Livvie continued talking.

"Rachel lives downstairs. We went to the lake with her this morning and I asked if she could come for tea." Livvie trotted toward the kitchen and Gemma set her book aside to follow, no doubt to help with preparations.

Being a resident in the Carthage might be why Rachel seemed familiar, but that didn't necessarily mean he wanted her around his daughter.

He'd talk about it with Gemma. She had good instincts, but might have been too shy to turn away their neighbor. Her lack of confidence at times had been his biggest concern about hiring her to care for his newborn daughter. But Olivia had liked her and the way she'd handled Livvie, so he'd agreed. Now, with his wife's death two years ago, he couldn't contemplate removing Gemma from Livvie's life; his daughter had already lost too much. It would still happen at some point… Gemma was nearly twenty-six now and couldn't stay forever.

Forcing his thoughts to the present moment, Simon nodded at Rachel and she nodded back. He regarded her dispassionately. Her eyes were almost turquoise, he thought idly, making him wonder if she wore colored contacts. She was stunningly beautiful with a cloud of long, dark hair. But he wasn't a kid, ready to fall for a pretty face.

Friends sometimes claimed that he needed a wife and a mother for his daughter. But while he'd dated casually over the past year, he was always clear that he didn't want anything permanent; he and Livvie were doing fine on their own. Unfortunately, the woman he'd seen most often in New York had begun hinting for more. Sandra, a well-known socialite, had been furious when she discovered he was moving away without offering a marriage proposal.

He carefully returned Rachel's smile to show neither openness nor caution. "Hello, I'm Simon Kessler."

"It's nice to meet you. I've seen you at the Java Train Shop next door."

"They serve decent coffee," he said.

"Yeah. I used to have one of those fancy machines that practically dances a cup over to the table. But I got rid of the contraption when I moved home. Since I was returning to one of the coffee capitals of the world, why bother making my own brew?"

"I see. What brought you back to the Northwest?" he asked, knowing he was doomed to a period of polite conversation. It was frustrating. He'd come home for quality time with Livvie and had to share it with a stranger.

"Business. My partners and I bought a talent agency."

"I've never known anyone in the talent industry."

Her lips curved again. They were full and sweetly shaped, with just a hint of gloss over a natural rosy color. "I've worked in the modeling field since I was fourteen, so except for childhood friends, I hardly know anyone outside it. What line are you in?"

"My business covers multiple areas, but these days I mostly focus on textiles for home furnishings."

It was a dismissive description of his varied enterprises, but he didn't see the need to go into detail. Through the years Simon had acquired and sold several companies, but he no longer did corporate takeovers; it required time and a callousness that didn't match the man he wanted to be as Livvie's father.

Livvie returned with a small tray, her upper lip caught between her teeth in concentration. Rachel reached up to help lower the tray to the table, and he wasn't thrilled to see her seeming willingness to connect with his child; it reminded him of the way Sandra had started dropping by, hoping to become cozy with his daughter. Her motives had been transparent and if he hadn't decided to leave New York, he would have bluntly told her that Livvie was off-limits. Even at his worst he'd never used a child to advance his personal or business goals and didn't appreciate anyone who did.

"Livvie didn't think you'd be home so early," Rachel said, breaking into his thoughts.

Was she trying to suggest she'd come to the tea party without expecting to see him? For pity's sake, he'd turned into both a cynic and an egotist. A woman could respond to a child's invitation without having ulterior motives. And if Rachel had anything else in mind, he'd figure it out soon enough.

"I had a couple of meetings with people who weren't available during the week. I expected to stay at the office longer to finish some work," he told her, "but changed my mind after the earthquake."

"Daddy works almost every day," Livvie said sadly.

Guilt struck Simon. His hours hadn't mattered as much when Olivia was there and they both could spend time with her outside their demanding careers. "I know about mommies and daddies who have to work a lot," Rachel said as she accepted the miniature cup Livvie handed to her. "My parents run a catering business."

Livvie looked puzzled. "What's that?"

"They prepare food for parties and special dinners and other events."

"Do they have to work awful hard like Daddy?"

"I don't know if it's the same as your daddy, but caterers work different hours than some parents, especially late afternoons and evenings. Us kids usually stayed with our grandmother when they were busy."

"I don't have a grandma."

"But you have Gemma, which is great, right?"

Livvie grinned and nodded, handing one of the tiny cups to Simon.

It wasn't entirely true that she didn't have a grandmother. Legally, she did. Olivia's family was gone and Simon's mother had died when he was nine, but when he was eleven, Richard Kessler had forced his wife to adopt his former lover's child. Karen had tried, in her awkward way, to treat Simon decently, but he'd been the living reminder her husband had never been faithful and that she hadn't given him the son he craved. Neither Karen nor Simon's father was a part of their lives now.

"Please have some cookies," Livvie said, holding out a plate to her guest.

Rachel took one of the cookies and ate a bite. "Delicious. Did you make them yourself?"

Giggling, his daughter shook her head. "We got them at a bakery. I don't know how to cook. Do you?"

"It's one of my hobbies."

"Did your mommy teach you how?"

Simon's throat suddenly closed with suppressed emotion. He tried not to remind

Livvie of how much she'd lost when Olivia died. Though, to be honest, cooking hadn't been one of his wife's skills. Instead she'd told their daughter about clothing designs and the way certain fabrics moved depending on how they were cut.

"My mother and father both taught me," Rachel explained. "Dad is the baker. He makes breads and desserts, while Mom does most of the other stuff. I enjoy doing both."

"My mommy can't teach me," Livvie answered with the curious frankness that seemed part of both her age and personality. "She went to heaven when I was five."

"I'm sorry. If she was anything like you, she must have been very special."

Livvie beamed, then turned and looked at him. "I hardly ever see you in the kitchen, Daddy. Can you cook?"

"'Fraid not, kiddo. I learned more about business stuff than cooking spaghetti when I was growing up."

His daughter giggled.

Simon loved it when she laughed. He loved it when she seemed to be happy instead of scared and pulled into herself. At times he worried that *he* frightened her. In more sensible moments he was sure that was ridiculous. But he also knew he was very much the man his ruthless father had molded him to be.

RACHEL HADN'T BEEN sure about accepting Livvie Kessler's invitation to a tea party, but the child seemed lonely and it had felt like the right thing to do. Still, it hurt when Rachel thought that if her marriage had succeeded, she might have a little girl or boy around Livvie's age.

She pushed the thought away. If she'd known that Livvie's father was Simon Kessler and that he would be coming home, she might have refused Livvie's invitation.

On the weekend she preferred keeping things casual and comfortable, and the brief glimpses she'd caught of Simon had suggested he was brooding and intense, ready to explode into action at any moment. There was nothing wrong with that. She'd known plenty of people with the same coiled energy inside, but sitting at a child's tea party with one of them unsettled her. Besides, the few times their gazes had connected in the past, he'd turned away as if he had no interest in other people…or even in common courtesies.

But she gave the guy credit for one thing—he was obviously a hardworking business-man, yet he was willing to sit on the floor and have a tea party with his motherless child. Whatever other faults he might have, she found that admirable.

Nonetheless, she quickly finished her tea and cookie as soon as Livvie was done with hers. She noticed that Simon did the same—perhaps hoping his daughter's guest wouldn't stay long.

"Thank you, this has been lovely," Rachel told her small hostess. "I enjoyed it, but I'd better go." She untangled her legs and stood.

"Do you have to?" Livvie asked plain-tively.

"Afraid so. I have things to do before going out tonight."

Nicole had invited everyone to her house for a barbecue and Rachel had offered to bring a couple of salads. Had Nicole and her fiancé, Jordan Masters, finally settled on their wedding plans? Of course, Adam was now engaged to Cassie Bryant so they might have a similar announcement. What's more, the agency's office manager, Chelsea Masters, who also happened to be Jordan's sister, was seriously involved with a grade school teacher. The next year could be busy with all the weddings of people at Moonlight Ventures.

Rachel had wondered if Nicole and Adam both getting engaged would change the dynamics of their friendship, but it was working out all right. After the couples were married, the four business partners probably wouldn't hang out as often in a group, but they had never spent every minute in each other's pockets, anyhow. Besides, Jordan and Cassie were great.

Cassie was the legal guardian to two of the agency's clients. She designed websites and had revamped Moonlight Ventures' website. Jordan was a reporter, which was how he and Nicole met, or rather met again. They'd known each other growing up, but hadn't been in contact until he was asked to do an article about her changing careers from modeling to being an agent.

"I'm really, really, *really* glad you came." Livvie walked her guest to the door, a proper little hostess. "Can we do things together sometimes?"

Rachel smiled at the sweet, hopeful face, aware that Simon had followed with a closed expression. "Maybe, if it's all right with your daddy."

"We're neighbors and neighbors should be friends," Livvie said with her oddly adult air. It probably wasn't unusual for an only child who'd been homeschooled, though earlier Gemma had explained Livvie was now enrolled in a private school with kids her own age. Maybe it would help her be less lonely.

"Thanks again for the tea," Rachel repeated when Simon stayed silent.

She took the stairs down, aware of the heavy security door snapping shut behind her. Nobody except the Kesslers could access the top floor of the Carthage. A special key was needed for the elevator and cameras monitored the third-floor staircase.

The setup seemed slightly paranoid, but maybe Simon Kessler was a fanatic about his privacy. Rachel understood, and the penthouse was undoubtedly a nice home. She'd only seen a small part of it, but visible from the living room was an actual garden, with a deck, flower boxes, a tiny area of grass and trees in large planters. High, spotless heavy glass enclosed the space, ensuring Livvie could play with no chance of falling.

Rachel let herself into her condo and felt as if she was reentering the real world.

She would have loved having a house and garden like the one Nicole had purchased, but the muscles in her left leg weren't as strong as they'd been before the accident, especially if she made unusual or twisting movements. So rather than hire someone to do the yard and other exterior work, she'd decided on a condo with a balcony large enough to host small groups. She couldn't have found a better location under the circumstances. The neighborhood was in a historic town, tucked into the greater Seattle area. It enjoyed some preservation from further development along the lake by protected green space on either side. There was even a mom-and-pop type of grocery store up the block, complete with an old-style deli.

While she vacuumed the living room, Rachel thought about Simon Kessler. Livvie must take after her mother, except for her eyes, which were as dark as her father's. But the little girl's eyes were eager and hopeful, unlike Simon's.

Rachel could understand. In pictures of her taken after the accident, her eyes had conveyed the same sense of bottled-up emotions she saw in Simon's gaze. Only slowly had she lost the self-conscious pain she hadn't wanted anyone else to see.

Simon's wife had died a little over two years ago. Maybe that was why he seemed so intense, struggling to keep himself under tight control... He was a man who had lost the woman he loved and was trying to navigate this new world as a single dad. Having a girlfriend in New York didn't mean he'd figured things out; it could just have been part of the process.

Rachel pushed the thoughts aside to prepare lettuce and other vegetables for a Thai noodle salad.

At five she drove out to Nicole's house. Jordan opened the door and took the box of food she carried.

"Mmm." Jordan sniffed. "I smell onions, peanuts, roasted sesame... Must be Thai."

"Is that your favorite?"

"Whatever you cook is my favorite. I haven't tasted anything you make that I haven't loved."

"That's for sure," Nicole agreed, overhearing them as they walked into the kitchen. "And I've been eating your cooking a lot longer than Jordan."

"I've been wondering if you'd like me to fix a meal for after your wedding," Rachel said. "Or the rehearsal dinner."

Jordan put the box on the counter and exchanged a look with his fiancée.

Nicole sighed. "Actually, we've decided against a formal wedding. We considered giving it a try, but there are too many George and Masters family bombs threatening to go off. It would be the Hatfields and McCoys, Seattle-style." She clutched her forehead in mock horror.

"Oh, dear."

Rachel knew that Nicole's mother didn't get along with Jordan's mom, a long-time feud that the engaged couple had hoped would be put aside, at least for their wedding. Obviously that wasn't going to happen.

Jordan shrugged. "The fight runs too deep, and neither side wants to give up being angry. Maybe someday. But if it doesn't, at least we live two states away."

"I hope the battle doesn't extend to the two of you."

"Nope. Mom has decided Nicole is perfectly wonderful—despite everything—and Nicole's mother says she can't figure how I turned out so well with parents like that."

"Yikes." Rachel could imagine the battle scenes if the two families got together.

"Right." Jordan put the salads she'd brought into the refrigerator. "It's our own version of the Cold War and we don't want it to heat up."

"Then what are you doing for the wedding?"

"We're going to our fallback plan. December or January, city hall, no friends or family except witnesses," Nicole said succinctly.

"We won't let them drag us into their fight," Jordan added.

It made sense to Rachel. "Then let me do a nonwedding party afterward. We can have it at my place... Unless you're planning to leave for a honeymoon immediately?"

"We're still making plans for our honeymoon." Nicole exchanged glances with Jordan. He nodded and she grinned. "But that sounds fabulous."

"Sure does," Jordan agreed. "Thanks. We wouldn't leave until the next day, anyhow, and it would make the wedding day more special."

Rachel knew Nicole didn't care if she had a fancy wedding. Being in love and starting her married life with Jordan was what mattered to her, and all Jordan cared about was being with Nicole.

It was probably natural that Nicole had recently questioned whether Rachel might consider marriage again—she was in love and wanted the whole world to be in love with her. But Rachel didn't think it was likely. Her life was good, and getting involved with someone could jeopardize the peace she'd finally found.

CHAPTER TWO

RACHEL DROVE TO the office on Monday morning feeling as if a hidden thought was nibbling at her mind. She'd experienced the sensation before and it often turned out to be something important she needed to consider.

Hopefully it would emerge in time.

As she pulled into the lot, she saw Matt Tupper stepping down from a transport van. He didn't have his guide dog and was using his cane. She walked his direction, and he turned at the sound of her footsteps.

"Hey, Rachel," he called. "Good morning."

"I didn't know my walk was that distinctive."

"It isn't hard to deduce. Not many people arrive this early and Nicole usually wears heels. You wear flats most of the time and walk with a different pace."

Rachel didn't explain that heels made her left leg ache.

She was learning about the importance of listening from Matt. Even if she hadn't seen the tension in Simon Kessler's face, his voice would have told her a great deal about him.

"Is Pepper all right?" she asked, trying to dismiss Simon from her mind. "She's usually with you." Pepper was Matt's guide dog and she was devoted to Matt.

"Pepper is fine, but she's due for her annual vaccinations. My brother offered to take her to the vet so I could get to the studio for an early recording. He'll bring her by later. I'd give her the day off, but she's restless when she isn't with me."

"How has it been going since you expanded?" she asked.

"We're still getting the equipment installed for the second live studio, but it's already booked ahead for months. Tara is coming in this weekend to ensure they finish the work."

"That's Tara Henley, your assistant."

"Right. With the schedule so full, it looks like I'll still end up doing books for the blind on Saturdays. Maybe it's just as well since my volunteer readers have more available time on weekends."

Matt owned a recording studio and had

been one of the renters Rachel and her friends had inherited when buying the building along with Moonlight Ventures. He recorded radio spots, music and audio books, often hiring his vocal talent through the agency. Instead of being off the atrium area, he was in a rear section of the building where they had few renters, so it hadn't been a problem to lease him additional space for the second studio. Ironically, their agency also needed to expand, but the space next to them was occupied, with several years left on the lease.

"That's terrific," Rachel said. "You may have to add a third live studio."

He chuckled. "Maybe. As my dad says, success is a two-edged sword. Have a great day."

ONCE INSIDE HIS STUDIO, Matt didn't really need his cane. His employees knew to leave everything in its place or to tell him if something had been moved. He walked around with assurance, occasionally putting out a hand if he sensed something wasn't right.

Even before losing his eyesight, he'd been aware of sound and how pitch and modulation changed in relation to everything else. He navigated relatively well for that reason, usually able to sense larger objects nearby, though he still stubbed his toes often enough. Losing his sight hadn't even changed his college plans—he'd always intended to major in electronic communications.

The phone rang and he hit the speaker button. "Tupper Recording."

"It's Conan, Matt." Conan's voice sounded gravelly, as if he'd just got out of bed.

"What's up?"

Conan started to say something, then broke into a fit of coughing. Obviously it was more than a rough morning voice.

"Got a cold," he finally choked out. "We can't make it today, but we'll still pay a full fee for the recording session."

"The cancellation fee in the contract is fine," Matt said firmly. It made him uncomfortable when people tried to pay more than their contracts required. Maybe he was being ultrasensitive, but it felt as if they were giving alms to the blind.

"When can we reschedule?" Conan asked. He was an account executive for a major bank...who also blew a mean saxophone. His jazz band played in local clubs periodically, and they'd decided to record a CD under their own start-up label.

"Let me check the schedule." Matt pulled it up on the computer. He used both a braille and audio reader, but preferred having the electronic braille device translate from the screen when other people might be able to hear. "I don't have an opening until three weeks from today, 4:00 p.m."

"That's—" Conan had another fit of coughing. "We'll take it," he said when he could talk again. "Sorry about this. My kid brought the bug home from preschool and must have spread it to the whole band when we practiced a few days ago. I've been getting emails from everyone that they're sick."

"Get well soon," Matt returned, entering the booking in the system and setting an electronic reminder to send a revision to the contract for signature.

"Thanks."

Matt disconnected and automatically reached to rub behind Pepper's ears, only to remember she wasn't there. He missed her. He'd resisted getting a guide dog for years, but Pepper had become a friend who sensed his moods better than any human had ever done.

Sitting back, Matt listened to the sounds coming from the street and the whisper of the HVAC system blowing air through the vents. This was his kingdom and it was exactly where he'd always wanted to be...even if his life hadn't been changed by a driver jumping the curb and plowing into a group of high school seniors.

RACHEL'S DAY PASSED quickly between desk work and site checks, which included visiting two photo shoots where new clients were booked. Everything was going smoothly in both locations.

Late in the afternoon she and Adam enjoyed rejecting a business owner who was supposedly searching for a model to represent his used-car dealership. The guy had raised alarm bells when they'd talked, so she'd checked him out further. Apparently he used what he called "casting calls" to meet and then try to date female models. Adam had wanted to be the one who told him to get lost but in the end agreed they could do it together.

She drove home in a good mood, encountering Gemma and Livvie when she stopped in the lobby to check her mailbox.

"Hi, Rachel," Livvie cried. "We're going to the lake. Can you come with us?"

Gemma nodded and smiled, but Rachel hesitated. When she'd mentioned spending time with Livvie if her father agreed, he hadn't responded one way or the other. But surely he would have told Gemma if he didn't approve.

"I'd love to," Rachel said. "Can you wait a minute for me to change into something else?"

"Okay."

She rushed up the stairs and slipped into casual clothes. Livvie's face bloomed with pleasure when she got back and they headed toward the water. Once there, the child concentrated on her boat, while Rachel chatted with Gemma.

"It's beautiful here in Washington," Gemma murmured after a while. "So green and fresh. I missed it in New York, though we were able to see things like the Statue of Liberty and museums. I especially enjoyed Greenwich Village."

Once again her clear, musical voice impressed Rachel, and she suddenly recalled the elusive idea that had been buzzing in her brain. She should have thought of it when she'd run into Matt Tupper that morning.

"Gemma, would you be interested in doing side jobs?" she asked. "At the agency we get calls for people to do narration or voice-overs and other vocal work. I'm sure you'd be great at it."

"Oh, I never thought of such a thing. I'm not... I mean, I don't have any experience and can't imagine anyone would be interested in hiring me."

"They might. I'm not saying you'd make a fortune or anything. You could even ease your way into it by doing volunteer reading. One of the tenants in our building has a sound studio and he records books and magazines for the blind—regionally published stuff that the National Library Service is less likely to do. He's always looking for readers willing to give time to the project."

The nervous clutch of Gemma's fingers relaxed. "I'd be happy to volunteer, only I doubt I'd be very good."

"Think about it. There isn't a deadline."

They stayed quiet after that, watching Livvie direct her boat in the water. It was a beautiful late afternoon, and Rachel enjoyed just sitting and watching the rippling lake.

"Hey, kiddo!" called Simon Kessler out of the blue.

"Daddy," Livvie cried, "come see how I make my boat move."

Rachel's pulse had jumped when Simon Kessler's voice intruded into her musings. She watched as he went to the water's edge, crouching to speak with his daughter—from what she'd read, getting down to eye level was the best way to talk with kids. At the moment, Livvie seemed to be pleading with him for something and Rachel restrained a grin. Livvie would be hard *not* to spoil with her funny adult manners and earnest eyes.

Gemma looked at her cell phone. "Oh, dear, we've been here longer than I thought. I need to go, I have a class tonight at the community center. I'm learning sign language."

She went over to speak with her employer, then waved and hurried away. Rachel stood to leave as well, thinking she needed to develop more hobbies or take classes. She loved cooking and reading, but having other interests would be good.

"Rachel, wait," Livvie screeched, dashing up the pathway. "Please come with us for dinner."

Wishing she'd made her escape earlier,

Rachel smiled. "That's nice of you, Livvie, but I have leftovers in my fridge that need to be eaten. I hate to waste food."

"Pleeeze? I want you to come. Daddy, please ask Rachel to come."

"Livvie, honey, get your boat out of the water while I talk with Ms. Clarion."

"Okay."

Rachel looked at Simon, whose face wore the same closed expression she'd seen before. He was darkly handsome, with chiseled features that might photograph well. Strange, now that she was a talent agent, it seemed as if she was always assessing how someone might look in an ad or appear on television or in film. She'd have to work on that, because she didn't want her view of the world becoming too narrow.

But maybe it wasn't just from becoming an agent. In all honesty, she would have noticed Simon's looks regardless.

He was a hard man to ignore.

SIMON HADN'T WANTED to agree to Livvie's request about inviting Rachel to dinner, but the little mischief maker had asked for a treat and he'd impulsively said yes before learning which treat she wanted.

His daughter had taken a strong, instant liking to their downstairs neighbor. He just didn't know why. While Rachel had an almost otherworldly beauty, it probably wasn't something that would influence a child. He'd questioned Gemma to find out if Rachel had done something special to catch Livvie's attention, but she'd said nothing unusual had happened aside from the minor earthquake. Rachel, it seemed, had been exceptionally calm during the event, which had really impressed Gemma.

"We would very much like having you as our guest for dinner," he said formally.

"Thanks, but as I told Livvie, I have food in my refrigerator that will go to waste," Rachel explained, her gaze seeming straightforward.

"I hope you'll reconsider," he urged. "She rarely asks for anything, so it's hard when I can't give her what she wants."

"Well…there's far more than I can eat, so maybe you could have dinner at my place."

He went rigid, recalling a few meals to which he and Livvie had been invited since Olivia's death where there'd been a clear ulterior motive.

"Really, Rachel? Can we eat with you?" Livvie asked from behind him.

Was it possible Rachel had seen his daughter coming and spoken when she did, counting on getting his child's support? Or was he being unreasonably suspicious again? He desperately missed Olivia's sensible way of keeping him grounded.

"It's up to your father," Rachel said.

"Thanks, that would be nice," he agreed finally. After all, one dinner didn't mean anything.

"Great. I'm going to head back to my place. I'm in 2B and can have everything ready in an hour. Does that sound okay?"

"It works for us."

He kept himself from watching her graceful figure walk away, and concentrated on spending a while longer with Livvie, putting the little motorized boat back into the water and sending it around in circles. Then they went home to wash up for the meal. Livvie wanted to put on the dress she'd worn for a Christmas party, but he talked her out of the frilly outfit before changing his business suit for less formal clothing.

Shortly before seven, he rang the doorbell to 2B.

Rachel was still wearing jeans and a T-shirt and had a dish towel tied around her waist instead of an apron. A delicious, faintly exotic scent wafted through the air.

"Welcome," she said, waving them inside.

Simon glanced around. It was the first time he'd seen one of the other condos in the building. This one seemed spacious and had a nice lakeside view. The living room was decorated with eclectic touches from around the world and an electronic picture frame shifted through scenes he recognized from his own travels.

Rachel had gone into the kitchen and returned with a tray holding serving bowls. She carried it toward the French doors opening onto the deck.

"I enjoy eating outside when the weather is nice," she said. "Is that all right?"

"Sounds fine."

"Sit wherever you're comfortable."

A minute later she reappeared with a large platter. "As I mentioned, this is all leftovers."

"I like leftovers," Livvie announced.

His daughter seemed determined to like everything connected to their neighbor, though Simon wasn't sure Livvie knew what Rachel meant. Neither he nor Olivia had bothered with leftovers much.

"So do I," Rachel said. "Since my parents were caterers, I grew up on food left from their catering jobs. Maybe I'm biased, but I think some dishes are better the second time around."

Simon looked at the platter of meat and roasted vegetables, alongside bowls of salads.

"You made all of this?"

"Just the salads. My friends grilled the meat and veggies for a get-together on Saturday. Fewer guests came than expected, so they sent a container of the excess home with me. I meant to share it around the office today and forgot."

"What's that?" Livvie asked, pointing to a vegetable.

"Eggplant."

Livvie giggled. "That's silly. Eggs don't grow on plants."

"No, but some types of eggplant have an egg shape, or at least that must be what people thought."

"Do I have to eat a whole serving if it's yucky?"

Rachel's lips twitched. "Simon, I don't

know your rules about food, so you should probably answer that."

"I want Livvie to try things, but she doesn't have to finish anything she truly dislikes."

"There's your answer, Livvie," Rachel said. "If you want to try it, fine, but I won't be upset if you don't want to finish."

"Okay," Livvie said, looking relieved. While she seemed eager to please Rachel, she was decidedly picky about her food.

Simon served his daughter before filling his own plate and taking a bite of the eggplant. He'd eaten it in eggplant parmesan, but this was different and quite delicious.

Livvie chewed a small amount of the eggplant and made a face before swallowing. But she ate another bite, so perhaps she was merely concentrating.

"This is excellent," he said, tasting a salad of noodles and various vegetables.

Rachel didn't appear flattered by the compliment. She simply shrugged. "Thanks to my parents, cooking has always been part of my life."

"But you didn't decide to become a caterer?"

She grinned. "I'd rather cook when I want, not on demand."

"To keep it a hobby, not a job."

"Right." Rachel cocked her head. "I was thinking about hobbies earlier. It's interesting that you mentioned them."

"How do you define a hobby?" he asked politely.

"I'm not sure. I used to think it was to create something lasting, but that isn't true of activities like mountain climbing. And food only lasts until you eat it."

"Perhaps it leaves lasting memories."

She wrinkled her nose. "Or a little extra on the hips."

Simon tried not to look at her figure; he'd already noted how attractive she was. Sandra's determined efforts to get him in front of an altar had left him suspicious of women, yet he didn't think Rachel was fishing for compliments.

He glanced at Livvie. She was exploring the food on her plate. Some dishes she obviously liked, but others she seemed less certain about. He decided it was best to let her continue experimenting without comment.

"Rachel, what other hobbies would you enjoy?"

"I'm still thinking about it. Gemma mentioned being in a sign language class, so I thought about taking classes, as well. I've always been fascinated by anthropology."

Simon was so busy he couldn't imagine needing a hobby. "I've never had to worry about it, but I suppose something like that would help fill your time."

She sent him a look tinged with annoyance. "I don't need to *fill* my time," she said crisply, "but I'm essentially self-employed now. It would be easy to lose myself in work. Instead I want to expand my mind and explore new things. But I suppose *some* people don't care about doing that."

It was a not-so-subtle gibe and Simon belatedly realized he must have sounded condescending.

"New things like eggplant?" Livvie asked, innocently breaking the tense moment.

Rachel smiled at her. "New foods are one thing to explore, and I want to find others. There are so many choices, I'll have to think about what to do."

He half expected a suggestion his daughter could "help" her figure it out, but Rachel merely served herself more vegetables, then spent a moment gazing at the view from the balcony. The sun had sunk behind the building and the lights of the surrounding community were beginning to glow.

"I love this time of day," she murmured. "It's an in-between moment, where maybe you can…"

She stopped and Livvie looked intrigued. "Do what?"

Rachel waved her hand. "Just a fancy of mine. It's silly. What's your favorite part of the day?"

As his daughter chattered about mornings and her daily activities, Simon focused on her face, rather than the lake and sparkling lights. Twilight wasn't *his* favorite time; it signaled the beginning of evening, a period that reminded him of his loss.

Olivia had worked hard, trying to build her clothing design business into something the world would notice. He'd worked equally hard, but they had set the evening aside for family. And once Livvie had gone to bed, they'd focused on each other.

Well, it had been that way a good deal of the time.

When Olivia had got an idea for a design, she'd wanted to capture it right away. Otherwise, she had explained, she risked losing the nuances. On those evenings, she had quietly disappeared into her work.

Their marriage hadn't been perfect, but it *had* been good. Since her death, he'd wondered if she had guessed her life would be short and whether that explained how determined and driven she'd been.

RACHEL SAW A faraway look on Simon's face and wondered what it might mean. Not that she needed to know. The Kesslers were merely neighbors, and based on her contacts with Simon, she'd rather not get closely acquainted. The only reason she'd offered the dinner invitation was for Livvie's sake.

"The part I don't like about mornings is when Daddy leaves," Livvie finally said.

Simon brushed a crumb from his daughter's cheek. "Sorry, Livi-kin-kinnie, but that's what daddies do."

Livvie let out a huge breath of air. "I know. When I grow up I'm going to work at Mama's place."

"Your mama's place?" Rachel asked.

"She made dresses and things. Daddy, you 'splain it." Looking sad, Livvie slipped off her chair and wandered to the end of the balcony to stare at the lake.

Rachel glanced at Simon and saw his expression had gone tighter than usual. "My wife, Olivia, designed a line of clothing. When she... Well, she left the business to Livvie and I've been trying to run it the best I can."

"Was it based in New York?"

"No, in Seattle."

Rachel straightened in her chair. "Good grief, are you talking about Liv'ing Creations?"

His eyebrow shot upward. "Yes. You sound familiar with the label."

"I should hope so. I know my agency used to provide models for their shows and catalogs. I've also enjoyed their clothes and have several items in my closet. Older ones, that is, not..." She stopped, aware she might be treading on sensitive ground.

"You mean nothing from the more current lines, not since Olivia's last designs were released," he said in a low, flat tone, possibly to keep his daughter from hearing.

"Basically." Rachel kept her volume equally low. "The line has radically changed direction over the past few seasons. It no longer has the vitality and style that originally caught my attention. In particular, the rich colors have become muted."

From the little she could read in Simon's expression, she didn't think he'd enjoyed hearing her opinion, even if he knew—or suspected—something was wrong with his wife's company.

"Maybe it appeals to other people, just not to me," Rachel added awkwardly.

"I hired Janine Jenkins, a clothing designer from New York, to keep things going. Sales have been indifferent," he said, "but the manager of Liv'ing Creations feels it's because consumers know Olivia is gone and are avoiding the label for that reason. She and the designer are convinced another season or two should turn things around."

"I see," Rachel said carefully, not sure how else to respond.

She hadn't been aware of Olivia Kessler's death; she'd simply lost interest when the designs no longer showed the unique flair she had first appreciated. It seemed unlikely that the original buyers would return if the current designer stayed in her conservative mode, though interest might pick up in a new market. The designs weren't awful, but they felt like something you'd find in any nice department store.

As Simon started to say something else, Rachel saw Livvie heading back to the table.

"Hey, Livvie, does your daddy allow you to have dessert?" she called in case he hadn't heard the soft footsteps.

Livvie brightened. "If I eat a good dinner. I ate a good dinner, didn't I, Daddy?"

"That's right, honey."

Rachel was relieved to be talking about something else. "In that case, I have strawberry sorbet, along with cookies that a friend made."

"Yum!"

Rachel began clearing the table and Simon got up to help, despite her urging to stay put and relax.

"Should I put these in the dishwasher?" he asked, carrying the tray into the kitchen.

"Just leave everything on the counter and I'll clean up in the morning. Would you like coffee? I got decaf at the Java Train Stop."

"Sounds good."

She filled two cups from the insulated carton and offered cream and sugar, but Simon declined.

"Is that homemade?" he asked as she served the sorbet.

"Yes. I made it for a gathering a couple

weeks ago. As promised, tonight's dinner is all about leftovers."

"Everything was excellent."

They carried the coffee and dessert to the balcony.

Livvie tasted the sorbet and grinned. "*Double* yum."

"Rachel made it," Simon told her.

The child's eyes opened wide. "I didn't know you could make ice cream stuff at home."

"You can make most things if you know how and have the right tools."

While they ate, the pink glow in the sky faded entirely and the lights from homes and streetlamps shone in the blackness.

When the dessert and coffee were finished, Simon smiled politely. "Rachel, thanks for a pleasant evening, but we'd better get going."

"I'm glad you could come."

"I like eggplant," Livvie said, her eyes shining. "And I looove strawberry ice cream."

Rachel chuckled and walked them to the door, where Livvie hugged her.

"Thank you, thank you, thank you," she exclaimed.

Unable to resist, Rachel bent and kissed the top of her head. "You're very welcome."

But when the door closed behind them, her shoulders sagged with exhaustion. Unlike evenings with her friends, spending time with Simon Kessler was far from relaxing. The way he looked at her, as if weighing her words for a secret meaning, his measured responses, his guarded expression…she felt as if she'd run a marathon.

SIMON WALKED UPSTAIRS with his daughter. They spent an hour playing games before she put on her "princess" nightgown and he tucked her into bed.

"Daddy, I like Rachel."

He brushed the hair away from her forehead. "Of course you do, honey. She's a nice lady."

"Can I go visit her?"

"I'll think about it."

Livvie yawned. "Okay. G'night."

"Sleep tight and don't let the bedbugs bite."

She giggled sleepily while he turned off the light and left the bedroom door ajar.

At his computer, Simon started looking through the files for Liv'ing Creations. Rachel's comments about the current clothing line were bothering him.

It no longer has the vitality and style that originally caught my attention. In particular, the rich colors have become muted.

The colors in Janine Jenkins's designs were undoubtedly more subdued, and he wondered if Rachel had put her finger on the issues that Liv'ing Creations was having. Though he hadn't wanted to admit it, he was starting to think Janine Jenkins was part of the problem, not the solution.

What had Rachel said—that her talent agency had once provided models for the design house? A search through the financial reports gave him a name, Moonlight Ventures.

At the agency's website, Simon found pictures and brief bios of the owners. His eyes widened as he recognized two of the partners, supermodels Nicole George and Adam Wilding. Logan Kensington was a world-renowned photographer, while Rachel had worked as both a model and a makeup artist.

Simon broadened his search on the internet and found something Rachel's agency biography hadn't mentioned—her modeling career had been cut short due to injuries in an accident at work. After recovering, she'd turned her talents to doing makeup on photo shoots and in the movie world.

He tapped his fingers on the keyboard. Liv'ing Creations' sales were lackluster and in danger of slipping into the red. He'd sold most of his holdings and split the proceeds between Livvie's trust fund and a donation to ovarian cancer research, seeing both as an investment in his daughter's future. Still, he could probably subsidize the design house for a year or two. But that wasn't what Olivia would have wanted. His wife had poured herself into the company. She'd often talked about wanting to leave a piece of herself behind for Livvie, and that had become especially important to her once she'd fallen ill. It wouldn't be much of a legacy if the fashion house became a joke in the industry and died an inglorious death.

Restless, he turned off the computer and went into the garden. While sitting on Rachel's balcony earlier in the evening, he'd realized he couldn't remember the last time he'd enjoyed the fresh air or appreciated the night vista. In fact, he could almost hear Olivia chiding him. She would have asked him if he wanted their daughter to grow up with such a limited sense of things. After all, kids often modeled how their parents behaved.

Simon shuddered. His father had been as ruthless and narrowly focused as a man could be. He'd dragged Simon out of a good foster home, made his wife sign adoption papers and set out to mold his son in his own image. He'd succeeded. Simon had learned his lessons well, cold-bloodedly pursuing a hostile takeover of Richard Kessler's business as an adult and then taking it apart and selling the pieces.

Justice or, more likely, retribution?

Because if his father had behaved decently, Simon's biological mother might still be alive. Instead she'd died, overworked and unable to get needed medical care. However happy Simon's foster home had been, it couldn't erase the memory of losing her so senselessly.

When he and Olivia had got married they'd both been obsessed with work until Livvie was on the way. That was when they'd taken a step back to review their lives and realized they wanted more for themselves and their child. Now it was time to revisit those values.

A crisp breeze swirled around Simon, carrying a fragrance that reminded him of Rachel's light perfume.

His senses went on alert.

Rachel's balcony was located below the penthouse garden and he realized she might be sitting outside as well, watching the moon over Lake Washington. He hadn't enjoyed hearing her opinion about the latest designs from Liv'ing Creations, yet that didn't mean they weren't valid. Perhaps he should call Moonlight Ventures in the morning and make an appointment with her. They could talk, and if her ideas seemed on target, he could try hiring her as a consultant—that would make it clear the contact was purely business.

CHAPTER THREE

ON TUESDAY, GEMMA woke early and contemplated how quickly the days were getting shorter. It was always that way in Washington—the long days of summer, shifting into the equally long nights of winter.

She turned over, thinking about being close to her family again…and wrinkled her nose.

Mr. Kessler—it was hard to think of him as Simon—had arranged for her to visit Washington every three months after they'd moved to New York, but after the first trip, she'd quickly found reasons not to go. She loved her parents, but it always felt as if they were looking past her to admire what her talented oldest brother was doing.

Drake looked like Adonis, had the social skills of a diplomat and was now a resident in cardiology at the University of Washington Medical Center. There seemed to be nothing he hadn't accomplished and probably done better than anyone else. When she and her other brother were growing up and wanted to try something new, their parents would say, "Drake is so good at that, find your own special gift." Once she'd been tempted to suggest fan dancing since she was reasonably certain it was one of the few things Drake hadn't tried.

No wonder Mom and Dad were so proud of him. They claimed to be proud of her and Sully, too, but Gemma often wondered if they were being completely honest. Sully didn't care. Dad's moodiness while drinking hadn't frightened him the way it had frightened her, though it was the reason they'd both been eager to get away from home.

Stop.

A deep sigh welled from Gemma's chest. Her biggest problem was shyness and a lack of confidence. It was easy to be with kids. They didn't judge, could throw themselves wholly into play and had wonderful imaginations. Studying childhood development and becoming a teacher had seemed an ideal fit, though the idea hadn't impressed her family. Nor had her slow movement through college while they pointedly mentioned her brother's breakneck academic successes.

So what about Rachel's suggestion of doing voice work? She knew people were hired to do narration for things like cartoons, but it seemed improbable that she could be one of them.

A faint knock on the door caught Gemma's attention, more a scratching than a knock.

"Come in, Livvie," she called softly. Mr. Kessler slept poorly now that his wife was gone and she didn't want to interrupt any rest he might be getting.

Livvie slipped inside and ran to the bed. "I had a bad dream. It made my tummy cold."

"I'm sorry." Gemma patted the pillow next to hers. "Maybe telling me about it will make you feel better."

Hugging the pillow in her arms, Livvie began relating the nightmare. It was about an evil sorcerer who killed the queen and was trying to cast an evil spell on the king and send the princess into the forest to live with a witch who didn't want her. There was a dragon who was actually a good dragon and a talking horse who could knock down walls, but the underlying theme was the same as in all of her dreams...the fear that her daddy would be taken away, just like her mother.

Yet a new element seemed to be emerging—Livvie was beginning to understand that she didn't have anyone in the world except her father. However frustrating Gemma's own childhood had been, she had an extended family—aunts, uncles, grandparents, cousins—a great big safety net. But Livvie didn't have anyone else except two grandparents who'd never made an effort to meet her.

"Maybe you should tell your daddy about your bad dreams," Gemma suggested.

Livvie shook her head in a definitive *no*. "I don't want to make Daddy sad. Promise you won't tell."

"I… Okay," Gemma promised reluctantly.

She'd tried to suggest a grief counselor to Mr. Kessler, at least for Livvie, but maybe she hadn't been forceful enough. Perhaps she should look for an opportunity to try again.

On Thursday, Rachel was startled when she found Simon Kessler's name on her morning appointment calendar. The discussion she'd had with Gemma about doing voice work was a possible reason for it, though surely it wasn't his business what an employee did on her off time. Or was there something personal going on between them?

At eleven, Chelsea brought Simon back to her office.

Rachel gestured to one of the chairs at the side of her desk. Even if her office had been larger, he would seem overpowering in it.

He sat and glanced around. "This is nice."

"Thanks. Originally we envisioned a small agency with specialty clients, but we've expanded beyond that. We expect to hire more agents within the next two years."

"I understand your blog is increasingly popular, both inside and outside the talent industry."

Rachel's senses went on higher alert. Now that she thought about it, she couldn't recall mentioning the name of the agency to Simon or Gemma. "I didn't realize you knew anything about us."

"I've been doing research on you."

She narrowed her eyes. Often when somebody brought up research it meant they were digging into details of her past that she didn't want disturbed. How had she felt lying under a piece of heavy equipment while rescuers figured out how to get it off without doing further damage? How had she felt when her husband walked out less than a year later? Was he obsessed with appearance, the way his ex-girlfriends claimed? Was he shallow? Did he leave because of her scars?

Rachel slowed her racing brain and focused.

"Why were you researching the agency?" she asked pleasantly, seeing no need to unload her emotional baggage on other people.

"Because of your comments the other evening about Liv'ing Creations. I mentioned the sales have slipped and you seem to have an insight into why."

"Oh." That *hadn't* crossed Rachel's mind as a possibility for Simon's appointment. "I was simply speaking from the point of view of a customer."

"But you have experience in the fashion industry. You're a former model and your partners are connected to the business. Not to mention the fact that you're still involved in supplying models for the fashion world."

"Perhaps, but the agency is mostly regional. At the moment we don't have any clients modeling in places like New York or Paris." Rachel didn't add that she'd once been Kevin's most successful client and had modeled all over the world, for most of the major designers. Eventually Moonlight Ventures would have that kind of profile again; they'd already had some of their clients cast for Hollywood projects.

"Liv… Olivia…" Simon hesitated for a moment. "My wife didn't want to be a clone of New York or Paris designers or of anyone else. She wanted to be unique and didn't care if a famous actress arrived on the red carpet in one of her creations."

"Yet you hired a designer from New York."

"Only because I didn't know where else to turn. Preserving the business for Livvie was desperately important to Olivia. It also connects Livvie to her mother. I *have* to keep Liv'ing Creations going for my daughter's sake."

It was a motivation that Rachel understood.

She didn't know much about Simon, though one of the Carthage residents had mentioned he was a successful businessman. But wanting to save the design house for his daughter—when it would be easier to sell or close the operation down—must mean he also cared about intangibles.

"I admire your goal," she said, "but I'm not sure what I can do to help. Are you trying to find models who might help turn things around?"

Simon sat forward in his chair. "Actually, I was hoping for your help in another way. I realize this isn't what your agency generally deals with, but I thought you could help address the situation at Liv'ing Creations. As a consultant."

Rachel didn't know what to think, though it was flattering that Simon believed she could offer something useful.

"I'm not a designer," she finally said. "I just shared a couple of comments. Why would you suddenly decide I might have answers your professional designer doesn't?"

"Because I trust my instincts. I don't know haute couture from a hole in the ground, but you might be able to recognize when a designer is creating styles that don't jibe with what Olivia was doing. I asked Janine Jenkins to study her work and try to emulate it, but I'm not sure she's done that."

"There's no guarantee I'd be successful," Rachel said gently.

"Maybe, but I can't tolerate the thought of Liv'ing Creations sliding into mediocrity."

Rachel gazed out her window, organizing her thoughts. In a way, Simon's idea was compatible with what Moonlight Ventures did—he wanted to hire talent. Besides, a number of young designers had come to the agency, hoping the partners' experience in the fashion world would help get them jobs.

"Is that all you want, for me to assist you in identifying a designer with a more colorful, innovative flair?" she asked.

"I'd also appreciate your opinion on other aspects of the operation. Any ideas you could offer might help."

Though Rachel sympathized, it seemed a big risk to offer advice on someone else's company when she was almost completely new to business in the first place.

"Frankly, I'm not sure I want that kind of responsibility," she said.

"The responsibility is mine. It will be my choice whether or not to agree with what you recommend."

That made it slightly easier, but it was still a lot to consider.

"I've reviewed the agency's blog and website," he continued. "The goals of Moonlight

Ventures seem clear—you want clients to perform at their best. Look at the design house in the same way."

"I'll need time to think about it," she said. "But there's something I want to say up front. You're here because of the remarks I made the other night, yet you got uptight when I made them. Are you ready for serious input, or would it simply frustrate us both? I'm not talking about taking my every word as gospel, but genuine listening."

A hot, dark emotion flickered in Simon's eyes. "Of course I'll listen. Can I take you to dinner tomorrow to discuss it further? We could also go by the design studio for you to look around."

Being able to investigate behind the scenes sounded interesting. Rachel had seen designers at work before, but had always wondered if they kept certain aspects of their designs hidden until the finished product was unveiled.

"No promises about accepting you as a client," she warned, "but I'd like to see the studio."

"Shall I pick you up here, or would you rather go home to change?" he asked.

"Work clothes are fine. It isn't a date."

SIMON HADN'T EXPECTED Rachel's calm, almost dismissive statement. He'd offered dinner without thinking, only to be immediately sorry in case she got the idea he had something in mind besides a professional arrangement. Truthfully, it had unsettled him to discover she'd picked up on his reaction to her observations of Liv'ing Creations. Either she was unusually perceptive, or he'd got sloppy about controlling his emotions.

"Is anything wrong?" Rachel asked. "You seem surprised about something."

Simon searched through his mind for an appropriate response. "Since my wife died, a few women have been aggressive in assuming I must be interested in them. They would have tried to turn a business dinner into something else."

Her lips twitched. "I thought that was a stereotype. You know, a widower being fair game."

"I'm not saying all women, just enough to make me wary. I doubt I'll ever get married again. It's too big of a risk." *A risk in every possible way*, he added silently. He'd been lucky to find Olivia and doubted that sort of good fortune could happen twice in a lifetime. Losing her had hurt more than he'd believed possible; if it hadn't been for Livvie, he didn't know what he would have done.

"You have my sympathy," Rachel said. "Everyone except my closest friends seemed determined to match me up with a guy after my divorce, and I didn't want to be matched. I've come to the very practical conclusion that friendship is better for me than romance, and it's worked great that way ever since."

If she was being genuine, then it was possible they could have a successful business relationship.

"All right, what time shall I be here tomorrow?" he asked.

"How about four? I'd prefer seeing the design studio first. That way we'll have more to discuss over a meal."

"That should work, because they close early on Fridays. I'll be here."

Simon left the agency, feeling encouraged. His decision to seek Rachel's advice about Liv'ing Creations had been pragmatic and logical, despite his attraction to her. Under other circumstances he would have avoided her as much as he could. But the design shop was too important.

There was somebody else he could consult, as well. While waiting for coffee one morning, he'd met Mark Revel, who had a first-floor condo at the Carthage. Mark had mentioned owning a clothing store that had once carried Olivia's designs. It was a reminder of how close the connections between people could be. Some people talked of six degrees of separation, but he often found it to be even fewer.

The downside of speaking with Mark was that Simon didn't want it known that Liv'ing Creations was struggling. If the news got around it could just make things worse.

THE NEXT AFTERNOON Simon arrived a few minutes before the agreed-upon time. The receptionist recognized him.

"Hello, Mr. Kessler. You can go directly back to Rachel's office."

"Thanks."

As he walked down the wide hallway, a woman was coming from the opposite direction. He recognized Nicole George. She was almost as beautiful as Rachel, though in a different way. While Rachel was ethereally lovely, Nicole was taller and exuded vitality.

"You must be Simon Kessler," she greeted him with a smile. "I'm Nicole George. Rachel told me about your interest in revitalizing Liv'ing Creations. I'm glad. Your wife was a wonderful designer."

"Er, thanks." Simon was faintly annoyed; the problems with Olivia's studio were his business, not to be shared. But he hadn't asked for confidentiality and it was natural Rachel would discuss the matter with a colleague. Besides, another opinion could be helpful.

Rachel's door was ajar and she stepped out. "Hello, Simon. I see you've met one of my business partners. Nicole and I have been coming up with a list of new, young designers we know who might be worth exploring."

"Excellent. Would you like to join us this evening?" he asked Nicole.

"Thanks, but I can't. My fiancé and I are…uh, having a conference call with our parents about wedding plans."

Little showed on her face, but Simon could tell it wasn't something she expected to enjoy. He also noticed Rachel's wince of sympathy, so figured there was a story behind the planned conversation. Or maybe not. He and Olivia had got married in Las Vegas, but he knew weddings could be stressful at the best of times.

Rachel locked her office and walked with him out to the parking lot. "I used alternate transportation this morning," she explained. "I assumed you wouldn't mind taking me back to the Carthage instead of returning here."

"That's sensible."

He opened the door and she slid into the passenger seat.

"Your colleague seems nice," he commented once he'd pulled out of the parking space.

"She is. I've been friends with Nicole, Logan and Adam for years."

"So you decided to go into business together."

Rachel shifted in her seat to look at him. "We were ready to make a change. For different reasons, I suppose, though we talked for a long time about starting a talent agency where we could pursue our individual interests."

"And what are those?"

"While we all have clients, Adam edits the blog and is making plans for developing a literary division for the agency. Nicole's specialty is teen talent, not only models, but actors and singers…that sort of thing. She recently placed a talented singer in a movie being shot up in Vancouver. Logan plans to work with both models and photographers."

"How about you?" Simon glanced at her, admiring the way every movement Rachel made seemed graceful and alluring. With difficulty he banished the thought—this meeting was business and had nothing to do with male-female attraction.

"I'm especially interested in clients who don't fit stereotypes of popular beauty, but have their own unique qualities."

"Aren't all advertisers looking for distinctiveness?" he asked, thinking it was ironic that a woman who looked like Rachel, and who was such a classic beauty, wanted to work with clients who were different in some way.

"Yes and no. There's a tendency for one type to become popular and suddenly everyone wants a version of it. But in recent years there's been an exploration of talent that's broader in scope." She laughed. "I should say a renewed exploration. It's cyclic, like the antihero in film and television or literature. You go through a period where a certain type is popular, then people start wanting something new."

It made sense. "Do the unique individuals get the big contracts?"

"Occasionally, though it's less likely, especially in modeling. People can find it challenging to recognize nontraditional beauty or good looks. But it's happening."

"Surely representing that sort of client isn't the most profitable choice for a talent agency."

Rachel cocked her head. "Perhaps, but we want to develop talent, whether it fits a certain mold or not. I never had the impression Liv'ing Creations was trying to compete with the huge designers, either. You said yourself that your wife wasn't interested in becoming a clone of other fashion houses. The same goes for Moonlight Ventures—we don't want to be a clone of other agencies."

Simon thought about his father's scorn at Olivia's lack of mega-aspirations. She'd laughed about it, unconcerned that her father-in-law had disapproved of her goals. "Liv used to say she wanted to fill a niche in the market, but didn't care about *being* the market."

"I would have liked your wife. It… Well, it must still be hard without her."

He managed a nod. Most of the time he could think about Olivia without being overwhelmed with pain, but it wasn't easy. "At least the pain no longer hits like an 18-wheeler the way it did at first."

Rachel straightened and stared through the windshield; her face seemed sad. "I'm sorry you lost what you had together. You were fortunate to have found someone like that."

"Thank you."

Strangely, for all the urging to "buck up," the platitudes and the sentimentality that had been poured over him, Rachel's quiet comment meant the most. Perhaps it came at the right moment, reminding him he *had* been fortunate. His life with Olivia hadn't been perfect, but perfection was overrated. They'd been in love and had enjoyed nine good years together, which was more than many people got.

He glanced at Rachel, whose face still wore a sad, distant expression. Her divorce must have been difficult since she claimed to no longer be interested in marriage or romance.

Simon recalled seeing something about the end of her marriage in various internet articles, though he'd skipped over the gory details. She'd overcome pain in a number of different ways; he admired that.

He fixed his gaze forward, frustrated that he kept thinking about Rachel in such personal terms. Even if he was willing to consider another long-term relationship, he simply wasn't ready.

Olivia was a ghost, haunting his heart and mind.

CHAPTER FOUR

RACHEL TOOK NOTE of several things as they walked into the reception area for Liv'ing Creations. The most interesting aspect was that it must have been redecorated during the past year.

"When did you redecorate?" she asked.

"How do you know we changed anything?"

"Because this place is as different from your wife's style as I can imagine. She had verve and originality. Now it's opulent and generic. Sorry, but those are the only words that come to mind."

Simon's mouth flattened into a straight line, but he finally shrugged. "You're right. I approved redecorating because the designer felt it was needed to keep up with the changing world of fashion. Except now I suppose it's generic decoration to fit a generic product."

"Some people may like that product. You

mentioned sales have dropped, but surely they haven't entirely vanished."

"We're still in the black. It's just that my gut tells me things aren't going the way my wife would have wanted."

Simon seemed to have a good business acumen, but this wasn't about making money; it was about saving something special for his daughter.

"Hello, Mr. Kessler." A woman had come out of the back room. "I didn't realize you were here."

"I'm showing an acquaintance around who's interested in fashion houses. I thought everyone would be gone since the shop closes early on Fridays."

"There were a few things I wanted to clear up."

Simon turned to Rachel. "Rachel, this is Miriam Timmons. She's the manager of Liv'ing Creations. Miriam, Rachel Clarion."

"Hello. Simon, I'd be happy to give Ms. Clarion a tour. You don't need to stay."

"That isn't necessary. Have a good evening. And weekend, of course."

Miriam seemed reluctant to leave. "Thank you. It was nice meeting you, Ms. Clarion. Is there any chance you used to be a model?"

It wasn't unusual for Rachel to be recognized by people, whether or not they were connected to the fashion industry, though she preferred anonymity.

"A long time ago. Now I'm a partner in the Moonlight Ventures talent agency."

"Really."

The look on Miriam Timmons's face wasn't especially friendly. Was she interested in Simon on a personal basis, or did she suspect the purpose behind the tour was his concern over how the shop was operating? Whatever the reason, she clearly wasn't thrilled when Simon firmly sent her out the door and locked it behind her.

Rachel gazed at a memorial photo on the wall with a tribute from the staff written beneath. While not traditionally beautiful, Olivia had been an auburn-haired, blue-eyed stunner, whose picture seemed to exude the same suppressed energy as her husband. They must have been exhausting to know as a couple.

"She looks so dynamic," Rachel said to Simon, who was also gazing at the large portrait. "I get the impression of tight springs, as if she was bursting to keep moving and even sitting still for a picture was hard for her."

He chuckled, though there was sadness in his face. "Liv had to do everything as fast as possible. Before we met, I thought I was the only one who was that driven. It was a struggle to make time for marriage and family, but we managed."

A wistful envy went through Rachel. Mutually demanding careers had also been tough on her and Hayden. In a way she kept wanting to blame the accident for her divorce, but she knew it had just precipitated the inevitable end. Their problems had begun practically from the day of their wedding.

It wasn't that she still loved him. The idea of love and partnership was appealing, despite her choice to stay single and focus on friendship. She was a modern woman, yet deep down she longed for the fairy-tale love she'd grown up hearing her grandmother talk about.

"Is something wrong?" Simon asked.

"No, of course not."

He hiked an eyebrow and she shrugged.

"I was thinking about the problem with

fairy tales. 'And they lived happily ever after' is really just the beginning of the story. Falling in love is easy, but staying in love and making things work is hard. You and your wife succeeded where a lot of people fail." Rachel squared her shoulders. "Enough of that. How about showing me where the designer does her thing?"

"Sure."

As they moved past the public area, Rachel studied what she could see of the operation. Sketches, fabric swatches, half-made garments. This was the heart of the process, where the creative production began.

When she tried to open a large wardrobe, she discovered it was locked.

"Are there valuables in here?" she asked.

"That's where Liv used to store her designs ready for production. I believe it's still used for the same purpose."

He took a key ring from his pocket. "Liv gave me this as a way of showing she trusted me. We got married rather quickly and it was kind of a wedding present."

Rachel grinned. "Does your designer know you have it?"

"Probably not. I've got the impression

she's slightly paranoid about her designs being copied, but I wouldn't give it to her, regardless."

Of course not. The key symbolized a relationship and it was endearing that Simon carried it with him more than two years after his wife's death. Hopefully it remained a working key.

He fitted it into the lock and it turned. "Let's see what secrets are hidden here," he whispered conspiratorially. "Maybe it's a dragon's lair."

Rachel hadn't expected the hint of whimsy. Perhaps, deep down, there was a little boy inside the stern man she'd seen so far. The doors opened to show a rack of clothes. She began pulling a garment out, then stopped. "Should we make sure they go back in the same order?"

"Frankly, I don't care. Under Janine's contract, her designs belong to the company."

One by one Rachel took the garments from the cabinet. The fabric was conventional and not unattractive, but far from distinctive. If possible, the clothes were even more blah than the last time she'd taken a look at a Liv'ing Creations collection. She didn't actually think another designer could capture Olivia Kessler's style, but surely someone could be found who'd use more color and innovation.

"What do you think?" Simon asked.

"It's more of the same," she admitted, deciding to be frank. If he didn't like what she had to say, he didn't have to hire her as a consultant. "A clothing designer may do something startling to be unique, which can work great for some people. But Liv'ing Creations made stylish and unusual clothing that everyone could enjoy. That probably doesn't make sense to you."

"I think I get what you're saying. What is your take on this collection?"

"Some of the designs are decent, even classic, but they're largely in the clone category. They should appeal to women who shop at department stores, wanting to look like other properly dressed midlevel business women, which often means not standing out or grabbing attention."

Simon gritted his teeth. "That definitely wasn't Liv's intention. How can it be fixed?"

"I wish it was as easy as pushing the designer to be more experimental with color and fabric. Besides, she might be planning to dress up these outfits with accessories we aren't seeing here."

He glanced at the clothes they'd taken from the wardrobe. "Would it make a difference to you if unique accessories were provided and you were shopping in this collection?"

"Not really and I think most women prefer to choose their own accessories. With these clothes, it's as if the designer you hired wants so badly to be successful that she's deliberately departed from Olivia's style and headed for the herd instead. How free a hand have you given her?"

Simon winced. "She had initial instructions, but after I hired Ms. Jenkins, I asked my business manager to stay in touch with Miriam Timmons. It's only recently that I've got more involved."

Of course. After his wife's death, he must have been far too distracted to pay much attention to anything.

"Then it's possible that Janine Jenkins actually *is* a department store clothing designer," Rachel said carefully.

"I'm afraid so. Miriam spent years working with Liv, so I thought it would be all right when she recommended a designer."

Rachel recalled the less-than-friendly expression in Miriam Timmons's eyes. Perhaps she was under pressure because the designer she'd suggested wasn't working out well.

They continued through the studio. Pushed to the back of storeroom shelves, gathering dust, were bolts of fabric Rachel recognized. "I have a dress made out of that one," she said, pointing.

"The colors would be great on you."

"Thanks. It's a shame such lovely fabrics aren't being used."

His words about the color had sounded like a compliment, but she doubted that was what he'd intended. This was entirely about business and there was nothing else between them.

SIMON CAUGHT HIMSELF watching Rachel as she sorted through the fabric bolts. He'd spoken without thinking, but she hadn't followed up with the kind of remark or attitude that might have turned it into a personal moment.

She tugged at a bolt on a high shelf and he helped lift it down, trying not to notice her curves or the faint, sweet scent of her perfume. It was an old-fashioned scent, with a hint of gardenias. Since that evening in the garden he'd often imagined smelling it out there, but she couldn't possibly be on her balcony every single time he was outside, too.

After examining the fabric, Rachel glanced over her shoulder. "*Kessler* is printed on the end of the bolts. Are they from the textile company you mentioned at Livvie's tea party?"

"Yes, produced to my wife's specifications. We'd just started making them for Liv'ing Creations when… Well, it wasn't an issue any longer. There's a warehouse full of the stuff and Liv left dozens of fabric patterns that were never used. What about having Janine substitute them, instead of the neutral fabric she's using now?"

The corners of Rachel's mouth twitched as if she wanted to laugh and was restraining herself. "I don't think it's that easy. The fabric patterns were probably for specific designs your wife had in mind. They would need to be combined in a creative, dynamic way."

Rachel took the lids from a number of dust-covered boxes and looked inside, her face growing more somber as she inspected the contents.

"What?" he asked.

"It looks as if they just stuck everything in here that wasn't finished."

"Out with the old," Simon added, grimly recalling something that had happened during a recent visit to the design house. Janine Jenkins had suggested creating her own label and changing the name of the company to JJ's Designs. He'd wanted to fire her on the spot. Now, after hearing what Rachel had to say, he was certain the designer had never intended to honor the commitment she'd made to emulate Olivia's unique style.

Anger filled him and he had to struggle not to reveal it. He was a businessman and expected people to do what they were paid to do, but what bothered him the most was Olivia's memory being disrespected. It was ironic. He'd never felt sentiment and business could coexist and yet here he was, willing to do everything possible to preserve Liv'ing Creations for his daughter.

"I'm sorry. It must be hard to have your wife…" Rachel stopped and Simon hated the look in her eyes—sympathy was bad enough, but pity was untenable.

"It is what it is," he said shortly. "Do you

think the half-finished designs should go into production?"

She shrugged. "It's hard to say. When the timing is right, offering them as a classic Liv'ing Creations collection might be a good idea. The original drawings for the designs must be somewhere. Designers don't work from nothing."

"Liv made extensive notes and story-boards of her designs, with views of the fronts, backs and each side. I don't know at what point she scanned everything into the computer, but I told Miriam not to discard anything without my authorization. So if they aren't in the computer records, the original storyboards had *better* be here."

Rachel nodded. "Good. If nothing else, Livvie might find a way to use them some-day. From what I've seen of her drawings, she's bursting with creative ability."

"She's going to be a designer like her mother."

A shadow seemed to cross Rachel's finely sculpted features. "She's young. Has that always been her ambition?"

"What do you mean?"

"Sorry, I shouldn't have said anything. It's

none of my business and I don't know the situation."

"You've opened the can, you may as well let the worms out," Simon said impatiently.

"Fine. I have a colleague whose parents wanted him to be a lawyer in the worst way. When he ended up with a career that didn't fit their image of a highbrow professional, they couldn't let it go. They nagged him for years about it. The family has resolved their differences now, but it was a long, painful process."

"I've never pushed Livvie to do anything," Simon insisted, offended by the idea. "She's the one who says she wants to design clothes like her mommy."

"As I said, I shouldn't have spoken in the first place."

This wasn't the first time someone had offered unsolicited advice about the needs of a child being raised by a single father, though the advice wasn't entirely unsolicited in Rachel's case. Apparently, she hadn't intended to say anything more than her initial words, but he disliked hanging statements or suggestive comments. In his opinion it was best to get everything into the open and deal with it immediately.

MATT TUPPER SUPPRESSED a yawn as he ran his fingers over the equipment and made minor adjustments. The Sound Worthy band was doing the final track for their single and it had been a long session. He'd have to call a break if it continued for another hour, because Pepper would need to go outside. Pepper had amazing control over her bodily functions, but Matt didn't think it was right to let her be uncomfortable, particularly in a week when she'd gone through the stress of vaccinations and her annual exam.

Luckily they were done ten minutes later. "Thanks for letting us do everything today," the lead vocalist told him. "The guitarist has a two-month gig with another band, six nights a week."

"It sounded good, Bernadette," Matt assured her. "I'll start the mixing and mastering tomorrow."

"Do you think you'll find any problems?" He heard strain in her voice. "I don't think we have enough money left in the budget for another recording session."

"I'm not anticipating any, but there wouldn't be a studio charge if I find a technical problem. The rest depends on how happy each of you are with your performances."

They were hoping to get a big record producer interested in their single. From what Matt had heard of them, he thought they had a better chance than some of the other singers and bands he'd recorded. One of the hard parts of his business was working with a group that seemed to be fooling themselves about their talent. He often felt bad about charging them, but who was he to stomp on someone's dreams? People had tried to do that to him when he lost his sight, and he'd proved them wrong.

Bernadette left to speak with the others.

A few minutes later, heavier footsteps approached.

"Hey, Matt, thanks for staying late." It was the guitarist. Matt's mental image of Eddie Harcourt was of a tall, skinny guy with long hair and a scraggly beard. The reality was probably quite different, but even before losing his sight he'd hear a person's voice and get an instant picture in his brain of their appearance. The same thing still happened, now with little chance of correction.

"You're welcome."

"I really wanted to do this recording,"

Eddie said, "but I couldn't pass up a pay-ing gig. Music gig, that is. My dad pays me to work at his company during the day. He says I'll never make it in music and should just give up."

"I suppose parents think they're being helpful when they tell us to take the safe road," Matt replied.

"Don't they remember what it's like to be our age? You can't get anywhere if you don't take a chance."

"They probably remember it in a differ-ent way."

And hate seeing their kids disappointed. Matt knew his folks felt that way. But there was more than one kind of disappointment, and surely it was better to give your dreams a shot and fail than not try at all.

The band left and Matt shut off the equip-ment. Last of all he called for the access van. The operator said it would take around forty-five minutes to arrive.

Pepper seemed eager to get outside, and they went to the grassy area the landlords had set aside for animals to do their business. After Matt took care of Pepper's "deposit," they walked up and down the sidewalk by the longest section of the building. The van driver knew where to look if they weren't in their usual spot. She didn't mind. As a dog lover, Vanessa understood both he and Pepper needed to stretch their legs.

Soft footfalls approached.

"Hi, Matt." The voice belonged to Nicole George. "You're here late tonight."

"A recording session went overtime," he explained.

"Your clients are fortunate to have someone so patient."

"Aren't you late leaving, as well?" he asked.

"Just trying to work down a backlog, though it's never completely done. But it's getting better with Rachel here."

His landlords were nice people. Not that the former owner would have sold the agency and building to anyone he didn't think would do a good job. Kevin McClaskey could be a pain with his desire to help everyone, but he was honest and loyal. Still, Matt appreciated not having to constantly defend his self-sufficiency with the new owners. Unlike Kevin, they respected the boundaries he set and didn't try to cross them.

"Rachel seems pleasant," he commented.

"She's terrific. By the way, she said to

let you know that she found someone with a great voice who's interested in volunteering to read books for the blind."

"I appreciate Moonlight Ventures keeping an ear out for volunteers."

"It helps some of our clients, too," Nicole assured him. "This way they get a professional credit, even if it's unpaid."

Matt heard footsteps that sounded like a tall man walking toward them.

"Hey, Jordan, I didn't expect to see you here," Nicole called. Jordan was her fiancé, and her tone was filled with the warm timbre of pleasure. "I thought we were going to call our folks at the house."

"I heard from your mother. She came down with a migraine, so we'll have to delay, since we need to speak to everyone as closely together as possible. I've already let my parents know we've postponed. Since we won't be talking to them, I wondered if you wanted an evening sail and dinner on the lake?"

"Sounds terrific. I'll follow you over to the marina. Night, Matt."

"Have a good evening."

Jordan said good-night as well, and Matt listened as their cars departed. Jordan and

Nicole seemed to be a good couple, though he didn't know them well. And now that they were engaged, Jordan came around often.

People in love did that sort of thing, though it wasn't something he knew from personal experience. So far, love had eluded him. Just as well. He kept a busy schedule and probably shouldn't add anything on top. Besides…when it came to romance, many women couldn't deal with him being blind. It wasn't a criticism, just reality.

RACHEL SPENT AT least an hour exploring aspects of the design house, but it wasn't easy to concentrate around Simon. She couldn't fault his behavior, but didn't appreciate the way his expression could turn hard and almost suspicious. While it might just be mixed feelings about bringing in an outsider to consult on his wife's creations, she suspected it was more.

Of course, you had to be wary in the business world, and she knew nothing about the forces that had shaped Simon's nature. Nonetheless, she felt on edge around him. Admittedly, part of it was a heightened awareness—he had an intensity, even a magnetism that pricked at her senses.

"Anything significant?" he asked as she looked through the current production notes they'd found in the studio.

"I'm hardly an expert, but there seems to be more concentration on cost cutting than top-quality design. That's the kind of business decision every company makes and might be in keeping with your instructions, but it doesn't fit with my sense of Liv'ing Creations in the past."

Simon actually chuckled. The humor lit up his face and made him appear almost joyful.

"Liv considered herself an artist first, and a businesswoman second." His smile faded and he frowned. "She'd hate a cheap product going out under her name."

"Not cheap, it's just that the choices always appear to bend toward reducing costs. For example, here's a note about two similar fabrics. One was preferred, but the other was chosen because the supplier offered a better deal."

His frown deepened. "I'm no designer, but that doesn't seem to be an artistic way to make a decision. Miriam must be aware

Liv'ing Creations isn't doing as well as in previous years, but I haven't asked her to cut costs, and my business manager would have consulted me before talking to her."

Rachel's feelings about Simon were mixed, but she appreciated the way he was holding on to the design house. A man who cared so much about his daughter and the memory of his wife couldn't be all bad.

Simon pointed to the fabric swatches attached to the notebook page.

"Which one would you have chosen?"

"My opinion isn't important," she replied. "It's more about the way the decision was made, not which fabric was best."

"In other words, you wouldn't have wanted either one."

She smiled ruefully. "No, but I'm not a designer, either. I just know what I like."

Another thing was certain, Simon was as smart as they came. Perhaps she should look him up on the internet. It wouldn't be out of line to do so. After all, he'd done research on her.

Suddenly she felt even more uncomfortable. Simon couldn't have looked her up without reading about the accident and the scars that had ended her modeling career.

Yet it wasn't logical to feel vulnerable. She'd grown accustomed to the way people seemed to search her face, as if to see where the damage had been done. Okay, she hadn't actually got used to it, but she'd stopped thinking it was the only reason they looked at her.

Rachel straightened her shoulders. Most days she didn't give a thought to the accident. She was happy. It would be impossible to feel grateful for what had happened, but she was thankful for the way things were now.

"Do you need to see more?" Simon asked.

She shook her head. "I've seen enough for the moment. It might be helpful to talk with members of the staff, too, but not if they're as defensive as the manager."

"Then let's go to dinner."

"That isn't necessary. I should think for a while before discussing my impressions."

"Come anyway. I've made reservations, and it's the least I can do in return for taking your time this afternoon."

The problem was that she didn't want to spend time with Simon; her awareness of him set her on edge. It was ridiculous. If she accepted the design house as an unusual sort of client, then she'd be seeing him even more often. Of course, that might be reason enough for not accepting the assignment. Then again, she'd never backed away from a challenge and wasn't going to start now.

"All right," she agreed, pleased with her decision.

CHAPTER FIVE

SIMON LOCKED THE door of Liv'ing Creations and turned toward Rachel. She stood with her back to him. Her dark hair was caught in a silver clasp at her nape and cascaded down her back in soft curls. The early-evening sunlight glinted against the burnished waves and it was one of the most appealing sights he'd seen in a long while.

He sucked in a breath.

Fortunately, he had a personal distaste for mixing business and pleasure…though admittedly, he'd never been seriously tempted before. He couldn't say he'd never found another woman attractive—marriage hadn't dulled his senses—but he would never have cheated on Olivia. He'd seen too much of the pain that infidelity dished out to its victims.

"That's an unusual clasp in your hair," he commented, walking to Rachel's side. "Native American, right?"

Her hand strayed to the silver clip. "Yes.

It's a style distinctive to the Hopi, but Navajo artisans are now doing something similar. I've always loved the artistry."

"I see you have several pieces," he said, noting her pendant and earrings. "They aren't as eye-catching as some Southwest jewelry I've seen, but the style is compelling."

"I agree. They aren't colorful, but they're very tactile. Even organic. Anyway, I wear things for me, not for other people."

Perhaps, but the jewellike color of the turquoise silk jumpsuit she wore was a perfect foil for both the jewelry and her fine complexion. He couldn't take his eyes off her.

"Something wrong?" she asked.

"Nothing, I just have a lot on my mind."

Back in the car he focused his attention on the road.

Fifteen minutes later, he parked at the restaurant and hurried around to offer a hand as she rose from the seat of the car.

A faint smile lifted the corners of her lips.

"What's so amusing?"

"Nothing, I was just thinking that it's a nice gesture, helping a woman from her seat. I appreciate thoughtfulness, especially with getting in and out of a low-slung car. Was your father old-fashioned?"

Simon controlled the visceral reaction that came with any mention of Richard Kessler. "What does he have to do with it?"

Rachel's expression turned cautious. "My dad says it's a father's responsibility to model behavior for his sons. He claims that even if it isn't a popular viewpoint, he'd rather err on the side of good manners."

"Perhaps, but my father has no acquaintance with courtesy *or* decent behavior, particularly in regard to women," Simon returned crisply.

"Oh."

"You don't have other questions?" he pushed, unable to resist prodding.

"None I plan to ask. It's your private business."

"Yet you wanted to know if my father was old-fashioned," Simon pressed, wondering why he was intent on prompting a reaction.

"I was just making casual conversation," Rachel answered. "But there was an edge in your voice when you talked about him, and I don't enjoy prodding old wounds."

In the early-evening light, her eyes matched the turquoise of her outfit. They were fringed with lush dark lashes that looked natural, and held no hint of guile. That proved nothing. He prided himself on being able to spot a cunning business associate, but then, he wasn't sure if his normal instincts were working for him when he was around Rachel.

"You've never heard of Richard Kessler?" Simon asked.

"Not that I recall. I assume he's your father."

"Yes. I met him for the first time when I was eleven. My mother had died two years earlier and I was living in a decent foster home when he decided to acknowledge me as his son. It didn't go down well with his wife. They'd just celebrated their twentieth wedding anniversary. Apparently they couldn't have children of their own." The bald explanation wasn't anything Rachel couldn't find on the internet, either directly or by inference.

Rachel nodded slowly. "It sounds as if your relationship with him went downhill from there."

"There's no love lost between us."

"Understandable."

Her head turned as she glanced toward the

lake, so it was even more difficult to guess what she might be thinking. Simon usually didn't persist this way. His father was a fact of life and there wasn't any point in bemoaning reality.

"Are you hungry?" he asked to change the subject.

"I didn't have time for lunch, so food sounds good."

As they headed toward the restaurant, another thought circled Simon's brain... Why had Rachel tried to cancel their dinner if she'd missed lunch?

He searched for something to say that would get his mind back in a business mode. "Becoming an agent seems like a major change from your previous career. For you and each of your partners."

Rachel shrugged. "Not really. We've all worked in the fashion industry. Also in Hollywood to a certain extent. And we have all had agents. Now we've just flipped our perspectives."

"Are you happy with the change?"

"That's an interesting way to put it...in terms of being happy. Mostly people have asked if I like my work."

"No deep psychological motives."

She smiled, and the way it lit her face was breathtaking. "Whatever it means, I *am* happy. That doesn't mean life is perfect, but I find more positives than negatives. Most of all, my work seems meaningful. I especially appreciate knowing I'm helping people succeed."

"That's why I thought you might be able to help get Liv'ing Creations back on track."

"I still haven't made up my mind about taking on the design house as a client," she cautioned.

"Right. You need time and I shouldn't have brought it up."

He held the restaurant door open for Rachel and saw a nod of appreciation.

Doing the gentlemanly thing had nothing to do with his father, who didn't have a chivalrous cell in his body. Nor was Simon trying to be the opposite of Richard. But Simon had once had a teacher who'd asked how he would have wanted his mother to be treated. The more he'd thought of his gentle, hardworking mom, the more he'd wanted to be courteous to other women in her memory.

The restaurant served excellent food, but Simon had chosen it because he didn't have memories of eating there with his wife. He could stay focused more easily if thoughts of Olivia didn't keep intruding. But he hadn't taken into consideration that restaurants often tried to create a sense of intimacy during evening hours. In the daytime this was an excellent location for business lunches; now it was the kind of place where couples came, either because they wanted to get closer or because they wanted to celebrate being in love.

And there was Rachel.

Her ethereal beauty made him think of old tales about fairies getting trapped in the human world, a bit of imagination his mother would have said was the Irish coming out in him. Whatever it was, he had to keep it under control while dealing with this particular fairy.

RACHEL SAW SIMON stiffen and his face regain a formal expression. Plainly it was the mask he used to put up barriers between himself and other people. Setting protective emotional perimeters was something she had experience doing, but she wasn't sure what had prompted Simon's withdrawal.

"This is pleasant," she commented as the hostess seated them.

"It isn't a family-friendly location, so I don't bring Livvie here to eat. Actually, I've never been here for dinner, just for professional lunches. The evening atmosphere isn't as businesslike as I expected."

"You're right, this definitely isn't a place for kids." Rachel eyed the delicate stemware and snow-white table linen. It was lovely, but if she had a young child or even a teenager, she'd see it differently.

"You mentioned your parents are caterers, so you have experience in the food industry."

"That's right. When I was a kid, I helped in the kitchen and with serving food."

"I didn't know kids could be employed."

She made a noncommittal gesture. "Mom and Dad followed the laws for minors working in a family business. When my grandmother was busy, we went with them. They made sure we had a place to study or play, but once I was old enough, I preferred helping. It also added to my college account."

"I see. The family that works together stays together." A hint of sardonic skepticism laced his voice and Rachel struggled to keep her expression neutral. She couldn't imagine living with someone who had such a negative view of the world. It made her wonder if his wife had shared his attitude, or simply had been very tolerant. At any rate, she felt bad for Livvie, who was going to grow up seeing other people through her father's jaded eyes.

"That's one way to look at it," she demurred, feeling she had to say *something*.

Given what he'd told her about his father, Rachel figured his childhood must have been really strange, and anyone else's life might seem alien in comparison. What would it be like to have a father who'd ignored you until two years after your mother was dead? She shivered. Not a pleasant thought.

The waiter arrived to fill their water goblets.

"Your youthful habit of saving sounds disciplined," Simon said when they were alone again. He opened one of the menus the hostess had left on the table.

"We knew we'd have to save and apply for scholarships since our parents couldn't afford to give us free rides through college. But they wouldn't have paid for everything, even if they'd had the money."

"Oh?"

"Sure." Rachel gave him a practiced

smile, the one she'd used as a model on photo shoots. "They believe you get more out of things when you have to invest in them personally. I didn't understand at the time, but I do now."

She glanced at her menu and then closed it. The waiter must have been watching because he appeared seconds after Simon had set his own menu aside. They ordered and Rachel looked at Simon, who still seemed to be mentally at a distance.

He cocked his head. "You think parents who give too much or make things too easy for their kids are doing the wrong thing?"

Rachel wasn't sure whether he had a personal ax to grind or was simply continuing the conversation, but wished she'd tried harder to cancel dinner with him.

"I suppose every parent has to decide that for themselves," she said carefully. "But isn't it a truism that we get back what we put into things? When we're invested?"

"I agree, though being *invested* has become a cliché."

"No question. In my parents' case, they helped us. They just didn't pay for everything."

"But did they use what they gave as something to hold over you?"

Now Rachel was certain a personal devil was behind Simon's questions. For a man who wanted to keep their relationship strictly business, he stepped into personal territory quite often. "No," she replied casually, "except we were expected to work hard and refrain from too much goofing off."

"That isn't unreasonable."

She didn't explain that in her case she'd been making plenty of money from modeling by the time her college years arrived. The threat to her grades had come from work assignments, not partying, but she'd managed to graduate. She'd also offered to help with her siblings' university expenses. Her parents had refused...out of pride, as well as for the reasons she'd already described to Simon.

Thinking about the prosaic past wasn't natural in this setting, anyway. Simon had alluded to the restaurant not being as "businesslike" in the evening as he'd expected. He was right. The understated lighting was designed to induce a romantic atmosphere. She didn't want to think in those terms, so she focused on the mechanics of how the atmosphere had been created. Lighting wasn't something her parents handled as caterers, but they'd talked about its impact on social interactions, mood and even the way food was perceived.

"You seem curious about something," Simon commented.

"Excuse me?"

"You keep looking around."

"I was interested in the way they've lit the place. Lighting has an unconscious effect on how people view food or other products, for that matter."

"Positive or negative?"

"Both, of course," she answered. "My folks say that bright fluorescent lights make people believe food is more economically produced, whereas subdued lighting enhances the opinion that it's gourmet. They have to be aware of the impact because customers might value the same menu completely differently, depending on how it's presented."

"Doesn't that bother them?"

"It's just the way things are. People are influenced without even realizing what's happening."

"Perhaps that's a life lesson," Simon suggested. "At the very least, being aware would help the rest of us avoid being conned."

She clenched her jaw. He was skating close to insulting her, her family and everyone in the food or advertising business.

"Someone isn't a con artist just because they present their product in the best way," she enunciated slowly and distinctly.

"I apologize. Your tone suggests I've offended you."

As she'd noted before, he was smart, although his IQ in human relations appeared to have hit rock bottom.

Rachel lifted her chin. "You can't tell me that as a businessman, you don't advertise and you don't have people put together catalogs and other promotional materials to represent your product at its best. Does that make you a con artist?"

His chiseled face was remote and hard. Then he smiled ruefully and her pulse fluttered at how compelling that made him.

SIMON KNEW HE'D been impolite. It might not have been so bad if he hadn't made his conned remark while discussing Rachel's parents and their work. Nor had it been fair. She was absolutely correct that quality food would be seen differently depending on how it was displayed.

The discussion was a reminder that he'd been schooled early in distrust and cynicism by one of the biggest con artists on the planet. How else could his mother have been taken in by such a jerk? Besides, there were plenty of victims who could testify to Richard's style in the business world. He was callous and utterly lacked a conscience.

"You're correct, of course," Simon acknowledged, hoping he sounded gracious. "As long as someone is selling a decent product, there is nothing dishonest in presenting it well."

Emotions flitted across her face, too fleeting for him to read. "It sounds as if you've been burned by enough con artists that you look at everything with a jaundiced eye."

"The man who fathered me was a con artist extraordinaire."

Rachel regarded him with an intense focus. Was she congratulating herself on getting him to open up about his father again? If so, she was wrong. When it seemed appropriate, Simon deliberately made his opinion of Richard Kessler very clear. He didn't approve of that kind of business practice, or want to be associated with someone who did.

"What was that look for?" he asked bluntly.

"I was thinking that it seems out of character for you to say something like that," she replied. "Even though you mentioned your father earlier, that comment seems particularly harsh."

"He casts a long shadow. I lay my cards on the table early so people know the score—I do business, but *not* his way."

"I never had the impression you were dishonest or ruthless, if that's what you're suggesting."

"At one time I *was* ruthless. That's how my father trained me to be, though I've never cheated anyone, which I can't say for him. But changing that aspect of myself doesn't mean I put up with anything. If someone tries to pull garbage, they get taken out, from a business perspective, of course."

"I see." Rachel paused to sip her ice water. "You know, you mentioned doing research on me, but I haven't had a chance to do any of my own on you."

He found it hard to believe, though it was possible that she'd been too busy to check him out. His instincts said she was basically

honest and he'd learned nothing to make
him believe otherwise. But he also kept reminding himself that his judgment wasn't
a hundred percent at the moment. While
he'd dated in New York, it had been mostly
as a distraction. Since meeting Rachel, his
awareness of women had reasserted itself
with a vengeance...or at least his awareness
of her had asserted itself.

Did that mean he was being disloyal to
Olivia's memory?

The thought bothered him. When she was
sick, they'd mostly talked about their hopes
for Livvie. He hadn't been able to envision
life without his wife, and would never have
asked how she'd feel about him moving on,
even casually.

"Do you regret not doing research on
me?" he prompted when Rachel didn't say
anything else and appeared to be studying
the fresh flowers on the table with undue
fascination.

She lifted her amazing eyes to him; in
the low light they appeared almost green-
ish blue.

"Yes. If I'd checked on you, I could have
saved us both some time. Frankly, I think
this may be a mistake. It was just such an

interesting proposal for a talent agent to take a fashion house on as a client. I was intrigued."

Simon gazed at the flowers himself as he sorted through what she was saying.

"Anyway," Rachel continued, "you asked me to give your idea serious consideration, but I'm not sure it could work out. Your primary—"

Simon's cell went off, interrupting whatever she'd started to say. It was the special ring he'd programmed for calls from the condo phone. "Sorry," he muttered, taking it from his pocket. "Normally I'd let it go, but this is from home."

"NOT A PROBLEM," Rachel murmured as Simon answered.

Clearly the caller was his daughter and he talked with her for a while, explaining "the schedule" she was supposed to be following. Their dinner salads were delivered while the conversation went back and forth, with Livvie apparently trying to negotiate an additional hour of television to watch a program coming on after her regular bedtime.

Rachel was getting a strong impression that the seven-year-old led a regimented life.

She knew kids needed routine, but how far should it go? Her own childhood routine had varied, subject to her parents' catering jobs. At the same time they'd also been very strict, while her grandmother had loved indulging her grandchildren—the classic situation of "if Mom and Dad say no, ask Grandma."

The corners of Rachel's mouth twitched as she recalled the hot-fudge sundaes and movie fests she and her siblings had enjoyed as kids. They'd all turned out okay, and she remembered her childhood with fondness. Surely a little indulgence wasn't the end of the world on a Friday night.

"What's so amusing?"

The question startled her; she hadn't noticed Simon getting off the phone.

"Just remembering something. Did you and Livvie come to a compromise?"

"My daughter may have finally figured out that I have a hard time saying no to her," he admitted. "Yet my wife wasn't a fan of television and I promised not to let Livvie watch too much. Now, about your agency being a consultant for the design house, can you tell me what your concerns are?"

It was a reasonable request. "I'm not sure that the ways we approach life and people are compatible." That was the diplomatic way of saying he was too cynical for her comfort.

He frowned.

"Please don't make a decision tonight. Remember that technically you wouldn't be consulting for me. You'd be consulting for Livvie."

Rachel wavered.

The way Simon had talked about his business dealings troubled her, yet she was already fond of Livvie, and a part of her wondered if she could genuinely offer something to Liv'ing Creations. Should she allow her mixed feelings about Simon to play a part in her decision?

Finally she squared her shoulders. "I'll give it more thought and let you know."

CHAPTER SIX

ON TUESDAY MORNING, Rachel glared at the computer screen after discovering Simon Kessler had made an appointment for later in the week.

She'd only had a few days to consider consulting for his late wife's design shop and didn't appreciate being pushed. Adam and Nicole were intrigued by the idea, but they were leaving the decision to her, perhaps realizing she was ambivalent about Simon.

Ambivalent?

Rachel almost snorted. Her research on the internet had shown Simon was an aggressive businessman. None of the articles she'd read suggested that he used underhanded tactics, but he was regarded warily, possibly because of his father. Richard Kessler's reputation was appalling. He'd gone to court for every imaginable financial offense, and it was considered a miracle that he hadn't landed in prison. Yet he was still wealthy and powerful. One interesting note was that he'd slid out of a few lawsuits supposedly through sheer charm alone.

A wry smile twisted her mouth. Plainly Simon hadn't inherited his father's charm. That was okay. She had trouble trusting people who were excessively charming—it made her wonder what they might be hiding, or if there was any depth behind the smiling face. In Simon's case... She didn't know what to think. He was like an injured grizzly bear, snarling and lashing out at the world.

The phone rang for the tenth time that morning, and Rachel answered to find one of her teenage modeling clients in an ebullient mood. "Please don't think I was trying to eavesdrop," Katie declared, "but I was getting coffee from the catering cart during a break in the shoot and heard someone say, 'We're getting her for our Christmas ad campaign.' Oh-mi-gosh, isn't that incredible?"

"Yes. I got a call this morning. They're offering an excellent deal," Rachel said. She hadn't contacted Katie earlier with the news, not wanting to interrupt filming on the furniture store ad.

Katie's excited shriek was so loud that

Rachel jerked the receiver away from her ear. She didn't want to spoil the model's excitement, but would have to look for an opportunity to warn the young woman not to get her hopes up over errant conversations. While it had turned out all right this time, that wasn't always the case.

"Calm down," she ordered firmly. "You have today's shooting to get through and don't want to mess up."

"I know, I know. I'll be careful," Katie said, still sounding excited. "Uh… I appreciate you getting me this job. You must know I wasn't thrilled when I got reassigned to you, but it's going great. Sorry about the way I acted in the beginning."

"You weren't that bad," Rachel assured her.

It was true. Besides, she understood how Katie had felt about getting a new agent so soon after signing a representation agreement with Moonlight Ventures. But it had been necessary for Nicole and Adam to redistribute part of their client lists now that another partner was full-time at the agency. Shifting new clients—with whom they hadn't already built a strong relationship—had seemed best.

"Ooh, gotta go," Katie said hurriedly. "The director gave us a fifteen-minute break, but I want to be the first one back."

Rachel was pleased. They didn't need their clients to develop diva traits, and being punctual was important. "All right. I don't know if I can make it to the set today, but have a good shoot, Katie."

"I will. Bye."

Rachel put the receiver down, cheered by the conversation. Her irritation with Simon had faded, though she wasn't any more eager to meet with him. She honestly didn't know what to make of the guy. He'd revealed intimate details of his childhood, but she didn't have a real sense of how it had affected him.

There's no love lost between us.

That was what he'd said about his father… a flat statement, his voice devoid of emotion, as if he was talking about the weather. Most of what she knew about Simon as a man, other than the bare facts he'd revealed, was from seeing him interact with his daughter. Of course, she knew he didn't want to get married again—he'd been very clear about that—though his comment about it being too big a risk was ambiguous. A risk? To what…his heart, his daughter's happiness, his bank account?

His bank account, Rachel promptly decided, then chided herself. Devotion to his wife's memory was one of the few things she felt certain about when it came to Simon Kessler. He probably just didn't want to take the risk of loving and losing again.

But he was still a cynical mystery. She didn't want to miss an interesting opportunity for the agency, but how could she agree to be a consultant for a man like that?

GEMMA CLUTCHED THE business card Rachel had given her and pushed open the door to the Moonlight Ventures talent agency. She saw a woman with dark hair busily typing at a computer to the right side of the reception desk.

The woman looked up. "Hello. I'm Chelsea Masters, the agency's office manager. Can I help you?"

"I'm Gemma Paulsen. Rachel suggested I come down to talk about volunteering for reading books."

Chelsea smiled. "She told me about you. I'll let her know you're here."

A few minutes later Rachel came into the

reception area. "Gemma, I'm glad you came. I called Matt and he'd like to meet you. I'll take you down there."

Glad that she wouldn't have to go to the recording studio by herself, Gemma followed Rachel outside. The day was beautiful, dominated by a brilliant blue sky and fluffy white clouds. With Livvie in school, she was usually free in the mornings. She'd been tempted to just walk down by the lake and read, but then she thought about how she wanted to do something different with her life. This seemed like a good beginning, if an unknown one.

Around the corner at the end of the building, Rachel led the way into another reception area. It had a totally different atmosphere. Rather than the refined elegance of Moonlight Ventures, there were photos of singing groups and book posters. Mismatched chairs were scattered around and the girl at the small computer desk had black spiky hair, black leather pants and a dragon tattoo down her arm.

"Hey, Rachel," the girl said.

"Hi, Sherrie. Matt is expecting us."

"Great. Go on, he's in the control room. I gotta keep working on these stupid invoices.

Man, I thought working at a recording studio was going to be so cool. Instead it's boring and lame."

Rachel winked at Gemma. "Don't let her fool you. She loves her job."

"Don't go around saying that," Sherrie ordered. "I want a raise."

Gemma laughed and tried to relax. They went down a hallway and Rachel knocked on a door marked Control Room. She opened it at a muffled "Come in."

A tall man was seated in front of an electronic board with all sorts of switches and things that Gemma didn't understand. It was a small area with a huge glass window that looked out onto a larger room with microphones hanging from the ceiling. A woman stood in front of one and gazed expectantly at the window.

The man wore headphones and seemed to be listening intently. After a minute he nodded and spoke into a mike on his instrument panel. "It sounds good, Bryce. We'll call it a wrap." Then he spun his chair in their direction. "Hey, Rachel."

"Hi. Matt, this is Gemma Paulson, the volunteer I told you about."

"Good morning, Gemma," he said.

"Hello. It's nice to meet you."

"The same here. Can you tell me a little more?"

"I...I'm not sure what you mean. This is kind of weird."

He shrugged. "You don't have to recite the Gettysburg Address. Just tell me something about yourself."

Hoping to calm her nerves, Gemma smiled. Matt didn't return the gesture and she wondered if something was wrong. "I, uh, was born and raised in Seattle. My folks live here and it's always been my home except for two years in New York. I'm a nanny, but I'm studying early childhood development. That is, I'm going back to college in January to finish getting my degree. It's taking a while. I have two brothers. My mom works part-time and my dad's job is in the aircraft industry." She stopped and looked at him uncertainly. "Um, how much more should I say?"

"That's enough. You've got a good voice. We'll get something recorded and see how you sound electronically. Just try to slow down and not talk so fast. Can you do the recording now? I had a cancellation this morning, which means my next two hours are free."

"That would be okay."

"Excellent." Matt turned toward Rachel. "Rachel, are you signing her as a client? I can make a CD for your files, if you like."

"That would be great. Gemma hasn't decided whether she wants to go in that direction, but in the meantime, we'll have the recording if it's needed."

It seemed surreal to Gemma that she might be hired simply because she had an okay speaking voice. Of course, she didn't want to give up on getting her college degree, but working as a volunteer shouldn't interfere.

"Then we're in business," Matt said.

Gemma thought he was nice-looking with his sandy hair and warm blue eyes. But it made her uncomfortable when his gaze seemed to pass over her as if she wasn't there. Maybe his eyes weren't as warm as they appeared, except he really *had* seemed pleased to meet her.

"See you, Matt," Rachel said. "Gemma, come by when you're finished. If you have the time. I know you have to work around Livvie's school schedule."

"Sure."

"Thanks, Rachel," Matt called as she left. "Gemma, let's get you set up in the live studio."

He reached for something behind him, and from underneath the table came a dog wearing a harness.

A guide dog.

Gemma drew a quick breath. So that was why Matt hadn't responded the way she might have expected: he was blind.

Feeling odd, she stepped through the control room door and waited as he emerged, his dog seeming to know where he wanted to go. Matt directed her to a microphone hanging down in the middle of the live studio and pulled over a heavy podium.

"I could help with that," she offered.

His expression tightened. "I've got it. Do you need a stool, or do you prefer to stand?"

"Stand. I've read you should stand when doing phone interviews because you sound more energetic and alert. The same must apply to reading aloud."

"You're right. When I signal, start reading from the papers on the stand. The mike is sensitive, so you don't have to be on top of it."

"Um, I brought a book if you'd prefer." Gemma held up her purse, then felt her face go red. He couldn't see her gesture.

"That's okay," Matt told her. "The material I've given you will give a good sense of your pronunciation and how you do with unfamiliar material."

"Oh."

He left, and a minute later she saw him re-enter the control room, though she couldn't hear anything. It was eerie. The live studio was utterly silent. He did something with some switches, then raised his right hand and waved. At the same time, a green sign lit up, saying On.

Trying not to think about being recorded, she started reading.

ON HER WAY back to the agency, Rachel stopped at the Crystal Connection for a cup of espresso. The shop was run by a tenant of Moonlight Ventures and sold an eclectic mix of goods that included fabulous coffee. Yet sadness permeated the air and Rachel was reminded that one of the owners, Eric Parrish, had passed away from a heart attack shortly after her own move back to Seattle. While his wife was considerably younger than Eric had been, she still must be around seventy.

"How is everything, Penny?" Rachel asked, generously stirring cream into her cup. She made the question intentionally vague, knowing Penelope might not want to be reminded of her loss.

"I'm managing. It helps that my granddaughter moved here a while back with her little girl. Imagine, me a great-grandmother!" Penny's smile was determined. "How did I get this old?"

"You aren't old, Grams," Jessica Parrish declared, coming out from the back room with a stack of boxes. "You're just well seasoned." Apparently it was a standing joke and the two of them laughed.

Rachel had frequently encountered the elder Parrishes when she'd flown into Seattle to spend time at Moonlight Ventures. They'd been a loving, devoted couple who'd spoken often about their family. Rachel had briefly met Jessica at Eric's funeral and got the impression that she was more standoffish than her gregarious grandparents. As she recalled, Jessica was a single mom, with a child around five or six. Perhaps that explained her reserve. Penny had mentioned her granddaughter was a wonderful mother, but proud and stubbornly independent.

Rachel's thoughts arrowed back to Simon. He was a single parent, too. In a way, raising a child might be easier for him since he had enough resources to hire a nanny, but he was still alone.

Simon's disdain for the women who'd chased him since his wife's death was impossible to miss, yet Rachel wondered if it was entirely deserved. Livvie was a wonderful child, highly intelligent, older than her years and anxious for love. Wasn't it possible that some of those women had genuinely believed she needed a mother and that Simon needed someone to draw him out of his grim solitude? She felt the pull herself, the desire to offer solace in the face of grief and loss.

Rachel shook herself and took a small drink from her cup.

She could be a friend to Livvie—as much as her father would allow—but must not cross a line.

"You made a face. Is something wrong with the coffee?" Jessica asked.

Rachel blinked. "Er, no. I was just thinking about a prospective client."

"Your thoughts couldn't have been very pleasant."

"They're mixed," Rachel admitted. "It's tricky whatever I decide, because he also lives in my building."

"Ouch." Jessica looked sympathetic. "I once did day care for a family in my old apartment complex. The situation didn't go well."

"Then you understand." It was on the tip of Rachel's tongue to suggest trying to set up a playdate between Livvie and Jessica's daughter… And she realized she was already at risk of stepping over the line she'd warned herself about. "Anyway, the espresso is great as always. I'd better get back to my office. Nice seeing you again, Jessica. Take care, Penny."

"You, too."

Rachel remained deep in thought as she returned to Moonlight Ventures. Having Gemma show up, interested in reading books for the blind, had been a welcome distraction from her deliberations about Simon. Gemma was interesting. She seemed quite shy, and Rachel wondered if there was a history behind the nanny's lack of confidence, or if it had always been an aspect of her personality.

It isn't your business, she reminded herself. She might have to address it if Gemma wanted to become a client, but not before.

Rachel sat at her desk, determined not to allow Gemma's boss to interrupt her day any further. Well, except to consider ideas for the design house. As she sipped her coffee, she added to the notes she'd made, though it was partly a list of pros and cons about accepting Liv'ing Creations as a client. No matter what Simon said about it really being for Livvie, she'd be dealing with him—a seven-year-old child didn't make business decisions. But was Livvie too young to have any creative input? It seemed so, but she couldn't assume.

After an hour or so, Gemma returned to the agency, her face pink with excitement.

"How did it go?" Rachel asked.

"Okay. I'm coming in on Saturday morning to start recording a novel printed by a local publisher. Matt seems awful nice. He said to give you this." She handed a CD case to Rachel.

"I'll put it in my file. If you decide to try picking up extra work as a voice artist, we'll be almost ready to go."

"I can't believe people would want to pay just to have me, uh, talk."

Rachel grinned. "You'd be amazed at how much work there is for voice artists—radio ads, voice-overs for television, documentaries, all sorts of things. I'm not saying you'd necessarily earn a living, just have the potential to earn extra cash."

"That doesn't matter. I don't want to leave my job."

"Of course not. Taking care of Livvie must be a delightful way to earn a living. She's such a sweetheart."

"She is." Gemma's voice was fervent. "Um, I didn't realize that Matt was blind at first. It was only when I saw his guide dog that I figured it out."

"To tell the truth, I don't think of him that way. He's just Matt. He lost his sight when he was a teenager—some guy lost control of his car and hit a group of teens. Most of them were pretty lucky, but Matt had damage to his optic nerve. As for Pepper, she's a beautiful animal and I always want to give her love, but I have to resist when she's on duty."

"I know what you mean. She's the prettiest golden retriever I've ever seen. Matt obviously takes great care of her." Gemma shifted her feet. "I'd better go. I have some things to do before picking Livvie up at school."

When Rachel was alone again, Simon inevitably wandered back into her thoughts. Hopefully she'd hidden how attractive she found him, his sardonic qualities notwithstanding.

There had been something in Gemma's tone when she'd mentioned Matt that suggested she found him attractive. The young woman was unguarded enough that she didn't even realize what she could be revealing.

Rachel remembered when she'd been as unguarded as Gemma. She wasn't that much older, but it seemed like forever ago.

MATT USED THE remainder of his unexpected break to work on mixing and mastering the Sound Worthy band's new song. His concentration wasn't at its best, though, and his thoughts kept returning to Gemma Paulsen.

She had a terrific voice, low-pitched and well modulated. Once she'd started reading his sample material, she had relaxed, slowed down and got absorbed in the short story. *An instinctive oral storyteller,* he'd concluded, the kind who drew the listener in because she sounded genuinely interested in the tale herself.

On the other hand, Matt hadn't appreciated the offer to help move the podium, as if his inability to see made him incapable of simple tasks. It was possible her initial reticence might have stemmed from not knowing how to act around someone who was blind. That was a common situation—after all, nobody was required to take classes on the subject.

Matt reached out a hand and Pepper got to her feet, yet she seemed to understand he was just offering affection.

"You always know what I want, don't you?" he murmured as she pressed against his leg and put her muzzle on his knee.

He stroked her neck, searching for the spots she liked best.

His family claimed Pepper rarely took her gaze off him, always watching in case she was needed. And he knew that if he stepped away by himself, she quickly got restless and came looking, as if she was worried he couldn't manage without her.

"Why is your protectiveness okay, when

anyone else's drives me crazy?" Matt whispered.

Pepper let out a faint whine and nuzzled his hand.

"I know, girl."

She grew anxious when he was moody. He wasn't even sure what had put his tail in a twist, though he suspected it was Gemma Paulsen. From her voice he'd got a mental picture of an attractive young woman, probably close to his age…and thoroughly uncomfortable. He'd been tempted to say if she was *that* uptight around a blind guy, she could donate her time elsewhere—he wasn't a charity. But he hadn't, partly because Pepper had liked her. The golden retriever was a good judge of character and it was clear when she didn't trust someone.

Blast.

Matt removed his headphones, annoyed with his lack of focus. He shouldn't care whether Gemma was uneasy around him, or why she'd volunteered to be a reader. His goals were to make a living and help make books from local presses available to people who were blind or sight impaired.

That was all.

CHAPTER SEVEN

RACHEL COULDN'T GET to sleep that night and finally went out to her balcony with the notepad she'd been using to keep notes about Liv'ing Creations. She scribbled a few additional thoughts, but soon turned off the light and just stared at the view. Moonlight sent a soft glow across the lake's surface and the effect was achingly beautiful.

It was also romantic, but she hastily reminded herself that she wanted to deal with reality.

After another hour she went to bed, forcing herself to relax and finally sleep. In the morning she retrieved the notepad, which had got damp from falling dew. She set it on the kitchen counter to dry while she ran next door to the Java Train Shop.

"Hello, Rachel," Simon said, stepping behind her in the line of people waiting to order.

Hmm. Perhaps she should switch to tea

for her morning wake-up juice. Tea was something she could easily make in her own kitchen and she wouldn't risk running into Simon Kessler while doing it. Still, he was there and unless she sold her condo and moved, she was going to encounter him occasionally, whether or not he became a client.

Rachel straightened her shoulders. "Good morning, Simon. How are you?"

"Fine. I planned to call later to see if you were okay with the appointment I made. Have you had enough time to process your impressions about the design house?"

"I've been making notes, but something has come up for tomorrow morning. Chelsea planned to contact you today about it."

"Now she won't have to." A muscle ticked in his jaw. No doubt he wasn't accustomed to following someone else's timetable...or having calls delegated to an office manager.

The line moved forward and Rachel turned toward the counter, pretending to study the menu mounted on the wall.

"Actually, there's something else I'd like to discuss," Simon said, interrupting her thoughts.

She swiveled, wincing as the motion caught her leg the wrong way. "Yes?"

"Gemma mentioned you'd arranged for her to do volunteer reading for the blind, and maybe the possibility of paid voice work in the future?"

"That's right," Rachel agreed. If he objected, he'd get an earful about what was his business and what wasn't.

"Is it a healthy situation for her? While Gemma's my employee, I've known her since she was eighteen and care about her welfare."

Rachel narrowed her eyes. "Do you honestly think I'd get her into anything I didn't think would be safe?"

"It isn't that," Simon denied, "but she had a difficult childhood and I don't want her hopes raised if things don't work out."

Still angry, Rachel met his gaze squarely. "This is a public location and hardly the right place for this discussion. But I'd like to know…if you don't trust my judgment, why would you ask me to consult on the design house?"

A hint of chagrin crossed his face. "I apologize. That was stupid and officious."

"You got that right."

A voice came from behind her. "Your usual, Rachel, or do you want to be adventurous?"

Rachel turned and nodded at the barista. "No adventure today, Palmer. My usual espresso, thanks."

She handed over the travel mug she'd brought and waited for it to be filled. When it was returned, she nodded at Simon and walked out of the shop.

"Wait." He caught up with her.

She gestured at his empty hands. "What about your coffee?"

"I'll get some later. Look, I shouldn't have brought up Gemma." He ran his fingers through his brown hair. "I'm not even sure why I did."

"You don't need to worry," Rachel told him crisply. "I've made it clear that it's hard to make a living doing voice work, so I doubt you'll lose your nanny because of me."

"I wouldn't stand in Gemma's way if she wanted to do something else."

"Glad to hear it. Livvie won't need a nanny forever. Good nannies are in demand, but there's no guarantee Gemma can get another position when the time comes. Or that the job would be what she wants."

Simon's expression turned harried. "I realize that. Originally it was only going to be until Livvie was in school. But things changed."

Plainly he was referring to his wife's illness and death, and Rachel nodded. The situation was hardly normal and it wasn't as if Gemma was miserable. Simon seemed to treat her generously and she loved taking care of Livvie.

Besides, Rachel knew it was none of her business. She just had a fix-it mentality. As a makeup artist she'd listened to people talking about their lives and careers. Sometimes they'd paid her the compliment of saying her questions or suggestions had benefited them.

And now she was an agent, in the business of helping people succeed. Yet she needed to be wary of helping *too* much. It was a trait Kevin McClaskey possessed in abundance, something she'd experienced when he'd represented her as a model. Kevin was a special guy, which was one of the reasons she'd been so pleased when she and her partners had bought Moonlight Ventures from him, but she also knew the importance of taking care of herself.

Independence was like a muscle that needed to be regularly flexed.

SIMON GAZED AT Rachel's face as various emotions flew across her features. He wanted to get a handle on what made her tick. That way he might be able to keep his thoughts about her in a manageable category in his head.

"You have an odd look in your eyes. What are you thinking?" he asked.

"That I need to control my impulse to fix things for other people."

"I don't need fixing." The denial came out more harshly than intended. As a kid, a number of people had figured he needed help because of his strange childhood. Lately it was more about encouraging him to "move on" now that he was a widower.

"I never said *you* needed fixing," Rachel said tartly.

"Perhaps, but that's what many people have meant when they said something similar."

"And you have a habit of jumping to conclusions, especially about the opposite sex. Most of us need something fixed in our lives, but my comment had nothing to do with you. What you need, no one can fix, because no one can bring back what you've lost, and if they could, it still wouldn't restore the past because you've become a different person."

"What do you mean?"

"Our experiences change who we are. You've gone through the loss of your mother, a hard childhood and now the loss of your wife. You're a different person because of it. You have to build something new without Olivia, because life can't go back to the way it was."

"You seem to have done a lot of thinking about me and my situation."

Rachel's brilliant blue eyes opened wide. "Don't flatter yourself," she advised in a dry tone. "I was simply applying what I've learned from my own experiences. Once upon a time I used to keep thinking about everything that's happened to me and what I'd lost. I dreamed about getting it all back. Life got easier when I accepted that both the world and I had changed, and my only choice was to move forward."

Simon wondered if she was subtly suggesting he sell the design house and allow his wife's legacy to become no more than a memory. But he didn't ask if that was what she meant—she'd probably retort with something even stronger than *don't flatter yourself.* Most likely it would be an accusation of massive arrogance. And she'd be right—after all, why should everything she said be a special message directed at him?

For the first time he tried to see himself from Rachel's point of view, and it was humbling to realize he might not seem like such a prize. She was beautiful and talented and could probably have her pick of Seattle bachelors. But what had she said, that friendship worked better for her?

"I suppose with Livvie you don't have much choice except to move forward," Rachel added. "She's a growing child with new needs and interests."

A rueful sensation swept through Simon. "In a way, but I've discovered Livvie is huge on tradition. I can't tell you how many times she's explained that we can't change how we do something, because that's how we did it when Mommy was here. The Christmas tree is a prime example. Liv loved fresh evergreens and wanted to put a tree up the day after Thanksgiving. Do you know how dry those things get after a week or two?"

Rachel winced. "Yes, even when they're new cut."

Instead of standing and talking, they'd somehow begun walking together toward the lake.

"I suppose tradition is in a special category of its own," she continued. "Doesn't it become a living part of the present?"

"In a way, but what if it stands in the way of making new memories and traditions? I hate hearing people say you need to move on when you've lost someone. At the same time, how healthy is it for children to stay stuck in the past? It's one thing for me to know Liv was the love of my life and to choose my memories over something else, but I don't want my daughter to think her best days ended when she was five years old. Or to believe when she takes over her mother's business someday, she can't make it what *she* wants because she has to keep doing everything the way Liv did."

The words burst out, astonishing Simon. Since losing Olivia, he hadn't discussed his parenting woes with anyone. In fact, he kept everything to himself; in the beginning he'd even done that with Olivia. Perhaps the relationship had worked because she'd been the same—instead of getting angry and frustrated, they'd forgiven each other for any failures to be open.

"Never mind," he said gruffly. "We're having to adjust to being back in Washington. I just didn't expect it to be this hard." He looked away at the lake, not wanting to see sympathy in Rachel's eyes. He didn't feel sorry for himself. He wasn't any different from other parents who were worried about their kids and the future.

"What about joining a support group for single fathers?" she asked in the silence. "It might help to hear how someone else is handling various parenting questions."

A support group?

Simon shuddered. Not a chance. If he'd struggled to confide in Olivia, he couldn't imagine discussing anything with strangers. The same with a grief counselor. Gemma had suggested one not long after Olivia's death, but he didn't need anyone explaining the "stages" of grief and advising him how to deal with them.

"I appreciate the suggestion," he muttered, "but I'm managing. The question of Christmas trees is on my mind because Thanksgiving comes early this year, which means the tree will be up for a longer time than usual. Dousing it with fire retardant is an option, but I also dislike bringing chemicals into the house."

Rachel nodded. "At least we have the overhead fire sprinkler system at the Carthage. I thought it might seem too industrial, like a hotel room, then discovered it gave me peace of mind."

Simon was glad to have the discussion shift to something less personal. "I feel the same way. The Carthage is a solid building. Old, but retrofitted to the highest standards. I had it checked out before buying our condo."

"Me, too. And I love this little town, though I'd prefer to be even farther out of the urban area, maybe up in Enumclaw or Buckley."

He cocked his head. "Then why did you choose the Carthage?"

"I just thought it would be easier with my… With everything. And the commute is better this way."

Her hesitation made Simon wonder what "everything" might be, but he didn't want to pry. They reached the lake and he tried not to envy Rachel's travel mug of coffee.

It was his own fault for walking away from the barista waiting for his order.

Her eyes suddenly twinkled and she held out the mug. "I have a feeling you need this more than I do. Besides, I try not to drink coffee more than two or three days in a row before taking a few off. This is my fourth day, but I went to the Java Train Shop this morning without thinking."

"I couldn't," he protested.

"Of course you can. You aren't in danger of getting cooties from me…if that's your concern. I haven't drunk any, and the cup was clean." Humor danced across her face.

Cooties?

He hadn't heard that expression since he was a kid and had nothing worse to worry about than imaginary germs.

"I'm not five years old, so I don't think cooties are an issue," he returned with a grin.

Rachel had gone from outraged indignation to sympathy to poking fun at him in just a few minutes. It was reassuring that she didn't seem to hold grudges. Wasn't that what friendship should look like?

"But you're probably right about it being healthy to limit caffeine intake," he added.

"In that case, I'll just pour this out."

Simon grabbed for the cup as she began unscrewing the lid. "That's all right. It would be a shame to waste good espresso."

Her laugh sent warmth coursing through his bloodstream. The sound was musical and he suddenly recalled an Irish folktale his mother had once told him. It had been about a fairy caught in the human world, her memory of fairyland gone. Then a simple soul came along with no better sense than to fall for her.

Shaking the memory away, Simon gulped the coffee down. He usually drank his black instead of with cream, but it was strong, unsweetened and tasted great.

"Is the Seattle area very different from New York?" Rachel asked after a quiet minute. The silence had been curiously companionable. Even restful. "I've visited New York many times, but never stayed long enough to have a real sense of the city."

He shrugged. "I prefer the weather here, but I needed to get away. We came back because it was what Livvie wanted. I bought a new place because I couldn't see moving into our old house. This one is better, anyhow—close to the lake and with more square footage."

"You have a nice outdoor garden for her."

"She likes it."

They'd turned and were making their way back to the Carthage. Ahead he saw Livvie and Gemma heading their direction.

"Daddy," Livvie cried, racing forward.

Simon pulled her close. An hour earlier they'd passed in the hallway by her bedroom and she'd given him an enthusiastic, if sleepy, good-morning kiss. It always melted his heart to know she was so happy to see him.

"Hi, Rachel." Livvie twisted in his arms to lean over and smacked Rachel's cheek. She smiled warmly in return.

"It's nice to see you, Livvie." Rachel snagged her mug from his hands. "I'd better take this, you've got an armful."

"Daddy, did you and Rachel eat breakfast together?" Livvie asked.

"No, we ran into each other at the coffee shop."

"Oh. Gemma made Mickey Mouse pancakes and they were really good. She made enough for you, too, but now they're cold."

"Sorry, sweetheart. Rachel and I forgot the time. Aren't you supposed to be in school?"

"It's an in-service training day for the teachers," Gemma explained.

"That's right, I forgot. Go ahead on your walk. I'm going to be late for work if I don't get moving."

"Okay." Livvie hugged him hard again, and he set her down. "Bye, Rachel. Bye, Daddy."

Gemma took her hand and they continued toward the lake. He should have remembered it wasn't a school day for Livvie and arranged something special to do with her. Ironic. He'd protested that his life didn't need any fixing, but in all honesty, he *did* have broken areas, including tunnel vision about his work responsibilities. The last thing he wanted was to inflict them on his daughter. Making time for her was important.

"Is something bothering you?" Rachel asked.

"I was just thinking that I should have planned a treat for Livvie, such as a trip to the Seattle Center with just the two of us. But I've got meetings scheduled and didn't think ahead."

"You could still take her to a big-girl lunch. Surely it wouldn't take too much time."

"That's a good idea." He shook his head.

"So, earlier you were saying that everyone needs some sort of fixing?"

Rachel chuckled. "Sure. No family is completely functional, no job is perfect and Elvis isn't coming back in the near future."

Simon decided to play along and let go of his darker mood.

"What if you're wrong about Elvis?"

"Then I'll dust off my blue suede shoes and buy a ticket to his first concert. In the meantime, I have a new client who is a bona fide Elvis impersonator. He sounds just like the King and blends music with humor. I've already got a booking for him—four weeks, five nights a week. He starts tomorrow."

It wasn't the sort of thing Simon normally enjoyed, yet he was intrigued. "Maybe I should see his act. Where is he performing?"

"At a comedy club in downtown Seattle. I'm going to his first show tomorrow night. If you'd like, we can attend together and talk about Liv'ing Creations. That way I'll have today and tomorrow to finish organizing my thoughts. Still no promises, though."

"That's fine. When do you want to leave?"

"How about meeting me at seven thirty, in the garage by my car? I drive a silver Toyota Camry."

Simon suspected Rachel was the type to arrive early and wait for him. There wasn't much crime around the Carthage, but he still didn't like the idea. "Maybe it will be better if I come by your place."

"If you prefer."

GEMMA HAD BEEN surprised to see Rachel and her boss together. Was it possible they were getting involved? It seemed unlikely. Rachel was very different from Olivia Kessler. Besides, Mr. Kessler didn't want to get married again. He'd talked about it one night, soon after they'd moved to New York. She'd stayed up late to read, then gone into the living room of the apartment to find him staring into a half-full brandy snifter.

As far as Gemma knew, it was the first and last time he'd consumed enough alcohol to become even slightly intoxicated.

"This isn't much of a painkiller," he'd told her, rolling the amber liquid around in the snifter. "It hasn't changed a thing except cause a headache."

At first Gemma had been alarmed, remembering the times her dad had got drunk and angry and loud. Then Mr. Kessler had gone to the kitchen sink and emptied the snifter and bottle.

"My daughter deserves better than having me like this," he'd said. "It's just that Livvie's private tutor told me today, oh, so delicately, that I might consider getting remarried. Nobody can keep their noses out of my business, but I don't want another wife, and the busybodies of the world may as well get used to it."

If he'd been her brother, Gemma might have hugged him, but that wouldn't have been right to do with her employer, so she sat down and listened to him talk about Olivia. After that he'd gone to work in his home office, while she'd returned to her book. Nothing like that had happened since then.

She and Livvie walked by the lake and played with her motorboat before going back to the condo. Mr. Kessler had left for work, but there was an envelope on the door addressed to Miss Livvie Kessler. Inside was a letter.

My beautiful daughter,
Would you do me the honor of being my guest at lunch today? I can pick you up at noon.
Daddy

"Ooooooh," Livvie cried. "I want to get all dressed up."

"Of course," Gemma agreed. "Let's go choose something right now. One of your really special dresses."

Gemma loved her job, especially at moments like this, when she saw a father acting the way she'd dreamed her own father would act someday. Her dad loved his family, but his affection was usually drowned by alcohol. And no matter what, her mother just made excuses.

A sigh welled up from Gemma.

If she ever met the right guy and got married, she didn't want someone with big problems or someone who was fighting personal demons, who might try to find a solution through booze. She wanted a man who was decent and kind, who'd put their marriage and family first.

Surely that wasn't asking too much.

RACHEL FOCUSED ON her computer, typing and organizing her notes about Liv'ing Creations. She entered the list of designers that she and Nicole had come up with, thinking a casual comedy club might be the best place to talk with Simon. An office seemed a sterile environment for something as creative as a design house.

Funny, she'd almost decided against accepting Liv'ing Creations as a client, especially after the way Simon had annoyed her at the Java Train Shop. Honestly, his ego was enormous. But then he'd revealed an aching vulnerability. Angst over the safety of a Christmas tree versus his daughter's memory of her mother? It was endearing. As for the way he worried about his daughter getting stuck in the past? She could have cried.

Simon Kessler was a complicated man, with edges as sharp as carbon steel knives, alternating with soft spots that could seduce a woman into thinking those edges weren't that dangerous.

"Rachel?" Adam's voice said, breaking into her thoughts.

She looked toward the door. "Hi, Adam. Is something up?"

"Sort of. I've been meaning to ask if you'd be interested in representing Tiffany and Glen Bryant? The twins are easy to work with and I'd transfer all agency residuals to your account."

Rachel hadn't expected the request. His fiancée was the twins' guardian and Adam might not have met Cassie if her niece and nephew hadn't become his clients.

"You don't want to continue as their agent?"

"Their careers are booming, but it might be best for someone else to take over since I'm no longer impartial. Better for the agency, too. Cassie is fine with me continuing, but I'd prefer just taking care of them as my family."

It was understandable that he wanted to simplify the relationships with his family-to-be and Moonlight Ventures. Things were already convoluted because his fiancée had designed the agency's website.

"In that case, I'd be happy to represent Tiff and Glen," Rachel assured him. "How is the house hunting going?"

"We're looking for a place outside the city that won't be a huge commute. For me, that is. Cassie runs her business from home."

Rachel grinned. "I can't imagine you living in a small town. You were the one who couldn't wait to get a place in the heart of Seattle, while Nicole and I wanted something less urban."

Adam grinned sheepishly. "It's a compromise since Cassie used to dream of living in the mountains. Anyhow, this way we'll have the advantages of small-town life and still be able to enjoy what Seattle has to offer."

They chatted another few minutes, and then he left to meet with a prospective client. Rachel opened the agency files on Glen and Tiffany Bryant to study their profiles and the jobs they'd got to date. They were going to be busy since the TV pilot they'd appeared in had been picked up as a mid-season replacement series.

After a while she sat back, unable to stop picturing the happiness in Adam's face. She was really pleased everything was going so well for him. He didn't seem anxious about becoming an instant father figure for Cassie's niece and nephew, though it couldn't be easy with teenagers.

Instant parenthood would probably be simpler with a child Livvie's age.

Rachel bolted upright. *No way.* She didn't have any business with idle musings about Livvie, because they might lead to musings about Simon.

He was a potential client, and that was all.

THE NEXT EVENING Rachel was ready to leave immediately when Simon knocked at her door. Fortunately, the club wasn't that far away and they got a table toward the back.

The show started and went on for nearly thirty minutes.

"I'm impressed," Simon said after the last song. "He's funny and looks and sounds the part. Why didn't he want to do a strict Elvis impersonation, without the comedy routine?"

"Elvis impersonators are relatively common, so Nelson decided to mix it up with humor." Rachel handed Simon a sheaf of papers. "Here are the notes I've made about Liv'ing Creations. Why don't you take a look while I say hello to my client?"

Standing, she made her way toward a curtained door, though she couldn't resist a backward glance to see Simon reading the notes, his brow furrowed in concentration.

She'd already noticed a couple of women gazing at him appreciatively, and now one of them leaned toward him and said something. Simon's response must have been chilly, because her bright smile vanished and she turned back to her two female companions.

With a sigh, Rachel continued to the backstage area and found Nelson in his dressing room.

"Great job," she said.

"It was awesome," he declared. "I didn't realize a comedy club would be okay with me singing, too, so it never occurred to me to audition at one. That's what getting an agent does for you. Do you think I might get a gig in Las Vegas someday?"

"Time will tell," Rachel returned lightly.

She couldn't make promises, particularly with such a specialized performer. Nelson had one interest and one interest only, *the King*. "In the meantime, I'll leave so you can focus on your next show," she added.

"Okay. Thanks."

Back at the table, Rachel found Simon with a steaming cup of black coffee.

"Do you expect to sleep tonight?" she asked, gesturing to the cup.

"Probably not, but I didn't want to order a beer or wine. Or a soft drink."

The server approached again and Rachel told him she'd have a mineral water with a twist of lime. Unlike Simon, she hoped to get some rest that night, and even decaf coffee had a fair amount of caffeine.

"Your notes are excellent," Simon said when they were alone again. "So, are you interested in becoming a consultant for Liv'ing Creations?"

Rachel had halfway hoped that he'd look at her material and decide he didn't needed her services, or that they'd be enough to nudge him in the direction he wanted to go. Part of her wanted to accept the project; part of her believed it wisest to stay away from him.

But she threw back her shoulders and nodded. "I think it would be interesting."

CHAPTER EIGHT

RACHEL HAD ENDLESS second thoughts about working with Simon that kept her from sleeping well for the next two nights. Through the years she'd met people from all walks of life, but she'd never met anyone like Simon Kessler. How could she deal with someone who could twist her emotions so easily?

Sunday morning dawned blustery and cold, the kind of exhilarating autumn day she'd missed when living in Los Angeles. She yawned, hoping the storm wouldn't blow too many of the fall leaves from the trees. It was before the full peak of autumn color, so maybe she'd still be able to head over to the University of Washington. She loved wandering around the campus when the fall colors were in full display, scuffing through the leaves on the ground and enjoying the mix of old and new architecture.

Reading in front of the fire was appealing, so she curled up on the couch and was soon lost in a nonfiction book about the Italian Renaissance.

Two hours later she swung her feet to the ground and stood. "Yikes," she muttered, stumbling at an unexpected stab of pain.

Sitting again, Rachel rubbed her leg. Maybe she needed to go back to doing strengthening exercises. She'd figured regular walking would be enough, but it didn't work all the different muscles. The specialist had hoped she might get to the point where she didn't have any functional differences between her injured and uninjured legs, but so far it hadn't happened.

The phone rang and the caller ID showed S. Kessler. She hesitated, then picked up the receiver. "Hello."

"Rachel, thank goodness you're there. This is Gemma."

"What's up?"

"Mr. Kessler left this morning on a business trip and my dad just got rushed to the emergency room. It probably isn't anything serious. I mean, this has happened before… but I hate taking Livvie to the hospital with me. Is there any chance you could—"

"I'll be happy to watch her," Rachel interrupted. "Do you need to borrow my car?"

"Oh, that's nice, but I have mine."

"Okay. Try to relax. I'll be right there."

Gemma was waiting at the Kesslers' door, already wearing a jacket and clutching her purse. "Thanks," she said; holding out a large envelope. "The house key is in there if you want to take Livvie to your place, along with Mr. Kessler's contact information and my cell number. For lunch there's a list of restaurants that deliver. It's next to the phone. Mr. Kessler doesn't expect me to cook all the time and he has accounts with each of them. Thank you *so* much."

"I'm sure everything will be fine. Here are my other numbers in case you need them." Rachel gave her the business card she'd grabbed as she was racing out the door. "Are you all right driving yourself?"

"Yeah. I was just… That is, I didn't know the best thing to do about Livvie," Gemma explained, her voice dropping to a whisper. "She gets awfully upset about doctors and hospitals. She still associates it with…um, bad stuff."

Bad stuff? Rachel recalled from her research that Simon's wife had died of ovarian cancer. It wouldn't be unusual for a child to blame doctors and hospitals for losing her mommy.

"I understand. Drive safely."

"I will. Bye, Livvie. I'll be back as soon as possible."

Livvie hovered on the other side of the foyer, looking solemn and ready to cry. Rachel gave her an encouraging smile. They'd got along well so far, but being alone with someone was different than when family or a third party was around.

"Hey, Livvie, would you like to learn to make cookies? We can have dessert first, then eat lunch."

The seven-year-old brightened. "Gemma showed me how to make pancakes, but she says her cookies come out like hockey pucks. What's a hockey puck?"

"It's a hard rubber disc that hockey players use. I know a simple sugar cookie recipe that always turns out right. If you don't have all the ingredients in your kitchen, we can go downstairs to my place."

"Yippee!"

They explored the cupboards together and found that everything needed for basic sugar cookies was stocked in the Kesslers' kitchen, though the baking sheets looked untouched. In fact, practically *everything* was pristine, as if it was a display kitchen where no one really cooked.

Maybe Simon wasn't the sentimental type when it came to belongings. Or maybe he hadn't bothered moving the contents of his New York kitchen and had a decorator stock this one for him. Rachel couldn't imagine giving up her favorite measuring cups. She also had her favorite pans, a bit dinged from years of use, yet all the more trusted because of that. Her bowls, mixer and other tools had followed her from home to home, as well. On the other hand, Simon had said he didn't cook. Perhaps his wife hadn't, either, and that was why the stuff looked untouched.

Rachel wrinkled her nose. She sure wasn't going to ask Simon about it.

It wasn't long before the kitchen was filled with the sweet, warm smell of fresh sugar cookies.

"Are you enjoying those cookies, or are you just eating them to be polite?" she asked Livvie teasingly.

The little girl giggled. She was munching cookies and drinking a glass of milk. Her face suggested she'd achieved nirvana.

"I never had warm cookies before. They're gooey *and* crunchy."

"It's my favorite way to eat them. But you don't have to make them fresh all the time. You can microwave a cookie from the bakery, or heat them in the oven a few minutes. A scoop of vanilla ice cream on the top tastes good, too. Does your daddy let you eat ice cream?"

"Uh-huh." Livvie put a finger to her lips and leaned forward. "Daddy's favorite is mint chocolate chip. I used to wake up awful late and find him eating some. Then he'd get me a bowl, too. We weren't supposed to tell Mommy we were the midnight mice, but I guess it's okay to tell you."

Rachel's heart skipped a beat. It was curiously easy to envision Simon sneaking a midnight snack with his daughter. She could almost hear them whispering their agreement that they wouldn't reveal their secret.

She washed the mixing bowl and other utensils and put them away, thinking Simon probably wouldn't approve of her having made cookies with Livvie. Well, too bad. She didn't have marital designs on him, and her friendship with his daughter was free of ulterior motives. Anyway, surely having her nanny rush out on a possible family emergency warranted a little indulgence.

When everything was tidy, they went down to her condo, where Rachel made salad and toasted cheese sandwiches for lunch. It seemed absurd to order a restaurant meal when she could make something.

"I like this, too," Livvie said, "almost as much as warm cookies and milk." She was obviously referring to the sandwich, not the salad, which she warily poked with her fork without eating any. "Rachel, is this a yuppie salad?" she asked finally.

"I'm not sure. What's a yuppie salad?"

"Daddy calls it that. He says it has funny-shaped green stuff and he doesn't like it. But this is all cut up, so I can't tell if it has a funny shape."

Rachel bit the inside of her lip to keep from laughing, yet it was also sad. Every now and then Simon revealed hints of whimsy. It made her wonder what he would have been like if his mother had lived and he hadn't been exposed to a hard, selfish man like Richard Kessler.

As for the salad?

Her parents offered a spring mix at their catering business and *yuppie* might be a good nickname for the varied contents. The mix tended to be somewhat bitter, and since foods could taste more intense to children, they often disliked greens such as escarole, beet leaves and dandelion. Apparently Simon wasn't any more fond of the stuff.

"If that's the definition, then this *isn't* a yuppie salad," she told Livvie. "It has romaine lettuce. Do you see vegetables in there that you like?"

"I like carrots." Livvie pulled out a carrot slice and ate it. "And cucumbers." One by one she sampled the various veggies and soon the bowl was empty except for the radishes.

Rachel's own parents had never insisted they clean their plates, though they'd ensured a balanced meal was on the table. "Just taste it," they had encouraged, while plainly enjoying the food themselves. The method might not be successful with all children, but she'd learned to love vegetables and cuisines from around the world.

"What do you want to do now, Livvie?" she asked.

"Let's read. I have a bunch of storybooks in my room."

"Sure."

Together they headed to the condo upstairs and settled in for a cozy afternoon.

GEMMA SAT IN the waiting room with her mom, unable to stop thinking about other trips to the emergency room when she was a child…such as the time her father had got drunk and fallen down a flight of stairs. The doctor hadn't intended her to hear, but he'd told the nurse if the patient hadn't been so relaxed, he might have done worse damage. Then the doctor had made a joke about getting high from the whiskey fumes.

"Mom, how much did Dad have to drink this time?" she asked finally. "What did he trip on, fall over or cut himself with?"

"How can you ask that? You always think the worst of him," Helene Paulsen said tearfully. "I told you, he got breathless and his chest hurt. It must be a heart attack. He's going to die and leave me alone."

Gemma's heart rate jumped. "Take it easy, I'm sure he'll be all right. Maybe it was indigestion. His stomach is always acting up and the symptoms can be similar."

Helene wiped a tear away. "It's more than that. If only Drake was here," she wailed. "He'd know what to do."

It was probably true. Drake was the golden child who could do no wrong. And since he was finishing his residency in cardiology, he'd also be able to go into the treatment room and be given real information. "I'm surprised he isn't here by now."

Her mother looked even unhappier. "He's backpacking in New Zealand. You know how he's always wanted to go there. He'll be devastated when he finds out his father is gone."

"Stop borrowing trouble," Gemma said in as firm a tone as possible. If Matt Tupper could be so strong and self-assured despite not being able to see, she should be able to deal with her parents. "Even if it's Dad's heart, we don't know that his condition is serious. This could just be a warning sign from his body to slow down."

Her mother always expected the worst, except when it came to her husband's alcohol consumption. As far as Helene was concerned, her husband was just under stress or needed something to help him sleep. She completely ignored the fact that he got moody and loud after a couple of shots.

Helene rose and walked jerkily around the room. Life with a hard-drinking husband had taken its toll on her, but she was still a beautiful woman.

"How about Sully? Did you call him?" Gemma asked, knowing the question would be a distraction.

"*Sullivan* didn't answer his phone." Helene hated the nickname Sully, just as much as Sully hated his given name, Joseph Sullivan. He'd stubbornly refused to answer to Joseph after getting chosen to play Joseph in three consecutive Christmas pageants. Mom and Dad had finally given in, but they were the only ones who called him Sullivan. To everyone else he was Sully.

Sully fitted her tall, laconic brother.

"I can never reach Sullivan directly. I'm starting to think he's avoiding me." Helene sat down heavily. "I left him a message, but haven't heard back."

Gemma knew Sully ducked calls from their parents. He claimed he got enough drama on the job and didn't need more from his family. True enough. Sully had worked himself up from patrol officer, to detective, to captain, and was now a sheriff in Wyoming. He'd received multiple awards for valor and service, though Gemma only knew about them because she'd briefly dated one of his fellow officers.

"Sully must be busy rounding up bad guys," she said noncommittally. "He can't drop everything to answer personal calls."

"Oh, please." Her mother scoffed. "That town where he insisted on moving is just a speck on the map. Sullivan probably sits around all day drinking coffee, his feet up on a desk. He has no ambition. And isn't it time you did something with your life instead of babysitting someone else's daughter? You don't even have your degree yet."

Why can't both of you be more like Drake?

The silent question was hard to miss—Helene had implied it often enough. To her parents, nobody could ever measure up to their eldest son. Sully didn't care, but it was hard for Gemma to let the criticism roll away without cutting into her confidence.

"Mom, I'm going back to school in January. And I love taking care of Livvie. She's a—"

"Mrs. Paulsen?" a voice interrupted. The speaker was dressed in a suit and had a stethoscope hooked around his neck.

"I'm Mrs. Paulsen. How is Clyde?" Helene

asked frantically. "Please don't tell me he's gone."

"Far from it. I'm Dr. Roth, the on-call cardiac specialist here at the—"

"Cardiac. Then it *is* his heart."

"I believe your husband had a mild angina attack. Angina is often a symptom of coronary heart disease," Dr. Roth explained. "However, there can be other causes. We're admitting Mr. Paulsen to continue our tests and to monitor his condition. I just came out to tell you that he's doing well. He's resting and his vital signs are excellent."

"Thank you," Helene said fervently. "Drake, my eldest son, is a resident in cardiology. He's in New Zealand right now. It may be a while, but I'm sure he'll want to talk with you once we're able to reach him."

The doctor nodded. "I've worked with Dr. Paulsen on a couple of cases. Your husband has signed a release, so a consultation won't be a problem. In the meantime, a nurse or aide will let you know when Mr. Paulsen is settled, and then you'll be able to see him for a few minutes. He'll be in urgent care, but don't let that worry you, we're just being careful. And you are…?" he asked, turning to Gemma.

"Gemma Paulsen. Clyde is my father."

"Nice to meet you. Your dad thought you might be here. He said to keep an eye out for a platinum blonde who looks like him, but is considerably prettier. I'll have to tell him that he was right."

Gemma blinked, unsure how to take the remark. Her father rarely complimented her about anything. "Thank you."

"Not at all. I'd better get back to my patients now."

He gave them both a kind smile before going back through the swinging doors into the emergency room. He seemed a quietly competent physician, though she didn't doubt her father would be transferred to the University of Washington Medical Center as soon as Drake could arrange it.

Still looking worried, Helene sat down, turning her wedding ring around and around on her finger. Sadness tightened Gemma's throat. One of her parents' wedding pictures was of her mom's left hand, proudly displaying that ring. Shining and new, it had symbolized hope and anticipation for the future. What would Helene Sullivan Paulsen have done if she could have looked ahead through the years to see her new husband become a man who found solace for life's disappointments in a bottle?

The truth was, nobody knew how life would turn out. The one thing Gemma had learned was that she could try to avoid getting involved with a man who had problems and the kind of personality that might lead him to start drinking. But there weren't any guarantees.

"How about tea?" she asked, jumping up. "I'll see if the hospital cafeteria is open."

"I suppose."

The woman at the information desk said the cafeteria was available until 2:00 p.m. and gave her directions. They stocked her mother's favorite brand of English breakfast tea, so Gemma carried a tray with two cups and an order of the daily lunch special back to the waiting room.

"I brought you some food, Mom."

Helene shuddered. "I couldn't."

"It won't help Dad if you don't eat. Relax and tell me more about what happened this morning." Gemma put the plate on her mother's lap and handed her a fork.

Helene poked at the spinach lasagna and finally ate a bite. "Well, your father has been unhappy the past few days. He got passed over for another promotion and it's terribly unfair. Nobody values experience any longer—out with the old, and in with the new. They've even suggested he consider retiring. Can you believe that?"

"Things have changed since Dad got his engineering degree. Didn't his company suggest he take a series of refresher courses a few years ago?"

Varied emotions struggled for supremacy in Helene's face. One thing Gemma admired about her mother was the way she loved and believed in her husband, despite everything. Unfortunately, it also made her extremely unrealistic.

"Clyde didn't need those courses. He's a senior engineer and ought to be in upper management by now. The nitty-gritty of engineering isn't a manager's job."

Meaning Clyde Paulsen hadn't taken any classes and had resented the idea that he needed them.

"So he was upset about not getting a promotion...?" Gemma prompted.

"Yes. He found out last Wednesday. We were talking about it this morning and suddenly his chest started hurting."

"There are treatments for angina, Mom."

"If only Drake was here."

Gemma patted her shoulder. Even in other families, her oldest brother would be the preferred child during a health crisis.

At any rate, her mom was eating. The lasagna and vegetables steadily disappeared, along with the slice of French bread that had come with the entrée.

It wasn't until every bite was gone that Gemma got up and collected the tray. "I'll take everything back to the cafeteria."

Her mother suddenly grabbed her wrist. "Thank you, dear. I know... Well, thank you. It's so good you could come right away. I don't say it often enough, but you know that we love you."

"I know, Mom." Her parents' love had never been in question. Gemma just wished her father's drinking hadn't loomed so large over her childhood.

After dropping off the tray and utensils, she took the opportunity to call Sully. He answered on the second ring.

"What's up, sis?"

"You didn't listen to Mom's message?"

"Nah. I delete most of them. It's always something with her. At the moment she's nagging me to come for Thanksgiving or Christmas and it isn't happening."

"Okay. Well, uh, Dad got taken to the emergency room earlier," Gemma said awkwardly. "It might be something with his heart. Maybe angina. The doctor doesn't seem too worried, but they're admitting him to urgent care to monitor his condition."

"I'm amazed the old goat didn't have a heart attack ten years ago."

"Sully, that isn't nice," Gemma couldn't help protesting.

"Sorry, sis, but you know it's true."

She leaned against the wall. "Yeah, I know. He stresses over everything and nothing. Is there any way you could call Mom? Drake is in New Zealand right now and she can't reach him, either. Hearing from you might reassure her."

A long silence followed. Gemma hated asking Sully to contact their parents. She was close to him, but he went his own way and did his own thing.

"I'll give her a call," he said finally. "But I can't come. Half my deputies are out with the flu and the rest of us are working double and triple shifts. I swear, next September we're having a vaccination clinic at the station the day after Labor Day, even if the cost comes out of my own pocket."

"Their family members should get them, too."

"You bet. How are *you*, sis? Is Mom driving you crazy?"

Gemma gazed at a painting on the opposite wall, a peaceful scene of the Puget Sound. "I'm managing. By the way, I'm now a volunteer, recording books for the blind. The man who owns the sound studio is really amazing."

Her admiration for Matt had increased even further after her first session with him. He'd been very patient, helping her to relax and be more effective. He was blind, yet she got the impression he saw better than most people.

"You'll do a great job."

"Thanks." The affirming statement made her shoulders straighten. She understood why Sully had decided to live so far away, but she missed him and the way he could make her feel better about everything. "Since you're so busy, I'll mostly send texts when I get updates on Dad's condition."

"That would be a big help. We can talk after my deputies are better."

"Don't get sick yourself."

"You know me, I'm never sick."

It was annoyingly true. Sully had the constitution of an ox. They said goodbye and Gemma then phoned Rachel with an update. Rachel assured her that Livvie was having fun. They'd made cookies, eaten lunch and were reading.

Finally, Gemma steeled herself to call Mr. Kessler and leave another message. His plane wouldn't land for a while, but the first thing he'd do was turn on his cell phone.

His brief greeting came through the speaker, followed by a beep.

"It's Gemma again," she said. "You probably haven't heard my earlier message about me needing to go to the hospital because of my dad. Livvie is fine—she's with Rachel." Gemma added that part hastily, realizing she should have led with the news that Livvie was in good hands. "I hope you don't mind me asking Rachel, but it seemed better than taking Livvie to the emergency room and getting her upset about the medical stuff. Right now I'm waiting with my mother to hear more about Dad's condition. I'll, um, call back in a minute with Rachel's number in case you don't have it with you. Bye."

Gemma fumbled in her purse for the business card Rachel had given her before calling back and leaving yet another message with both the personal and business numbers. She should have thought to have the number available ahead of time, but instead she'd tucked it away.

Back in the waiting room it was clear her mom was talking to Sully on her phone. Gemma was grateful. Her brother was a great guy. He'd just chosen to deal with his childhood by distancing himself from their needy parents.

She couldn't blame him.

CHAPTER NINE

RACHEL SAT ON the floor of Livvie's bedroom, looking through the picture books Olivia Kessler had created for her daughter.

Livvie hugged one of them to her chest. "Every night Mommy would draw the story and tell it to me at the same time. She told me bunches of stories. They're about us having adventures and wearing the pretty clothes she made. See? This is the first one. I can read it now."

Rachel turned the heavy pages of the book. It started as a simple tale of a mother and daughter looking for their lost cat, only to encounter strange and wonderful things along the way. Each drawing was vivid, especially the clothes worn by the characters.

The memory of what Simon had said at Liv'ing Creations went through Rachel's mind, that his wife had done extensive illustrations of her designs...from the fronts, backs and sides. The drawings in the books had each of the views and were highly detailed. Every couple of pages Livvie and her mommy would be in new outfits, each exhibiting the flair and verve that Olivia Kessler put into her fashion designs. The missing cat, when it finally appeared, was a Cheshire in brilliant rainbow tones.

"Me and mommy would talk about which color would be best for our clothes in the story. We talked about all kinds of stuff," Livvie said.

"'Me and Mommy' might be a good name for a clothing line," Rachel said, thinking out loud. "And there are enough designs here to last a year or two at least."

"Ooh, that would be sp-splendid." Livvie stuck her lip out. "Mommy said we'd make clothes together after I grow up. I don't know why she had to get sick."

"I don't know, either, honey." Rachel hugged Livvie close. "It doesn't seem fair, does it?"

"Uh-uh. Is Gemma's daddy going to die?"

Rachel tried to think of a way to explain. "The hospital is doing tests to find out the best way to help him get better. May I look at more of the books your mommy made for you?" she asked, partly as a distraction, partly because she was curious.

She listened as Livvie read the next story, revealing fresh sets of mother-and-daughter outfits on each page. Assuming the dress designs in Livvie's books had never been included in a Liv'ing Creations collection, they could be used until someone was found who could better capture Olivia Kessler's unique color sense and style. A complementary children's clothing line would add a whole new dimension as well, provided Simon was interested in pursuing the idea.

"I want to bring one of my books to show my class," Livvie said as she closed the cover, "but I don't want it to get dirty. Luis Sanchez brought his baseball hat to school and spilled chocolate milk on it."

"We could scan them on my computer," Rachel suggested. "The books come apart. That way you could take a printout to class and keep the original at home."

Livvie happily agreed. She wanted to copy all of the books, so it took several trips up and down the stairs to get them safely into Rachel's home office. She was a patient child, watching in fascination as Rachel methodically scanned each page. The phone rang as they were finishing the second volume.

"Hello," Rachel answered.

"It's Simon. Is Livvie there?"

He'd been so uptight about her contact with Livvie that Rachel instinctively tensed. "Yes."

"Is she okay?"

Her hackles went up. "Are you suggesting I can't take care of a—"

"Not at all," Simon said quickly. "I shouldn't have put it that way. I'm just worried. This could be reminding Livvie of her mother's illness."

Rachel wrinkled her nose. "Sorry, I'm being too sensitive. Everything is fine. We've been copying some of Livvie's books on my computer. Her homemade ones."

"Homemade?"

"Yeah. You know, the hand-drawn books from her bedroom. The ones with the clamps that come apart."

A long silence followed. "Olivia used to spend hours with Livvie, drawing and sketching and telling her stories. It was their special time together. Is that what you're talking about?"

"Yes. And they're giving me ideas related to our business discussions, if you know what I mean."

Simon recognized the careful tone in Rachel's voice.

"I'm getting the impression we should discuss this another time, when my daughter isn't around."

"Exactly. It can wait until you return. Do you want to talk to her?"

"Yes."

There was a brief, muffled discussion and Livvie came on the line. "Hi, Daddy. I'm sorry Gemma's dad's sick, but me and Rachel are having fun."

"That's great."

"For lunch she made me a toasted cheese sandwich with three different kinds of cheese! And a salad, but it didn't taste yucky. Ooh, and she made cookies. Rachel's cookies are the *best*. We ate them warm with big glasses of milk."

His daughter's enthusiasm bubbled through the phone and Simon grinned. "Did you help do the cookies?"

"Uh-huh. 'Cept I couldn't with the oven. Rachel wouldn't let me do that part."

"I'm glad you're having such a good time. May I speak to Rachel again?"

"Okay. Bye, Daddy. I miss you."

"I miss you, too, sweetheart."

The phone was exchanged again with the same sound of muffled voices in the background.

"Don't tell me," Rachel said when she came back on, "you think I have designs on your bachelorhood because I baked cookies with your daughter. Now you want to warn me away again."

"Have I really warned you away and now you're insulted?" he asked cautiously. "Or are you simply showing an interesting sense of humor?"

"A little of both, maybe."

"Well…the only thing on my mind is my daughter. I've got a couple of messages from Gemma about her father, but have no idea how serious things are, or how long she'll be tied up at the hospital. Naturally, she needs to stay for however long she wants, but the earliest return flight I can get won't have me back in Seattle until after midnight. And that's assuming the flight isn't full."

"No problem. I can put Livvie to bed and sleep on your couch. But don't you want to stay there until you know how Mr. Paulsen is doing? You might not need to come home. For all we know, the situation isn't serious and Gemma could be back any minute. If necessary I can take Livvie to school tomorrow and pick her up. We'll consider it a perk of my consulting services. Livvie *does* own the design house, after all."

The offer was both sensible and generous, a generosity that Simon was certain he didn't deserve. It had proved disconcerting to see himself through Rachel's eyes. He wasn't exactly a Prince Charming. He wasn't even an enchanted frog and she was well aware of his warts—he'd revealed them often enough over their brief acquaintance.

"Thanks. In that case, I'll try to reach Gemma for another update before making a decision." He stopped as an announcement came over the PA system, saying outgoing flights would be delayed for a few hours due to inclement weather, and incoming flights were being diverted to another airport.

After the announcement ended, he could hear Rachel laughing.

"I heard that loud and clear. Sounds as if you don't have much choice," she told him. "How long is this business trip supposed to last, anyhow?"

"Just until tomorrow. I'm scheduled for a flight back to Sea-Tac Airport that leaves in the afternoon." Simon hesitated. "Technically it isn't business. I told Gemma it was to keep things simple, but it's actually about an endowment to a medical research center. They're having some interesting results. I just don't like publicizing my donation."

He rolled his eyes in disgust, feeling like a kid, hoping to impress a pretty girl. He hadn't told anyone about the money he'd donated, but he'd acted like a jerk with Rachel so many times, he didn't want her to keep believing the worst of him.

"I understand," she assured him briskly. "Just come back the way you originally planned, provided your flight isn't canceled or postponed. Livvie's needs are covered and Gemma will be even more stressed if you return early because of her family emergency. Besides, changing your plans could upset Livvie more."

Disgruntled passengers were crowding the corridor, complaining about the connections they would be missing because of the weather.

Simon stepped closer to the wall. "You're right about that. Are you sure you don't mind?"

A low chuckle sounded. "I wouldn't have offered if I minded. But I've been thinking…

Gemma will be tired, even if she gets home today. Is it all right if Livvie stays with me?"

"That's fine. I'll call again this evening to say good-night. Contact me at any time if you need something or she gets upset. Or for any reason at all."

"Okay. Bye for now."

Simon put the phone in his pocket and rubbed the back of his neck. Adrenaline had charged through him after getting Gemma's messages and the weight of being a single father had descended like a truckload of bricks.

Having someone to share the responsibility of child rearing wasn't a good enough reason to consider marriage again, but maybe he shouldn't have so deeply resented the people who'd suggested that Livvie needed a mother. They weren't entirely wrong.

BY THE END of the afternoon, Gemma had trouble thinking straight.

She'd talked to Mr. Kessler, and he'd been so nice she could have cried. He didn't seem to mind that she'd asked Rachel to babysit; he'd even told her it was the most sensible thing she could have done and that Rachel had offered to take care of Livvie until he got home so she could rest and concentrate on her family.

As for her oldest brother, there was a chance Drake would be unreachable for the better part of two weeks.

"He should have brought a satellite phone," Helene said resentfully. "Why did he have to go hiking in the wilds of another country in the first place?"

Whoa. It was the first she'd ever said something remotely critical about her eldest son.

"Drake is a doctor, Mom. That's stressful. He deserves a vacation. And he'd be just as unreachable if he was backpacking here at home in the Cascades or Sierras."

"I know." Helene looked apologetic and Gemma squeezed her hand.

They'd only been allowed two brief visits in urgent care and had moved to the nearest waiting room to be available for any updates. Gemma was considering whether she ought to order a pizza or some other takeout meal when Dr. Roth came to see them again. He appeared much wearier than he had that morning.

"Mrs. Paulsen, we've given your husband

something to help him sleep," he said. "He's stable, so you should go home and get some rest. We'll run more tests tomorrow, and I've scheduled an angiogram for later this week."

"Why can't it be done right away? Surely it's better to do it sooner than to put it off."

"I understand your concern, but we have to wait because of the blood thinner Mr. Paulsen has been taking."

Gemma had forgotten her father was on a medication to prevent blood clots. "Will you do an angioplasty at the same time?" she asked. "If it's needed, that is."

Dr. Roth smiled. "Yes. Have you been looking up treatments for angina on your phone?"

Gemma shook her head. "I had a friend whose grandfather went through it when we were kids. He's in his nineties now, and still very active."

"Excellent. I hope you both get some rest tonight. Try not to worry. Mr. Paulsen is in safe hands."

"Thank you," Gemma and Helene said in unison.

When they were alone, Gemma turned to

her mother. "I'll drive you home. If you'd like, I can stay the night."

"Don't you have to get back?"

"Mr. Kessler told me to stay as long as needed. A neighbor is watching Livvie."

Helene pursed her lips. "You've worked for that family since you were eighteen and you still call him Mr. Kessler?"

"It's my choice, Mom. He's okay with it, either way."

Gemma urged her toward the exit, not wanting to hear what else she might say about the Kesslers or her work situation. It was understandable that Helene wanted her children to make a success of their lives, but success wasn't necessarily measured by professional status. What about personal success?

Being happy and contributing was important, no matter how many college degrees you got or the amount of money you earned. It was one of the reasons she was excited about being a volunteer reader for Matt Tupper's recording studio. Maybe she wouldn't change the world that way, but it was doing something for other people and a good way to spend her Saturday mornings.

Besides, getting to know Matt might be interesting.

SIMON'S WEEK WAS hectic after he returned to Washington. To make things easier on Gemma, he had insisted she take extended family time, which meant he needed to take Livvie to school and work from home after picking her up. His daughter loved the novelty of having her daddy around more, and he found it difficult to refuse when she wanted to take walks or do something else together.

Rachel's help had been invaluable and he was trying to think of an appropriate thank-you gift. His biggest problem was deciding if she'd be insulted by the gesture. It was hard not to be embarrassed whenever he thought about the stupid things he'd said in the past, trying to warn her away from getting ideas about him.

Warn off a woman like Rachel Clarion? *Ha.* She didn't seem conscious of her appearance, but she had to be aware, on some level, that she was stunningly beautiful. She was also thoughtful and intelligent. He must have sounded ludicrous, suggesting she look elsewhere if she was husband hunting. The most likely scenario was that she had men lined up at her door and was warning *them* off.

Thinking about Rachel reminded him of what she'd said when he was on the East Coast, about having an idea for Liv'ing Creations. Midafternoon, he picked up the phone to dial Moonlight Ventures and heard her voice come over the line after a short wait.

"Hello, Simon."

"Hi. We didn't have time to discuss your idea for the design house after I got back. Should I make an appointment, or is now a good time?"

"We should meet face-to-face so I can show you. Gemma called and said you'd be home with Livvie all week in the afternoon after school. Why don't I leave the office early and we can talk today in my home office? I have a few art supplies she could play with while we're meeting."

Simon glanced at the clock. It was a good plan, but he hated inconveniencing Rachel. At the same time, she'd made it clear that she didn't offer something she didn't want to do.

"Sure," he agreed. "I'm picking Livvie up in a few minutes and should be home no later than three thirty."

"How about four, then?"

"Great."

The school was careful about who picked the children up, and a teacher was waiting with Livvie when he arrived.

"Hi, Daddy!" She ran forward and jumped into his arms.

"Holy cow. You're getting so big I won't be able to lift you before long."

Livvie giggled. "You always say that. Rachel told me a bedtime story about a girl who tried and tried to shrink into a fairy and grow wings, but it didn't work."

"What happened to her?"

"She had a bunch of adventures. Then she grew up and became a queen. Everybody loved her because she was kind and generous and wanted her people to be happy. It's a splendid story."

Splendid seemed to be her new word of the week. Simon nodded to the teacher and returned with Livvie to his Volvo in the school loading zone. She automatically buckled her seat belt, and he checked the traffic before pulling out on the road.

"We're going down to Rachel's after we get home," he said casually. "She has art supplies and I was wondering if you want to make a get-well card for Gemma's daddy."

Livvie's expression grew instantly solemn. "I hope he gets better soon."

"Me, too. Gemma's going to take a vacation, so even if we see her at home, we don't want to ask for anything. No Mickey Mouse pancakes or rides to school or walks to the lake. Okay?"

His daughter heaved a sigh. "Okay. What about Rachel? She likes walking and she knows how to cook *everything*, not just pancakes."

It was a question he didn't know how to answer. Not long ago, his hackles would have gone up and he would have said, "Absolutely not." Yet Rachel was a neighbor and had become a business associate. A tentative element of friendship was also creeping into their relationship.

The idea of becoming friends with a woman was new to him. And it was rife with hazards. They came from such different places. Rachel had enjoyed a happy, relatively uncomplicated childhood with both parents, and she had friends she trusted well enough to make business partners. Except for Olivia and his real mother, he'd never trusted anyone.

"We shouldn't impose too much," he

hedged. "Rachel is still getting settled into her new home and business."

Livvie stuck her lip out in a small pout but didn't protest. At home she changed into play clothes and they went downstairs.

Simon rang the bell and waited, then rang it again.

"Sorry, I got delayed," Rachel said from behind them.

He turned and saw her coming down the hall, dragging a medium-size pine tree in a pot. She was limping and he hurried to help. "Are you all right?" he asked in a low tone.

"I'm fine."

"Look, Daddy, Rachel already got a Christmas tree," Livvie exclaimed in excitement.

A silent groan went through him. It wasn't fair to expect Rachel to help when it came to his concerns about Christmas trees, but couldn't she have waited to bring the thing home another day? Maybe she hadn't remembered their conversation by the lake.

"In a way it's a Christmas tree, a living one," Rachel said, giving him a small wink. "I got it for my balcony. I can decorate the tree and enjoy it through the window, but this way it will keep growing and growing and be green all year long. When it gets too big, I'll have it planted in the forest and get another one."

Livvie's face fell. "You aren't going to have an inside tree?"

"I'll have several artificial trees for Christmas. I just don't like cutting a living one down every year. Oh, I also found out they're asking people to 'adopt' a tree at the park for decorating. It'll be fun. I'm going to put solar lights and ornaments on mine, but also birdseed bells, so the animals have something extra to eat for the holidays."

His daughter looked up at him. "Can we do that, Daddy? Adopt our very own tree?"

"Sure, sweetheart."

Rachel didn't say anything else, but he was in awe of how she'd planted the idea of having an artificial tree inside the house without addressing it head-on. She unlocked the door and Simon carried the tree out to her balcony. "Is this all right?" he asked, adjusting it in one corner.

"That's fine. Livvie, do you want to work on an art project while your daddy and I talk?"

"Daddy said I could make a card for Gemma's daddy."

"That's a terrific idea. I'll get everything." Rachel went out of the room, and shortly returned with a plastic storage box. "Here you go. Use whatever you want."

Soon Livvie was busily working at the kitchen table and Simon followed Rachel into her home office. She sat in front of a laptop and turned it on.

"Based on our conversation when I was out of town, I assume your idea has something to do with the books my wife drew for our daughter," Simon said, taking the chair next to hers.

"Yes. Livvie wanted to take one to school to show her friends, but was worried about it getting damaged. I suggested we scan one of them instead, which led to us scanning *all* of them."

Simon had never looked through the books. They'd seemed like a private matter between his wife and daughter. The movers were given special instructions to pack and unpack them carefully, but that was all.

"What's so interesting about them?"

"They seem to be filled with original Olivia Kessler designs. Take a look." Rachel turned the laptop toward him so he could more easily see the screen.

Simon's chest hurt as he clicked through page after page. The designs were vividly Liv, with her color and energy, loosely woven into a story. So this was what she'd been doing all those evenings during her "alone" time with their daughter. Despite their mutual promise to leave work behind at the end of the day and make family a priority, she'd been refining clothing designs for her company.

"You don't seem happy," Rachel said. "I thought you'd be thrilled. This is a treasure trove of designs for all seasons. You could even release collections of children's clothing based on these books. I realize a lot of work is still involved. For one, designers will be needed who can follow through on the process to faithfully recreate the original drawings, but that shouldn't be too difficult."

He shifted uncomfortably. "It's just disconcerting to discover Liv was working, at the same time she was supposedly spending quality time with Livvie."

RACHEL CAUGHT A glimpse of pain in Simon's face, or at least she *thought* that was what she saw. He was still hard to understand.

"I'm not sure creative people can easily

turn off that part of themselves," she said carefully. "My friend Logan Kensington is a photographer. It's nearly impossible for him to stop looking at the world around him without considering how to frame it in a picture. That doesn't mean he isn't paying attention to other things. It's simply the way he's wired. Surely your wife was the same way, her brain constantly popping with how a certain color or pattern would look, and she was sharing that with her daughter."

"I suppose." Simon seemed to shake himself. "I'll have to see if these designs have already been released by Liv'ing Creations. For all I know, Olivia may have recreated the sketches and done the technical flats the morning after drawing the pages in Livvie's storybooks."

"Technical flats?"

"That's what she called them. Basically, they're less artistic renditions of the storyboards. They show exactly where seams, et cetera, should be located. The pattern maker uses the technical flats to create a first draft of the pattern. Please understand I'm quoting my wife. This isn't an area where I have a shred of experience."

Rachel nodded. "I tried to research the

designs to see if they'd already been used, but it's been hit-and-miss."

"What about the Liv'ing Creations' website?"

"The only photos on the website are from the past eighteen months. My guess is that it was revamped to reflect Janine Jenkins's style. Since her work is so different than Olivia's, it's likely she wouldn't want any pictures online from prior collections. The contrast would be too obvious."

Simon muttered something she couldn't understand. "I'm sure you're right, though it was done without my knowledge. It looks as if both Janine and Miriam Timmons may be looking for work by the new year. Miriam is the one who would have ordered a change to the website."

Rachel didn't know what to say. She hadn't liked Miriam the one time they'd met, and she definitely didn't care for Janine Jenkins's clothing designs, but fair was fair. "Simon, how often have you conferred with Miriam Timmons over the past two years?"

"Rarely," he admitted. "I've had other things on my mind. But I was very clear that I wanted to preserve Liv's legacy for my daughter."

"Which could be interpreted as simply keeping Liv'ing Creations in the black," Rachel argued. "There has to be a reason your wife trusted her in a management position. Maybe Ms. Timmons needs to be assured she isn't going to lose her job for taking the same risks that Olivia used to take. Some of the early Liv'ing Creations collections were avant-garde, to say the least, and they could never be called conventional. Even high fashion has trends, and from my perspective, your wife refused to follow them."

Simon cocked his head. "Are you going to defend Janine Jenkins next?"

That was a little harder. Rachel suspected the designer had known she wasn't doing what Simon wanted, but had hoped her work would become hugely popular before he recognized the difference. "How does her contract read?"

"It's boilerplate, but my instructions weren't ambiguous. I asked her to design clothes the way Liv designed them."

A laugh escaped Rachel's throat. "Simon, I should have told you this before... If someone could easily design clothes like your wife, then other people would have copied her when she became so successful. But that doesn't mean you can't find someone willing to be more colorful and innovative than Janine. Conversely, Janine may have done you a favor. If Liv'ing Creations comes out with something new and different after such conventional offerings, it should generate huge interest in the fashion world. Kind of a new beginning."

He glanced at the computer. "And the designs in the picture books could be the answer."

"I believe so."

"Well, as I told you, Olivia left extensive records of all her collections, from the start of the process to the finish. She was meticulous. I'll start checking the designs in the picture books against the ones put out by the company."

Rachel smothered another laugh. She doubted Simon would be able to distinguish one outfit from another. He'd said himself he didn't know haute couture from a hole in the ground. "Why don't you give me access to the records?" she suggested. "It's something I can do in the evening or on weekends when I won't have as many interruptions. And, since I've shopped for clothes from Liv'ing Creations, I might have a better eye for comparing the drawings to the finished product."

"You're right, but I don't want to take advantage. You must have a number of clients needing your attention."

She grinned at him. "Don't worry, you'll get a bill."

"I'll expect it. Since you're willing, I can give you computer files of the different collections, including scans of the original storyboards and technical flats. They might help."

Rachel thought it would be interesting to see the original drawings and how the finished product had turned out.

A sudden twinge from her leg made her flinch and Simon's eyes narrowed. "What's wrong?" he asked. "I could tell you were limping earlier. Did you get hurt dragging that tree up the stairs?"

"No, it's an old injury. My muscles are sore because I've been working to strengthen them. That's all."

She didn't want to talk about it and hoped her dismissive tone would put an end to his curiosity. People close to her understood she had no wish to keep going over old territory. The accident had happened and she didn't want to continually revisit it, or the year and a half she'd spent having surgeries and rehab.

"I've noticed you usually take the stairs," Simon commented. "Like the night when we went to the comedy club. You automatically went to the staircase, bypassing the elevator."

Rachel tried to suppress her irritation. Why couldn't he leave it alone? So she had mild claustrophobia, it wasn't debilitating and it wasn't anyone's business but her own. "Climbing stairs is good exercise."

"I see," Simon said quietly. "Off the subject, thanks for that bit about the Christmas tree."

"I don't know what you mean. I've been planning to get an evergreen for my balcony since I moved into the Carthage."

"And you just happened to get it on the way home from work, on a day we're scheduled for a meeting?"

Simon was grinning and Rachel grinned back. "Sue me. If your tree catches fire, all the sprinklers in the building may go off. It was merely a question of self-protection. I like warm showers, not cold ones."

He laughed outright. "Thank you, anyway. You know, a real tree wouldn't have been so bad if Liv hadn't put it up so early and loaded it with so many light strings. The heat dries the needles out in just a few days. Not that I thought much about it until after Livvie was born and I read about a house fire, started by the family's Christmas tree."

"I understand the first year of parenthood can be filled with worries. And all the other years, as well."

Simon smiled ruefully. "Livvie seemed so small and fragile, my imagination went haywire. Thank goodness my wife was relaxed about everything. She'd laugh and tell me it was going to be all right, we'd learn to be parents as we went along. I'm glad one of us was calm and levelheaded."

"I understand."

Rachel focused on her computer screen. Sometimes Simon was appealing enough that she was in danger of seriously liking him. But she couldn't forget his sharp edges. Sooner or later one of them would show itself and she could get hurt. A man could be a caring, loving father, but cold and insensitive to the adults in his circle.

"I understand how your wife felt about having a fresh tree," she added. "I love the scent and look of a silvertip pine, and I know a lot of them are grown in commercial tree farms, but life *is* easier when you use the artificial variety."

"Do you really put up more than one?"

She bobbed her head. "Absolutely. I'm a Christmas fiend, just like my grandmother. I used to dream of having a big old house, the same as hers, with wonderful corners for reading and tucking decorations into. She also has little groves of live trees out in the yard to cover with lights. Decorating would take the entire weekend after Thanksgiving."

A FAMILIAR PANG went through Simon…the same one he'd felt each time Rachel spoke about her childhood. *Normal*, whatever that was, filled with family and traditions. No wonder Livvie clung to the customs her mother had started.

"Couldn't you have found a place like that when you moved back to Washington?" he asked. "If not a Victorian, maybe an old farmhouse with those big, wide porches?"

He noticed Rachel put a hand on her leg, the one she'd been favoring earlier. It seemed almost an unconscious reaction. There was more to the story than she was willing to reveal.

"Maybe I'll do that after I get fully settled at the agency," she said lightly. "It's hard to maintain a big house and yard at the same time you're learning the ropes in a new career. Speaking of which, I'd suggest a working title of 'Me and Mommy' for the Liv'ing Creations project, provided you're interested in adding a children's clothing line. There could be sufficient designs in the storybooks for two or three years. That should be enough time to find one or more satisfactory designers to take over."

Funny, Simon had never expected to be sorry a subject had been changed *back* to a business topic.

"A children's line sounds interesting, and I'm certain Liv never did any kids' clothes," he said. "I have an employee who does market research who can look into it. The rest will depend on verifying whether these are new, unreleased designs."

"I'll start with the comparisons as soon you get the information to me."

A noise caught their attention and they turned to see Livvie standing in the doorway of the office, holding something in her hands. "I'm all done. Do you want to see?"

"We sure do." Rachel waved her inside.

Livvie trotted over and showed them the get-well message she'd made for Gemma's father.

"That's terrific," Simon told his daughter. "Since Gemma is staying with her parents right now, we'll need to mail this to him."

"Okay, Daddy. I'm going to make a card for Gemma, too." Livvie dashed out again.

"Livvie is very talented. Her ability seems really advanced for her age." Rachel took out a large white envelope and gave it to Simon for the get-well card. "Gemma didn't say much about her dad's condition when we talked."

"She hasn't told me the details, but it sounds as if he's doing okay. I insisted she take all the family time she needs, and also a long vacation. She hasn't wanted to leave Livvie since my wife was diagnosed."

"I'm glad she'll have a chance to relax."

Rachel knew how upset she'd be if her father or mother became seriously ill. They were in excellent health and their catering business was busier than ever, yet Simon's wife had got sick in the prime of her life, so you never knew when something could happen.

She talked to her parents and the rest of the family on a regular basis, and they all got together once a month for a meal. But maybe she should visit more often. She no longer lived in Southern California and was less than a half hour away if traffic cooperated. Her mom and dad might enjoy meeting for lunch or being taken out to dinner when they were available. And Grandma would love having her spend the night now and then.

More than anything, Rachel didn't want to end up regretting missed opportunities.

CHAPTER TEN

GEMMA RANG THE bell at the recording studio on Saturday, flustered from an argument with her mother, one that had delayed her departure for over twenty minutes. Helene felt she couldn't manage alone and wanted her daughter to be with her 24/7 during Clyde's recovery. It was nice to feel wanted, but he mostly needed rest.

"I'm awfully sorry to be late," Gemma told Matt when he unlocked the door. "It won't happen again."

He shrugged. "No problem. Rachel mentioned your father was in the hospital. She was concerned you might be too busy to come in today."

"That was thoughtful of her, but I couldn't miss the recording session," Gemma said quickly. "Not under the circumstances. Everything is okay. Dad had an angioplasty and two stents inserted. He's home now, recovering. His heart seems to have escaped damage, so the cardiologist is optimistic."

"And you've been helping."

"Trying to. It isn't, um…easy with either of my parents."

She followed him to the control room. Unlike the previous Saturday, nobody else seemed to be working at the studio. Except for Pepper, of course, whose tail waved in a slow, graceful arc. She was a beauty, with long reddish-gold fur, a happy face and intelligent eyes. "You sound uptight about your folks," Matt commented.

"Dad doesn't want to cooperate with the doctor's orders, particularly about lifestyle changes. But it should be better when my oldest brother gets back. They always listen to Drake."

"Sounds familiar," Matt said wryly. "Anything my oldest brother says seems to carry more authority, too. Even when he's wrong. Frustrating, isn't it?"

Gemma blinked. It was good to be reminded that other families had similar problems to her own. "Yeah. Though in Drake's defense, he's also a cardiology resident at the U-Dub." U-Dub was the nickname a lot of locals used to refer to the University of Washington.

"You said he needs to get back. Where is he?"

"In New Zealand. Hiking or backpacking or whatever they call it there. It's a dream trip for him, but we haven't been able to do more than leave messages on his cell phone. Surely he'll have cell coverage soon. Mom usually talks to him a couple of times a week and she's going through withdrawal."

Matt chuckled. "Cell coverage might not be the problem. If I was a cardiologist and had a chance to visit a place like New Zealand, I'd leave my phone at home. It must be a relief for him to get away from it all. Even from his parents."

Even from his parents?

Gemma was so accustomed to her eldest brother being the favored child, she hadn't considered how Drake felt about it. He'd often taken advantage of the situation as a kid, but he was an adult now, with heavy professional responsibilities. It was entirely possible that he needed a break, not only from his work, but from the demands their mother put on him.

"I have to admit my folks can be overwhelming," Gemma confessed. "They feel that being a nanny isn't a worthy enough job for their daughter. They also don't approve of me wanting a degree in childhood development. I spent two years in New York and only visited once—it just didn't seem worth the drama."

"I wouldn't waste energy trying to get their approval. They're the ones with the problem."

"That's easier said than done. You don't know my mom and dad."

Matt leaned forward. "Yeah, but I know *my* parents. It drives them batty that I won't let them take care of me. If Mom had her druthers, she'd be doing my laundry, shopping, cooking and who knows what else. She can't accept that I've got Pepper and the access van and don't need her looking after me. It's her issue, not mine."

The conversation had been comfortable to that point, so it was almost a shock to be reminded that Matt was blind. He was so confident and capable that it was easy to forget.

"Maybe she just needs to feel useful," Gemma suggested. "My grandmother says that no longer being needed is one of the hardest parts of getting older. Not that my mom has that problem. She stays busy taking care of Dad."

MATT HEARD A distinctly bitter note in Gemma's tone that seemed out of character.

"Has your father been sick for a long time?" he asked.

"He…he drinks. A lot," Gemma admitted flatly.

Matt felt as if a light had turned on in his head.

The previous week he'd offered to take her for pizza and a beer at a joint down the street from the studio as a thank-you for volunteering. She'd instantly refused and he'd figured it was her discomfort from being around someone who was blind, even though he'd made it clear the invitation wasn't a date. But maybe the beer in the invitation was part of the reason. Some people couldn't think about eating pizza without a cold brew, but that was the only reason he'd mentioned getting one.

"I imagine alcohol could cause difficulties with him getting better."

"It already has. Mom actually sneaked a bottle of bourbon into the hospital for him.

One of the nurses nearly had a meltdown when she found out. Dr. Roth wasn't any happier, either, and it delayed the angiogram and angioplasty. Now Mom wants *me* to be the one to keep reminding Dad that he can't have a drink."

Matt couldn't imagine a mother trying to put her daughter in the role of enforcer because she couldn't do it herself.

"In that case, it's time for your big brother to come home and take the heat," he said.

"I wish. Mom didn't want me to come today," she explained, "but Dad's condition isn't critical, he just has to take it easy and recover. Anyway, I shouldn't have brought any of this up. I suppose I just needed to vent."

"Don't apologize. I'm the one who introduced the subject."

Gemma laughed, a light, soft sound that Matt enjoyed. "That's right. It's all *your* fault."

"I have broad shoulders. But why don't we get started on the recording? Afterward we could go for a cup of coffee from the Crystal Connection if you want to vent some more. It'll be a good excuse to delay your return."

"I'd like that. I just wish they had a sitting area outside the shop."

Matt realized he'd unconsciously held his breath after issuing the invite to coffee, and now he let it out, annoyed with himself. It shouldn't be important whether Gemma was willing to have coffee or pizza or anything else with him. He knew from experience that a number of women couldn't handle being with a man who couldn't see. It was a fact of life he'd accepted after a few difficult relationships.

Difficult?

He restrained a snort. With most women, things didn't get far enough to be defined as a relationship, but a few had wanted to "take care" of him. He already had one overprotective mother, he didn't need or want a girlfriend who acted the same way.

"I don't think the Crystal Connection bothers with an outdoor patio because there's an atrium in the center of the building," he said. "You have to walk outside and around to the main entrance, but it's open and has nice skylights."

"I, um, haven't been in there. Just Moonlight Ventures, the Crystal Connection and your sound studio."

"The studio isn't much to look at." Matt chose his words deliberately. "By the way, I don't expect people to modify their language around me. I still say things like 'I'll see you later.' I may be blind, but those are generic terms. And in case you're wondering, I know the atrium is a large, open space because of the way sound travels in there. I can also feel warmth on my skin coming through the skylights when it's sunny."

"I didn't... I'm sorry."

"Don't worry about it. I just wanted to make myself clear so you wouldn't be so uncomfortable."

OH, YEAH, THAT'S going to help, Gemma thought.

Granted, she was unsure how to act around Matt, but if she had any guts, she'd tell him she hadn't modified the words she'd used, she was too busy figuring out other stuff. He seemed to have forgotten that a whole lot of communication was conveyed through visual clues...facial expression, hand gestures, body posture. She wanted to ask if he'd ever considered giving people time to adjust, but confrontation wasn't in her skill set.

"O-okay. I wouldn't have said anything about the studio, I don't know how these places are supposed to look."

Gemma deliberately skipped over part of the conversation, hoping they could go back to the camaraderie they'd shared when talking about older brothers being treated as though their word was gospel. Maybe all family members felt a loving exasperation toward one another, mixed with a few darker corners they preferred not talking about.

"High-tech," Matt muttered. "Studios are supposed to look high-tech."

"It does, and I can't imagine knowing how to run all this equipment, or being able to match up the different tracks the way you do," she said, still on edge. "Who knew it was that much work to produce a piece of music?"

The previous week Matt had patiently spent time telling her how mixing worked and the way he could manipulate aspects of each track to get the desired effect.

But they'd also talked about other things, like the books they enjoyed and the music they listened to. Maybe it had been easier because of all the bustle in the studio then.

"I've had a lifelong fascination with

acoustics," Matt explained, "which makes part of the job easier. Go on into the live studio. I left the binder on the podium."

The book they were recording had been taken apart, with the pages enlarged, hole-punched and put into a binder.

Gemma sagged in relief and immediately headed for the door.

MATT WISHED HE'D kept his big mouth shut.

The previous week Gemma had done an incredible job cold reading the first four chapters. It wasn't just her clear diction. She put warmth and energy into her voice, with a genuine, unselfconscious quality. The technicians installing the second studio had even stopped to listen until Matt's assistant had pointedly cleared her throat and suggested they please get back to work.

Matt's mood lightened as he remembered. He'd gone to college with Tara and she wasn't a person you messed with. The guys had finished the installation in record time.

He'd been running tests in the new control room ever since. It was the latest technology, unlike the touchy secondhand electronics he'd bought when opening Tupper Recording. The older stuff worked okay, but the new setup would mean twice as many clients and taking fewer hours for the mixing and mastering process. Someday he might even decide to take his business further, producing CDs on a "Tupper" label. Or maybe he'd call it Northwind Recordings, unless that was too close to the name of an existing company.

He'd left the mike turned on in the live studio and heard Gemma rifle through the pages in the binder.

"Um, I'm ready when you are," she called after a minute.

Matt put his headphones on, made minor adjustments on the control board and switched on the recording. "Go ahead."

"'Chapter Five,'" Gemma started, and he settled back in his chair. Rachel Clarion had guessed right that Gemma would be great reading books for the blind. She made few verbal slips and he rarely had to stop her to repeat a section, except when he detected an electronic glitch. Hopefully he hadn't messed things up for the day— upsetting a reader right before they started probably wasn't the best way to get a stellar performance.

He'd only need to do minimal mixing and

mastering along with adding a brief musical intro to the start of each recording. Other than that, his time on the project wouldn't be demanding because of Gemma's skill. Once, Matt had spent long hours regretting that he'd accepted the offer of a local celebrity, who hadn't been able to get through a single page without stopping to say, "That didn't sound right. Can we redo it?"

If Gemma was interested in commercials or other voice work, he was sure she could get a decent number of jobs. He might even do his share of advocating for her, provided she decided to go that direction and he found the right opportunity.

IT WAS LATE Saturday evening before Simon found time to isolate the records of Olivia's design collection. He told the computer to copy them to a portable hard drive, including everything from when she'd first started out, crafting her creations in a garage apartment in Bellingham.

The graphics files were huge and copying would take a while, so he sat back and thought about how smart and dedicated Rachel was. She'd actually defended Miriam Timmons, and her attitude about Janine Jenkins was ambivalent. So it seemed questionable she had the killer instinct usually needed to be a top talent agent, or perhaps that was just his own perception about agents.

He rubbed his face.

After his wife's death, his brain had been lost in a fog. Things had got better in New York and eventually he'd begun dating again, making it clear he wasn't interested in anything long-term. In the back of his mind he'd figured he was over the worst of his grief.

But was he?

Olivia had been the love of his life, yet he hadn't felt particularly guilty about socializing with other women. Maybe because those relationships hadn't meant very much. Rachel was different and friendship seemed like a real possibility. Yet why should he feel guilty about something so innocent?

"Daddy, can I come in?"

"Of course you can, Livvie." Simon held out his arms and she ran into them. "I thought you were asleep. Is something wrong?"

She heaved a heartfelt sigh. "Just a bad dream."

"What about?"

"Um…I don't remember."

Simon touched her nose. "If you don't remember, how do you know it was bad?"

"It just was."

She snuggled against him, warm and trusting. If only he could protect her from all the ogres in the world, real or imagined. But he hadn't been able to keep her from losing her mother, and unpleasant dreams couldn't be stopped by daddies, locked doors or security systems.

"Is it because Gemma isn't here?" he asked. "Her father is going to be all right. I just thought she should have time with her family, or to do something else if she wanted."

"No." Livvie hugged him tight. "I love you bunches and bunches, Daddy."

"And I love you, bunches and bunches, Livi-kin-kinnie. Tell you what, let's go have a bowl of ice cream."

Livvie straightened so fast she nearly bumped his chin with the top of her head. "I told Rachel that we used to have ice cream at night. That's okay, isn't it? I never told Mommy."

Simon's throat tightened. Olivia had known

about the late-night snacks, but Livvie had enjoyed thinking it was their secret.

As parents, he and Liv had tried not to interfere with each other's special time with their daughter. It was one of the reasons he'd never looked at the picture books Olivia had drawn. And now that he *had* seen them, he didn't know what to think.

Rachel's comments about creative people crept into his mind. What did he know about creativity? He didn't have an artistic bone in his body. Even before he lost his mother and was forced to deal with grim practicalities, doing art in school had bored him. And despite the years he'd spent with Liv, he'd never really understood that side of her, or the highs and lows she'd experienced as an artist.

"What kind of ice cream do we have?" Livvie asked in the kitchen.

Simon checked the freezer. "Strawberry and vanilla. How about some of both?"

"Don't we have mint chocolate chip? You like it the best."

He hadn't eaten mint chocolate chip ice cream in over two years. "I like other flavors, too, though I don't think the strawberry will be as good as Rachel's sorbet."

"Uh-uh. Rachel can make anything." Livvie's eyes opened wide. "Even bread. It doesn't have to come from the store or a bakery. She showed me how she puts flour and stuff together and it starts puffing up. She said it was yeast, but I think it's magic."

Magic.

Would she have said that before meeting Rachel? Over the past two years Livvie had grown solemn and serious. Sometimes she sounded like a grown woman in a child's body.

Simon had a sudden flash of his early childhood and how his mother had made everything seem more special. Somehow, he didn't think it was *just* a mommy's job to do that. But how did a pragmatic guy like him bring magic and mystery into his daughter's life? While Rachel had created magic with yeast and culinary enchantment, he was a hardheaded businessman. Not much magic was needed to run a company.

"Daddy, hurry up," Livvie urged, hopping from one foot to the other. "I'm starving."

"You are, huh? We can't have that." Simon took the two containers of ice cream from the freezer. He lifted her onto the high stool in front of the breakfast bar and then scooped servings into bowls. He savored a couple of bites, then saw Livvie had stopped eating.

"Is something wrong with your ice cream?" he asked.

"N-no." Tears were dripping down her cheeks and she let out a small sob.

Simon pulled her onto his lap again. "What's wrong, baby?"

"N-noth-nothing," she finally gasped out.

"It doesn't sound like nothing. Can't you tell me?"

"I… Oh, D-Daddy, we haven't been midnight mice in *forever*."

Midnight mice?

He felt as if a giant hand was squeezing his chest. The last time he and Livvie had been midnight mice was before Olivia had got sick. Now when they ate ice cream together, it was for dessert after a meal. Not as a late-night snack.

"I know. I'm sorry." He cuddled her closer as she cried on his shoulder. "It's going to be all right," he whispered.

"But you're so sad about Mommy. I don't want you to be sad."

"I'll always be sad that Mommy had to go away. We both will. But that means we loved her, it doesn't mean we can't be happy. You make me very, very happy."

"Really truly?"

"Really truly. Cross my heart."

She cried for a long time, the ice cream melting into puddles, and Simon wondered if she'd been holding back tears since Olivia's death. At the funeral and gathering afterward, people had speculated why Livvie didn't cry. "It isn't natural," they'd muttered, thinking he couldn't hear them.

His daughter's silent composure *had* troubled him, but he'd understood. Sometimes pain was too deep for tears, too horrible to let it show.

Perhaps now she'd begin to heal.

CHAPTER ELEVEN

LATE IN THE WEEK, Rachel finished her research into the Liv'ing Creations files. Because Gemma was away, she called Simon and suggested they meet at his condo so Livvie would have her usual playthings to keep her occupied.

Simon stretched and yawned the minute they sat down in the office. He looked tired and Rachel remembered what he'd said about not sleeping as much as he would like. Sometimes he didn't look as though he'd slept at all.

"Rough night?" she asked lightly.

"Rough *several* nights."

"Sorry. I don't mind if you want to meet another time."

He yawned. "No, it's fine. I'm used to being sleep deprived. Things were better when I was married, but even then I would often be up at night when my wife was in bed, working in my home office or doing something else."

"Such as eating ice cream with Livvie in the wee hours of the night?" Rachel teased.

Simon seemed startled. "Why did you bring that up?"

"No special reason. Livvie mentioned it when you were out of town. Obviously being 'midnight mice' is a special memory for her."

"Yeah." He yawned again. "We haven't done it since before my wife got sick. The ritual was important to Livvie and would have given her continuity after Olivia died, but I was too buried in my own loss to realize I was letting opportunities like that slip away."

"You can make up for them now. Why does she call it being midnight mice?"

"Liv used to say midnight mice must have been eating the ice cream, so that became our code term. Liv knew what we were doing, I just pretended it was a secret. She didn't approve of sugary late-night snacks, but she didn't ask me to stop, either."

"She knew it was one of your special moments with Livvie."

Simon's face turned even more haggard.

"I'm starting to wonder if effective parenting and marriage are possible with two career-obsessed people."

The remark seemed out of the blue. A couple of weeks ago Rachel might have got annoyed, figuring it was yet another warning not to get interested in marriage, but he seemed to have accepted that she wasn't concerned about a husband.

"Oh?" she said cautiously.

"It's this business with the picture books—it really looks as if Liv was working when she'd promised to take time for home and family. Night after night. She even dated and initialed the pages, the way she did with her storyboards at work."

Rachel had seen the date and signature as the habit of an artist. Or perhaps a way for mother and daughter to look back and be able to remember a certain period in their lives. Essentially, it was a visual journal. Problem was, Simon might not be sentimental enough to understand.

"Simon, part of this was your wife telling Livvie stories about the two of them having adventures together. It was also a way of teaching her daughter about design and color and how fabric moves. Is that any different than my mom and dad teaching me to cook and bake? While teaching me, they were also experimenting with recipes. I never minded."

"I don't know. Truth be told, Liv and I were a strange match. It was hard for me to understand how she could be so intense about designing clothes, though I probably would have felt that way if she'd been a different kind of artist. I'm a practical guy and she was a dreamer."

Rachel winced. Discovering the storybooks had seemed like a huge windfall, a way to infuse the struggling design house with Olivia Kessler's original vision and vitality. But there'd been an unintended impact... making Simon ask questions about his marriage. Who knew an innocent set of picture books could stir up so many emotions?

"I don't know if it will help," she said, "but I've checked and rechecked, and none of the designs in Livvie's books were put out by Liv'ing Creations."

SIMON WASN'T BIG on sympathy, but the concern in Rachel's face was nice. And he understood what she was saying about Olivia, maybe because he wanted to believe his wife had kept her word.

"Is there a special reason this is so important to you?" Rachel asked.

"Liv is the one who taught me to reach for something beyond business and profit. So it's doubly hard to think she was just using her time with Livvie to keep working."

"But that doesn't change how much you loved each other, and Livvie cherishes the memory of those evenings. Anyhow, you mentioned Olivia was driven and had to do everything as fast as possible. Maybe slowing down and taking time for family is something you were teaching each other."

Perhaps, but Simon didn't think it was a conundrum he was going to solve in the next five minutes. He wasn't sure he could even stand *thinking* about it for another five minutes. Grasping for a lifeline, he recalled the flyer he'd seen about a cat shelter in the neighborhood saying they'd recently been inundated with kittens.

"I hate to say this," he said, making an effort to look apologetic, "but with Gemma away and things being so unsettled for Livvie, it seems like a good idea to get her a kitten. I'd like to do it this afternoon so they have the weekend to get acquainted. You said you wouldn't mind postponing our meeting and I don't know how late Hannah's Home of Cats will be open. It's a private shelter close to here."

Ironically, Simon might have been annoyed if a business partner had made such a request to *him*, but Rachel smiled. "No problem. I've walked past Hannah's House of Cats and never gone in. Livvie will love having a kitten. Oh, I've chosen my tree to decorate at the park. How about you?"

"They don't just put your name on a list and assign one?"

"It's more personal to choose your own. I mentioned it because a volunteer is going to be there until 5:00 p.m. Also tomorrow and Sunday. You could go and sign up if you're still interested."

"Sure. There should be time to do both."

He was interested in anything that kept him from chewing the past apart. Besides, Rachel was right. Olivia had loved him, and she'd loved her daughter. They'd both made efforts to put family first and sometimes they'd failed. If the situation was reversed, what sort of things would Liv be thinking about him now?

Abruptly Simon recalled that anger was one of the so-called stages of grieving. Was this some kind of illogical anger at Liv because she'd died? Or maybe it was subconscious bargaining, a challenge that she do the impossible and defend herself?

Rachel got up and stretched. "I'd better leave so you can get going."

She was so beautiful that his mouth went dry as if he was a teenager again, unable to come up with something clever to say to a pretty girl.

"Would you like to come with us?" He felt like an idiot blurting out the invitation. "I'm sure Livvie would enjoy having you there when she chooses her kitty."

Rachel didn't answer right away. "I... Sure. I'll change and meet you downstairs. The community park and animal shelter are just a few blocks away, but it might be best to drive if you're bringing home a kitten."

Simon sat for moment after she'd left, wondering how he had allowed his life to get tangled up with another woman. *Business associate*, his conscience mocked him. Yet his business associates were kept at arm's length and would never be asked to help his daughter select a new pet.

"Livvie?" he called, pushing the thought away.

She came running. "Yes, Daddy?" She looked around the office and her face fell. "Rachel left?"

"Just to change her clothes. We're meeting her downstairs, so put on your coat. I have a surprise for you."

She disappeared and he heard footsteps racing down the hallway, making him smile. He'd rather have happy noise than the cautious silence that had filled their home the past two years.

Simon called the cat shelter and found they were open until six, so there would be plenty of time. He pulled a hoodie over his head and made sure his wallet was in his pocket before they went down the stairs. Rachel arrived a moment later, looking classy in a pair of worn black jeans and a snug black jacket.

"I'm getting a surprise," Livvie told her eagerly.

"Really? I wonder what it could be."

"The other place is open later than I

thought," he said to Rachel. "Shall we go to the park first?"

"That sounds good." Livvie seemed puzzled, then pursed her lips in excitement, perhaps guessing that they were discussing her surprise.

Simon drove to the park, and Rachel led them across the sloping terrain.

"This is the tree I picked to decorate for Christmas," she told Livvie, showing them a scraggly six-foot pine. "The red ribbon around the trunk means it's already taken. A green ribbon means the tree is available."

Livvie looked at Rachel's tree and her face scrunched up. "It isn't very pretty."

Rachel crouched to look into her eyes. "All trees are beautiful, sweetie. This one has had a tough time, so it needs extra love. Until this last winter there were two very tall trees growing above it."

"What happened to the big trees?"

"They blew down in a windstorm. It's sad, but this little one is getting more light now and is going to grow much straighter and taller. I picked it because I didn't think anyone else would. I want to make it one of the prettiest Christmas trees in the whole park."

"Hello, folks," a voice interrupted. "I'm

Tate Longhorn from the fire station up the street. Are you here to adopt a tree for the holidays? Because I'm here to take names." He waved the clipboard he carried.

Rachel straightened. "Hi, Tate. I already adopted this one, but my neighbors want to participate, too. This is Livvie, and her father, Simon."

"Livvie, Simon, welcome to the community park holiday program. There will be a tree lighting ceremony on December 3, which means everyone is being asked to decorate between November 25 and December 2. This way you have six weeks to plan what you're going to do and a week to get it done."

"I want to 'dopt that one," Livvie said, pointing to a nearby tree, nearly as scraggly as the one Rachel had chosen. "Because it needs love."

"Wonderful choice." Tate consulted a large sheet of paper. "According to my map, it's a Sitka spruce. That's a very special tree."

Livvie beamed as Simon gave the volunteer his name and phone number and received a list of the guidelines in return, a description of each species of tree in the park and a flyer about the fire department. *Kessler* was written on the park map and on the red ribbon replacing the green one. Tate said goodbye when he spotted someone else looking at trees, hurrying away to talk with them, clipboard in hand.

"Daddy, I love my surprise," Livvie exclaimed, her eyes shining as she looked at the bedraggled spruce.

"There's another surprise, too," Simon told her. "But we need to hurry."

Livvie gave an excited squeal when the car stopped outside the cat shelter, located in a trim arts and crafts home. They went inside and he was immediately impressed— the place was clean and smelled fresh, even though there were cats everywhere, both in kennels and lounging in comfy beds around the various rooms.

Livvie dropped to her knees, trying to coax a kitten with Himalayan markings in one of the bottom kennels to come to her. "Kitty, kitty," she called, but it remained curled up, sound asleep. Her bottom lip quivered.

"Kittens sleep deeply," Rachel told her. "They can take a while to wake up. Call again and wait."

Livvie called and the small feline finally opened its eyes, yawned and strolled over to greet Livvie. They said hello to each other, but after a while it curled up again and Livvie began going to other kennels, greeting other kittens.

"This may take some time," Simon told the volunteer.

"That's okay. We have plenty of patience for true cat lovers."

AFTER WATCHING LIVVIE hopscotch between kittens for a while, Rachel found her attention caught by a long-haired black feline with a white chin, whiskers and paws. It was staring at the wall of its kennel as though it had seen everything there was to see and wasn't impressed.

She went over to read the information card.

Binx. Sixteen-month-old neutered male. All vaccinations up-to-date. Fastidiously clean. Found abandoned with broken leg. Possible history of abuse. Small limp. Trust issues.

Trust issues? At least the people at Hannah's House of Cats were frank about their animals.

"Beautiful, isn't he?" said a voice next to her.

Rachel turned and saw a woman around her own age. She wore a smock with Hannah's House of Cats Volunteer printed on the front, and a tag saying her name was Angie.

"He's gorgeous."

"Binx was brought here at around eight months old. He's been adopted and returned twice. Both times they said they couldn't keep him because he's too depressed."

"That's appalling. How can people be that cruel?" Rachel looked back at Binx. "I'd be depressed, too, if nobody wanted me."

She knew she couldn't take in all lonely cats, but she could give this one a home where he was wanted and loved. Cats had a protocol of behavior they expected from humans, so she opened the kennel and extended her hand to let Binx get familiar with her scent, calling his name. It took a minute, but he finally turned his head to look at her.

"Hey, Binx. I know what it's like to get hurt," she whispered. "Do you want to come home with me?"

The feline regarded her for a long moment before looking away again. Rachel was patient, talking to him in a low tone, offering reassurances she was certain he understood. Cats were far more intelligent than some people thought. Finally he rose to his feet, limped over and looked into her face for an endless moment...then pressed his forehead to hers.

"Oh, my, look at that," said the volunteer. "I'm going to get Hannah. She needs to see this."

Slowly and carefully Rachel stroked Binx, avoiding his right side, guessing from his uneven gait that it was his rear right leg that had been broken. It would take time to know if he could be touched on that side without causing discomfort.

A faint, very rusty purr came from his throat.

When he finally broke contact, she looked around and saw the volunteer had returned with another woman, who was around sixty. They were watching, delight on their faces.

"Hi, I'm Hannah, the official cat lady of the neighborhood," the newcomer introduced herself. "But you probably figured that out from the name of our shelter."

Rachel grinned. "Hannah's House of Cats? It shows you have a sense of humor."

"Thanks. So, Rachel, do you want to adopt

Binx? You got a reaction that doesn't happen very often from a cat with his history," Hannah said. "Cats choose their people as much as we choose them, but I never expected it with him. He's gone through too much."

"Of course I do. He's wonderful. I realize you may have a waiting period, but I don't want to leave without him. He might feel abandoned and never forgive me," Rachel said firmly.

Hannah patted her arm. "I quite agree. Let me get some information from you and your husband."

Rachel choked down a laugh and didn't dare look in Simon's direction in case he'd overheard. "Mr. Kessler and I are just neighbors. His little girl is here to look at the kittens and they invited me along."

"Oops. Angie thought you were a family when you came in together."

Still avoiding Simon's gaze, Rachel sat with Hannah and filled out the adoption form. It included questions about whether Binx would be allowed outside, or if she intended to have him declawed.

"I might have part of my balcony screened off so he can get fresh air, but that's all," she assured the other woman. "I grew up with cats, so I know declawing leads to bad arthritis. I'd never have it done."

Hannah smiled. "Excellent. Do you have a veterinarian?"

"I grew up in the area and just moved back a few months ago. The vet in my hometown is still practicing, but I'd prefer someone closer. Is the veterinarian on Chilkat Drive any good?"

"He does all the medical care for our cats. I trust him implicitly."

"Are you getting a kitty, too, Rachel?" Livvie asked. The first kitten she'd looked at was tucked into her elbow.

"Yes, I am."

"Goody. Me and Daddy are both getting a kitty. See? Rocky kept jumping onto Daddy's shoulder from the cat tree. Angie said he'd decided to go home with us and Daddy said he could."

Rachel put her hand over her mouth to hide a grin. Simon was holding a tiger-striped feline who lay back with a smug expression, head on Simon's upper arm, lazily licking a paw.

"Looks like we'll have to make a quick stop at the pet store to get supplies," he said, his expression both harried...and flattered.

"Angie, would you help Mr. Kessler with the adoption application?" Hannah asked.

"I'd love to." Angie seemed pleased and Rachel hoped Simon wouldn't be a grump.

Just to be sure, she gave him a warning glance and he rolled his eyes.

Once he was sitting across the room with Angie, Rachel leaned forward. "Tell me, did you train Rocky to jump onto people's shoulders?"

Hannah chuckled. "Nope, but he prefers strangers who don't make a fuss. The more someone ignores him, the more he works to get their attention. Your neighbor must have been the epitome of indifference for Rocky to be so determined. Still, I believe Rocky picked his forever home the way Binx picked you. Felines are very wise animals."

"I hope Binx will be happy with me. You don't need to worry. I'll never give up on him."

A smile curved Hannah's lips. "I'm not worried. You obviously love and understand cats, which is what he needs."

They chatted for a while longer, then Rachel signed the form and paid the adoption fee. Simon completed his paperwork as well,

Rocky draped across his legs. He seemed relaxed and content.

Maybe Rocky would be a good influence on him.

Hannah loaned them three cat carriers and they drove to the pet store, where Simon went in alone and purchased supplies for both households so the "new cat mommies" could stay with their babies. He'd sounded vaguely paternal, but Rachel let it pass since Binx was crouched in the carrier, panting and looking wide-eyed.

"I can't believe I came home with *two* felines," Simon muttered as he loaded everything into the Carthage elevator. "Three if I count yours."

Rachel didn't respond. She was struggling not to let her claustrophobia overwhelm her. The elevator was even smaller than she remembered.

At her floor, Simon insisted on carrying the supplies the short distance into her condo while she stayed with Livvie and held the elevator.

"Thanks," she said when he returned. She let go of the elevator door, but he stopped it from closing.

"No problem." Simon glanced at his daughter, who was crouched on the floor, communing with her new kitten. "You helped give Livvie a special afternoon."

A warmth was in his eyes that Rachel hadn't seen before, and her heart gave a curious thud. He leaned out and gave her a swift, warm kiss.

Through the rush of blood in her ears, she heard Binx spit. She was holding his carrier and he probably didn't like Simon being so close. Whatever the reason, she stepped backward.

"I'm glad Livvie had a good time. Have a nice weekend," she said, proud that her voice was reasonably steady. "Good night, Livvie."

The seven-year-old looked up. "G'night, Rachel."

Rachel hurried through her door with Binx and locked it behind her. Being kissed by Simon Kessler was the last thing she'd expected. But it didn't mean anything and he probably regretted it more than she did.

With a silent groan she carried Binx to the living room and opened the door of the carrier. Then she focused on choosing places for the litter box and food and water bowls. Binx would come out in his own good time, and coaxing might make him feel threatened. It was one thing for him to respond at the shelter, where he was familiar with his surroundings, quite another to be put into a carrier, travel in a car and be introduced to yet another home.

Finally she dropped onto the couch.

The kiss with Simon aside, spending time with Livvie was hard, however much she adored the child. It was a painful reminder that she'd been longing to start her own family when the accident occurred, quickly followed by her marriage collapsing.

Adopting or having a baby through in vitro was a possibility, but it was a huge decision.

She glanced at the wall where she'd hung photos of her family. Despite their parents and grandparents being great role models when it came to marriage, she was the only one of her siblings who'd taken the plunge…and it had been a disaster. Sometimes she worried her divorce had turned her brothers and sister off the idea of getting married at all.

There was a faint thumping sound, and Rachel saw Binx had come out of the carrier and jumped onto the far end of the couch.

Maybe she should become an "official

cat lady" like Hannah. She could fill her spare time with good friends and felines who needed special attention. It would be entertaining, if nothing else, and she had contacts for raising money to support the cause. Or she could use those contacts to help Hannah's House of Cats. Unless Hannah was independently wealthy—which seemed doubtful—she could probably use the extra donations.

SIMON DIDN'T KNOW what had come over him to adopt a cat—two cats—and wished he could blame kissing Rachel on his uncharacteristic behavior.

The shock in her eyes was his only consolation.

Disgusted with himself, he took off his hoodie and tossed it in his clothes hamper, then glowered at Rocky, who'd already planted himself on the bed and was giving himself a bath. Getting a kitten or even a second cat for Livvie was one thing, but Rocky had clearly demonstrated his partiality for adults. His paperwork had confirmed that while he was okay with children, they weren't his preference.

"I showed you the litter box," Simon said to the cat. "You know how to use it, right?"

Rocky yawned.

Simon scowled. Great, he was talking to an animal. But at least Livvie's kitten had already demonstrated he was familiar with proper feline toilet procedures. Rocky was an unknown quantity as of yet.

Livvie came into the bedroom, the kitten draped over her shoulder. It was purring so loudly he could hear it from across the room. "Daddy, why does Jelly Bean have to eat different food than Rocky?" She'd quickly picked the name for her new cat, though Simon didn't have a clue how she'd come up with "Jelly Bean."

"Because Jelly Bean is still a baby. She needs a special diet."

"But Angie says she can't have milk. Why? I drink milk and I'm not grown-up yet."

"I'm not sure."

"Can we call Rachel? She might know."

Simon groaned silently. Rachel probably *would* know, but getting in touch with her was the last thing he wanted right now. "Not tonight."

Jelly Bean jumped from her shoulder onto

the bed and danced over to sniff noses with Rocky, then playfully batted at the elder cat's ear. Simon tensed in case he needed to intervene, envisioning the small animal getting smacked for impudence, but Rocky rolled the kitten under his paw and began licking her face.

"Ooh, Daddy, do you think Rocky is Jelly Bean's papa?"

Livvie had been peppering him with questions since they'd got home and his head was spinning. "I don't think so. They must have become friends at the shelter."

She climbed up on the bed and petted Jelly Bean, giggling when Rocky's rough tongue tickled her hand. "Daddy, can I be a model like Rachel used to be?"

"When did she tell you about that?"

"Gemma told me. I want to be a model for the clothes Mommy drew in my books. Rachel says 'Me and Mommy' is a good name for them."

His head began to pound in earnest. "We'll talk about it another time. What do you want for dinner?"

Livvie gathered the kitten under her chin. "Cheese pizza."

"We had pizza last night. How about Chinese? I'll order chop suey and the chicken and snow peas you like."

"Okay."

She left and Simon ground his teeth. Rachel shouldn't have told his daughter about the "Me and Mommy" collection. It was still just a concept and might never happen. He wanted to confront her, but first he needed to calm down. The situation had got a whole lot more tricky now that he'd kissed her.

Talking business while angry was a bad idea. He'd use the weekend to reflect and make an appointment with her next week.

Otherwise he could make another mistake he'd regret.

CHAPTER TWELVE

RACHEL SPENT THE next two days trying to get acquainted with Binx. She only went out for an hour on Saturday to return the cat carrier to Hannah and get additional cat supplies, including a scratching post, catnip and an assortment of toys.

On Sunday she found the toys scattered around the condo, though Binx remained standoffish. You'd never know he'd butted foreheads with her at Hannah's House of Cats, but he had a troubled history and this could be his way of testing her. The following morning she woke to find him asleep on the bed—the far corner of the bed, but it was progress.

He looked at her reproachfully as she got ready for work, apparently recognizing it wouldn't be a short trip, ending with bags of cat toys and treats.

"I'll be back," she promised.

He turned and jumped on a chair to look

out the window as if he couldn't care less. Cats often seemed self-sufficient, but Rachel knew Binx was anything but indifferent. He just didn't want to take the risk of caring for someone, only to have it end.

Sort of like Simon.

She still didn't know what to think about that kiss. It had come out of the blue and he was probably devising excuses to squirm out of their business agreement because of it. Well, fine. They had a contract, but she was more than willing to tear the thing up.

As for the way the picture books were making Simon question his marriage? From her perspective, he and his wife had shared a unique, strong relationship. An artist and businessman might seem incompatible, but they'd both been dynamic, ambitious and willing to work out compromises for their personal lives.

In fact, the glimpses into *their* marriage were making her wonder how she'd ever thought things could work with Hayden.

Her ex had never compromised, and he'd loved the glitz and glamour associated with modeling. Image was far more important to him than comfort; even in private he'd dressed and groomed himself as if a camera was pointed in his direction. *She'd* grown up in a small Seattle bedroom community and had never been overly comfortable with high fashion. He'd hated it when she'd worn comfy jeans and an ancient sweatshirt and gone without makeup.

She hadn't changed her mind about sticking with friendship over romance, but accepted that she'd mostly just chosen badly when it came to falling in love and getting married.

Rachel pushed her melancholy away and put out fresh water and food for Binx. "If I get a chance, I'll come home and see you at lunchtime," she told him. He stubbornly remained focused on the street and lake in the distance. At least it was a more entertaining view than the one from his kennel at the shelter.

She was grinning when she drove out of the parking garage, thinking that if she *wanted* to be an official cat lady, she might not be that far from it. As a kid she'd always talked to her cat, confiding her woes and joys to JoJo's funny, furry face. Now she was talking to Binx.

At the agency she said hi to Chelsea. "Any messages?" she asked.

"No, but you have a new appointment for this morning. Ten o'clock. Mr. Kessler just called and was insistent about seeing you as soon as possible."

"Why am I not surprised?" Rachel murmured.

"Is something wrong?"

"Nothing serious, but I suspect I'm about to lose a client."

"Mr. Kessler? Why? He's the one who came to you."

Rachel shrugged. "It's complicated, particularly with us living in the same building and me knowing his daughter. She's an adorable child."

"I feel sorry for her. He's handsome, but cold. I swear, he can freeze you with a look."

Not cold, Rachel wanted to protest, then thought better of it. Her feelings about Simon were mixed and she didn't want to broadcast them. "You don't need to worry about Livvie. Mr. Kessler is very loving with her and she means the world to him."

"That's a relief to hear."

Giving Chelsea a smile, Rachel went back to her office and printed a list from the Liv'ing Creations file, then made several calls. It was still early enough that advertisers were looking for the right faces to represent their Christmas and New Year's sales; she wanted her clients to be seriously considered. At precisely 10:00 a.m. there was a sharp rap on her door.

"Come in," she called.

Simon marched inside with an angry expression on his face.

"Good morning, Simon."

"Hello. I thought I'd calm down over the weekend, but I didn't. Why did you tell Livvie about the 'Me and Mommy' project? Now she wants to be a model for the children's line. Do you know how crushed she'll be if nothing comes of it?"

Wow. Rachel had anticipated various scenarios, but nothing like this.

Quite deliberately, she leaned back in her chair, determined to look unperturbed. "In the first place, I didn't tell her about the project, though when I was looking through the books initially, I said something to myself about it. She's extremely bright and could have understood more than I realized. But I haven't said anything to her since then, nor has she asked."

"I see." Simon looked disconcerted.

"However, I know what's likely bothering

you," Rachel continued. "And it has nothing to do with me saying something I shouldn't have to Livvie."

She'd been right to warn herself against Simon's sharp edges. You never knew when you'd bash yourself against one of them.

He made a dismissive gesture. "I'm simply concerned about my daughter. She's lost enough and I don't want her to be disappointed. There's nothing else to it."

Rachel stood. "That may be, but you're also forgetting that Liv'ing Creations belongs to Livvie. You even said I'd technically be consulting for your daughter, not you. Or don't you remember that? You're simply holding the company in trust for her."

SIMON REMEMBERED, AND was chagrined.

"Sorry."

Rachel walked around the desk and gave him a challenging look. "Let's be frank. This has nothing to do with whether or not I told Livvie about the 'Me and Mommy' concept. You're angry about what happened at the elevator on Friday. Which *you* instigated, not me, may I emphasize."

He resisted the urge to loosen his collar. She was right. They both lived in the Carthage, so even if they were interested in casual dating, it would be a bad idea. The more he'd thought about that kiss and how he had risked Livvie seeing it, the more angry and frustrated he'd become.

"And I bet you spent the past two days looking for a reason to break our contract," Rachel continued.

"That isn't true."

Well, not entirely.

"Tell you what, I'll make it easy." She had a wickedly amused expression as she stepped closer, put her arms around his neck and kissed him. Electricity surged through Simon and he caught her close, savoring the embrace the way he hadn't been able to in front of his daughter.

For once in his life he didn't want to think, just feel.

Rachel was warm, kind, smart...desirable. A reminder that he was fully alive. Yet all too soon she pulled away.

"There," she breathed. "Now you can self-righteously tell yourself that you need to get out of the contract because *I* kissed *you*."

"I don't want out. That isn't what I said." How could such an innocent kiss be turning his brain into a confused mass of misfired signals? He was the one who remained calm through dozens of high-pressure business deals when others in his organization were panicking.

Rachel took another step backward and sat on the edge of her desk. "No? I find that hard to believe after your warnings not to get romantic ideas. Though to be perfectly honest, you aren't a fairy-tale hero. So the better I've got to know you, the more absurd those warnings have sounded."

Her comment was an eerie echo of what he'd already concluded. "In that case, what am I?"

"The ogre in the story."

"Then why did you kiss me? To see if I was under a spell and would turn into a handsome prince?"

"As I said, to give you an easy out." Rachel crossed her legs and swung them gently. She was so poised it was utterly annoying. "It's all right, you know. It isn't as if I don't have enough clients. We can shred the contract whenever you please."

Simon frowned. "I told you that isn't what I want." It might have been his subconscious intention, but the thought had vanished the moment he'd walked into the office and looked at her. It was rash and probably silly, but Rachel kept reminding him of the enchanted creatures in the stories his mother had spun. He half expected her to disappear like a wisp of light in the fog.

"You're the one who made the appointment. What *do* you want?"

"To be friends," he improvised.

Her face was skeptical. "Friends?"

"And business partners," he added. "But I'm not a man who's made that many friends, so it's awkward for me to know how to proceed. Regardless, I shouldn't have kissed you. I'm sorry."

"That's all right. We're even."

Rachel wasn't innocent enough to think the two kisses were equal. She hadn't had much time to participate in the first one, while he'd eagerly increased the intensity of the second.

Was that one of the frustrations smoldering in his subconscious? Rachel hadn't reacted when he'd kissed her the previous Friday, but she also hadn't had time to react. Today she'd kissed him and he'd kissed her back with great enthusiasm.

Déjà vu, Simon thought. He hadn't felt this out of his depth and self-questioning since he was fourteen and smitten with the daughter of his father's chauffeur. They'd giggled nervously through their first and only kiss. But they had never shared a second because when Richard Kessler learned his son was consorting with an employee's child, he promptly fired the man. Image was everything to Richard.

The injustice still galled Simon.

"What are you thinking?" Rachel asked softly. "You look upset again."

He smiled wryly. "You're getting too good at figuring me out."

"Beware, that's one of the risks of having friends. They see beneath the surface—even when we don't want them to. And they tell us things we don't want to hear, but need to."

"I suppose. My mind was wandering. I was thinking about the chauffeur who my father fired, just because I had a crush on the man's daughter and took her to a movie. Mr. Carson was a great guy. He didn't deserve that."

"Did you ever try to find him?"

"Right after I started my own company. He'd left his old address and the forwarding order had long since expired."

Rachel pursed her lips. "How about searching on social media?"

"Hardly. I'm not exactly a fan."

She circled around the desk to her computer. "Fan or not, social media is an essential tool in business these days. Friends and families also love it for sharing news and pictures. One of the things I appreciate is that it also can help reconnect old friends, depending on the information entered. What was Mr. Carson's first name?"

"Harry. He's originally from Savannah, Georgia. He always hoped to move back."

Rachel entered the name and spent several minutes navigating through the hits she'd got, clicking on various names, shaking her head, then moving on to the next. Finally she clicked on one and gestured to the screen. "Is that him?"

Startled, Simon stared at a group picture that included an older Harry, along with a woman standing next to another man and two children.

"That's him. And I'm sure the woman is Selena."

Rachel clicked on a link and pulled up another page, then another. "This is Selena's Facebook page. She's now Selena Mitchell.

It says she's an engineer, married with two children."

"What did the other page say about Mr. Carson?"

Rachel navigated around the various screens and smiled. "He went back to school and got a degree. He's the supervising horticulturist at a botanical garden in Savannah, Georgia. It's owned by a philanthropist and open to viewing five days a week. He's also won several awards for developing new breeds of orchids."

"That's good to hear." Relief went through Simon. He'd always felt responsible for Mr. Carson being unfairly terminated, but apparently he'd landed on his feet—no thanks to the Kesslers.

"If you sign up on Facebook you could send him a message," Rachel suggested. "You don't have to display your last name if you don't want to. It could show Simon K, or you could use an entirely different screen name."

Simon wasn't sure how Mr. Carson would feel about getting a message from his ex-employer's son, twenty-plus years after being fired. "It's a little late, but maybe I could send him a check to help compensate for what happened."

"Why don't you just talk to him?"

Simon was having trouble making up his mind about Rachel. "Are you sure? In my experience, money usually smooths out the rough spots." As he said it, he saw her put a hand on her leg again. Sometimes it seemed to be an instinctive gesture, and sometimes...

"Let me tell you a story," she said. "You asked why I don't use the elevator much. Since you looked me up on the internet, you may have read about me getting hurt on a modeling set a number of years ago."

He nodded, recalling the stories he'd seen. For the most part he'd skipped over them. Being someone who valued his own privacy, he hadn't seen a need to know the details. "I saw some headlines, but it wasn't pertinent to my research, so they didn't interest me."

There was doubt on Rachel's face. "The injuries were to my face and left leg. I spent a year and a half in and out of hospitals having surgeries. The plastic surgeon was brilliant, and so was the doctor who rebuilt my jaw. I didn't want to look different and they succeeded. A few faint scars remain, but my jawline is the same and the marks are easily covered with makeup. See?"

She pointed to the left side of her face, as if daring him to look closely. Simon wasn't an expert, but he could imagine how hard it would be for anyone to deal with extensive facial injuries.

When he didn't step closer, Rachel dampened a tissue with a water bottle and began swiping it over her jaw.

"Rachel, don't," Simon protested. A few scars couldn't make her less beautiful, but it had to be hard for her to reveal something she carefully concealed each day.

"Why shouldn't you see?" she asked impatiently, coming around to the front of the desk again. "Some of the paparazzi got into the hospital dressed as doctors and sneaked pictures after one of my surgeries. Then they used Photoshop to make me look like Frankenstein's bride and sold them to a scandal rag, the kind that's displayed at every grocery checkout in the country. Imagine how fun that was for my friends and family."

When she was done, Simon saw two indistinct lines that would probably only be noticed if someone was looking for them and knew what they might be. He traced the marks with the tip of his finger, knowing they represented a huge amount of pain.

"There is nothing in the world that could take away from how gorgeous you are," he said. "My mother used to spin tales about fairies dancing in silver glens and how human males would desperately chase them, hoping for love. You remind me of those stories."

He kissed the faint marks, then her mouth, not caring that he was again doing something he might regret. A hint of gardenias filled his senses and it was like a magical potion. When he finally lifted his head, he saw Rachel was breathing as raggedly as he was.

"You just made the count uneven again," she whispered.

"It isn't a contest."

"And I'm not a fairy, much as the idea appeals."

Simon reluctantly stepped backward. It would be helpful to remember he wanted friendship and a business relationship with Rachel, nothing else. "All right. Is there a point to the story you were telling me?"

"Uh, yeah. In addition to the scars, my leg has never fully recovered. I also ended up somewhat claustrophobic from being bandaged so often."

The elevator.

He was disgusted with himself and his big mouth.

"Rachel, I'm sorry. I shouldn't have said anything about the elevator. It was insensitive."

"No, it's fine. Anyhow, my agent put out feelers when I was close to returning to modeling, but nobody was interested. They said it had been too long and the public would only be thinking about my injuries, not the product being sold."

Simon couldn't see the point she was getting at, but he was convinced she rarely talked about the accident, the same way she rarely mentioned having been a model. "So your career as a model was over."

"Yeah. I got a check from the insurance company as compensation, but a part of me resented that money. It didn't heal my leg and I still needed makeup to cover the remaining scars."

Simon nodded. "You're also living in the Carthage, instead of a country house, which is what you'd prefer. I'm guessing that's because it would be hard for you to manage the yard, at least by yourself." He didn't know why he'd added the last part, possibly because he'd had a mental flash of them taking care of a garden together, which was absurd. He'd never done yard work in his life; his fee at the Carthage included maintenance of the private garden area attached to his condo.

Rachel stuck her chin out. "I'm not talking about now. I'm talking about how I felt getting that check. What I really wanted was a sincere apology from the workers who were responsible. Mr. Carson might feel the same."

Essentially Rachel was saying that money wasn't always the answer. Mr. Carson was doing well in his new career, but maybe he'd appreciate someone saying they regretted the events of the past. A check might even seem to trivialize what had happened.

"I understand."

"Yes, but having said all of that, it's also important to point out that you aren't responsible for your father's behavior and apologizing isn't your job."

Simon wasn't convinced. As much as he wanted to be a better man than Richard Kessler, he wasn't sure he'd succeeded. The concept of paying things forward was great, but maybe there were times to pay things backward, as well.

"I'll give it some thought," he promised. Then something else occurred to him. "Rachel, forgive me for being insensitive, but your marriage—"

"I don't think Hayden could handle the end of what he saw as a storybook life," she interrupted in a flat tone. "But it wasn't just that. We discovered we had almost nothing in common besides our work."

"I'm sorry."

"It's in the past. It's *all* in the past."

Simon seriously doubted that was true. Everything he'd learned about Rachel suggested her scars influenced how she saw herself. "Are you sure? All experiences leave scars. Yours are just slightly more visible."

Her eyes flashed. "Yeah, and your scars have hardened your view of people. I'll keep mine, thank you very much."

"Take it easy, I wasn't trying to start an argument. And I'm not disagreeing. The last thing I want is for Livvie to see the world the way I do, so I'm working on it."

"Fine." She reached across the desk for a file folder. "I've added to the list of designers for consideration. It would be a good idea to consider hiring one who does children's clothing. Their portfolios each show a flair that might meld well with Liv'ing Creations."

He accepted the folder. "I'll take a look. Incidentally, this morning I told Janine Jenkins that her next collection will be the last with Liv'ing Creations. She'll get a decent severance package, provided she satisfactorily completes her responsibilities for everything in progress at the moment. Her termination letter will simply say we're taking the design house in a new direction and wish her well."

Rachel's eyes softened. "That's very generous, Simon. It must have been hard not to get angry with her."

"You have no idea. I may not have been clear enough with Miriam Timmons, but my original discussion with Janine was specific. She knew she wasn't doing what I'd asked and even admitted it—she actually thought our meeting was to congratulate her for putting the design house on 'the right track.'"

"Ouch. That wasn't very bright."

Simon grimaced. "I was pretty steamed, but I didn't want to react the way my father would have, so I let it go. As I said, I'm working on it."

"What about Ms. Timmons?"

"Her employment is still in question. I explained how unhappy I was that Janine Jenkins has veered so far from the spirit of my wife's designs. Miriam instantly turned defensive and declared she couldn't be blamed for the falling sales. No matter what I said, she didn't seem to understand that my concerns aren't about sales, they're about Liv's legacy."

THOUGH RACHEL HAD defended the other woman, she couldn't help wondering why Olivia Kessler had hired Miriam in the first place.

Luckily the phone rang before she could say something Simon might take the wrong way. It was Chelsea notifying her that Lydia Kravitz, her ten-thirty appointment, had arrived. Lydia was an actress whose performance Rachel had caught at a local repertory company. Her stage presence had been so engaging, Rachel had made contact with her to learn if she already had an agent.

Rachel told Chelsea she needed a few

minutes and put the receiver down. "Sorry, I have someone waiting."

"Of course. I'll get going, but I'd like us to continue working together, especially on the 'Me and Mommy' collection. Shall I talk to Chelsea about setting up more meetings?"

"She knows my schedule better than I do."

When he was gone, Rachel took out a mirror and bottle of foundation and quickly smoothed a small amount on her jaw. What had possessed her to melodramatically reveal her scars to Simon?

The whole exchange held a surreal quality, as if it had happened to someone else. She'd kissed him? What had come over her? Then he'd kissed her. Again.

Most of the time, dealing with Simon was akin to a precarious game of baiting the tiger. He had claws and teeth and she'd felt them today before everything had got weird.

At least he wasn't stupid. He might have been angry, but when she'd shot a few home truths at him, he'd backed off and talked rationally. *This time.* He'd also held up a metaphorical mirror and challenged her perception of how well she'd left the past behind.

Rachel was tucking the makeup back into

her desk drawer when a soft knock sounded on her door. She squared her shoulders and fastened a smile on her face before opening it.

It was time to get back to work.

CHAPTER THIRTEEN

MATT WAS FRUSTRATED by Pepper's behavior. He'd taken her harness off, but even when she was off duty, she didn't respond to other people unless she perceived them as a threat. Today, the moment Gemma had arrived, she'd begun whining unhappily. Now she put her forefeet on the instrument console, apparently to look into the live studio where Gemma was reading.

"Down, girl," he ordered.

With another unhappy whine she dropped to all fours, but instead of seeking her bed under the table, she put her head on his leg and whimpered. It was her way of saying, *I don't think everything is okay.*

Gemma's performance *was* off, so Matt stopped the recording and flipped the two-way mike switch.

"Sorry for interrupting, Gemma. Pepper is upset. She thinks something is wrong." As soon as he said it, he winced. How professional was it to bring up his guide dog's emotional state? "Are you okay? Your voice isn't as a strong as usual."

"Oh." She didn't say anything for a moment. "Sorry, I'm a bit sore and achy today. I'll try to do better."

"Maybe you're coming down with the flu. We should wait until you're feeling better."

"It isn't the flu. I fell on my parents' front steps this morning when I went out for the newspaper. It was frosty and I didn't realize how slippery they'd be."

The things she'd revealed about her father's drinking instantly made Matt wonder if she was hiding something. A drinker, frustrated by a health crisis, might strike out at the nearest target.

"Are you sure that's all?" The question came out harsher than intended.

"I don't know what you mean. Maybe Pepper is unhappy about my wrist being wrapped. I sprained it when I fell."

"Have you been to the emergency room?"

Gemma laughed. "It wasn't that serious. I have bruises on my hip and my knee, and an even bigger one on my pride." The ease in her tone suggested there was nothing more to the tale.

"I've read it takes a year to get over a really bad fall."

"I read that, too. But does traditional or holistic medicine make the claim? Because I'd love to find someone to restore my energy balance, or whatever hitting the ground disrupts."

Matt chuckled. Gemma could be fun when she relaxed and wasn't self-conscious. "I'm not sure. Maybe both of them. Has your brother, the doctor, got home from New Zealand? He should be able to help."

"Drake will be back in a few days."

The sound of something being dragged came through the speakers. Aside from the reading stand for the manuscript, the only furniture in the recording room was a stool, reminding Matt he hadn't offered Gemma a seat. She'd turned it down in the past, so it hadn't occurred to him to offer it again, but she had to be sore after taking a tumble.

"I don't think it's quite the tourist season in New Zealand yet," Gemma continued, "but Drake found someone willing to act as guide on every well-known hike in the country. Then they were delayed by weather. His phone got soaked, which is why he couldn't get in touch with us earlier. I also think he didn't try that hard, so you must be right that he welcomed the chance to get away from everything."

"Not quite the tourist season? Oh, that's right, the seasons are reversed down there. We're heading into winter in our hemisphere, and it's their spring."

"So Drake tells me. He's always wanted to visit New Zealand. Now he's setting his sights on Australia—even told me that when he called. Mom won't appreciate the thought of him trekking into the outback. If he doesn't return safely, none of us will hear the end of it."

Matt chuckled. "Maybe she can talk him out of going."

"More like he'll convince her that it was her idea. Drake can charm bees out of their honey. He can't do any wrong in her eyes, unless you count going to another country and being out of cell range."

Matt stood up. "Why don't we go for something at the Crystal Connection? You can't feel up to reading this morning and I need to stretch my legs. I came in at 5:00 a.m. to catch up on work."

"All right," Gemma agreed after a moment. At the Crystal Connection he ordered black coffee while she had hot chocolate. Pepper's tail lashed back and forth against his leg and he grinned; she was hoping for a treat, but was too well behaved to ask for one.

"Penny, do you still have that jar of dog treats on your counter?" he asked.

"Naturally. I have one for cats, too, but we don't get many of them. Would Pepper like a snack?"

"I'm sure she would." He removed the golden retriever's harness. She eagerly moved forward, and he heard her teeth click as she caught the treat and chomped it down.

"Say thank you, Pepper," he instructed.

Pepper yipped and circled back so he could replace the harness.

"What a good girl. She's so polite," Penny said.

Matt was glad to hear Penny sounding more like herself. "Thank you. She rarely breaks discipline. Ready, Gemma?"

"Yes, thanks."

They returned to the studio and he detected the faintest hint of unevenness in her step. Odd that he'd missed it when she first arrived, but he was having trouble keeping his perceptions sorted out with her. She'd talked about her brother having great charm as if she didn't share his gift, but her voice and laugh were enticing.

"I should have gone to the Crystal Connection and let you rest," he muttered, feeling distinctly lacking in chivalry.

"Not at all. Moving around will help keep me from getting stiff. Besides, I didn't realize until we got there that I felt like having cocoa. This time of year makes me want to curl up with a cup of hot chocolate and play a corny movie."

Matt didn't play many corny films. Any sort of saccharine sweetness was too much for him.

"I'm mostly a fan of nonfiction. Historical biographies, interviews of interesting people, that sort of thing. Not always easy to find on television these days."

"I like that, too. A man after my own heart."

Matt grinned. "Afraid I'm not after anyone's heart. Few women seem to be able to handle me being blind."

Silence followed and he wondered what Gemma was thinking. Most of the time he was at peace with not being able to see, but there were moments when he'd do anything to read someone's expression.

"That...that isn't a very flattering opinion of my sex," she said at length.

"I'm not claiming men would do any better if the shoe was on the other foot."

"Well, I believe you're wrong. You'd just have to give someone a chance to adjust and learn. Give-and-take is needed in all relationships."

Matt unlocked the door of the studio. "Like the way your mother enables your father to drink? That kind of give-and-take I can do without."

There was another long silence and he started to regret the tactless comment. Gemma had confided about her parents' codependent relationship and he had no right using it to deflect an uncomfortable subject.

"You know, maybe I don't feel up to doing the reading today," she said before he could apologize. "Thanks for the cocoa. I'll get going now."

"Are you coming back?" he asked, worried the answer would be a resounding no. "It wouldn't be for two weeks. The studio is booked for next Saturday."

"Why not? I should be better by then."

FUMING, GEMMA DROPPED her cup in a trash can and hurried to her car, ignoring the protests from her sore hip and knee. For the most part she liked Matt, but today he'd proved he could be a complete jerk.

Predictable, Olivia Kessler would have said.

Gemma had learned a good deal about men and marriage from Mrs. Kessler. She'd been understanding of her husband's utter lack of interest in design, saying it was only fair, since she wasn't interested in high finance, his area of expertise. She'd seen her spouse for who he was, a generous, brilliant man with a truckload of demons from his past.

Matt had demons, as well. One thing was certain, he'd decided his lack of sight was an insurmountable barrier to a romantic relationship. And she'd been too polite to inform him that his attitude was likely the biggest reason he'd never get married or have a long-term girlfriend.

Sure, some people couldn't handle having a partner who had a physical challenge, but that didn't mean *everyone* should be painted with the same dismissive brush. Matt having a drinking problem would be a far bigger issue to her than his not being able to see. But she'd need to feel it was okay to ask questions and talk openly with him about his lack of sight—without being thought less of for not knowing everything already, or being judged for whether she had responded correctly.

Gemma pulled off the road at a supermarket and tapped her fingers on the steering wheel. She could return and tell Matt what she thought of his behavior, but it might reveal that she'd started to like him too much. Besides, she could be wrong and something else was bothering him today.

Or maybe she was just making excuses, the way her mom made excuses about her husband.

Gemma dropped her head back and closed her eyes, trying to sort her racing thoughts. Sometimes it seemed as if she'd spent her entire life trying to earn her family's approval. What Matt had said about it being *their* problem made sense, but she needed time to let go of feeling like a failure.

Finally she got out and went into the market to buy groceries. Once Drake got home, he could take over hand-holding their parents while she had a real vacation. But it wouldn't be relaxing if she just went back to the Kesslers' condo, so she needed to decide where to go and what to do...preferably not thinking about Matt Tupper.

Victoria, up in British Columbia, sounded nice. She'd grown up in the Seattle area, but she'd never had a chance to visit Vancouver Island. She could spend some solid time there and then come home to do another session at the recording studio.

Maybe by then she wouldn't be tempted to scream a few hard facts at Matt.

SOON AFTER THE awkward encounter in her office, Rachel began having daily meetings with Simon. Their work together was relatively fruitful. She loved being busy and productive, but the ongoing tension was stressful. Or maybe it was the way he made her feel.

Toward the end of the first week she noticed he seemed preoccupied, but he denied it when she asked if something was bothering him.

He plainly wasn't becoming more conversant with fashion, but he supported doing a children's clothing line, and even brought Livvie to a couple of their work

sessions. Together they'd selected a target
set of designs for the next collection and
discussed his impressions of the designers
he was interviewing.

Curiously, Rachel was coming to the conclusion that deep down, Simon resented
Liv'ing Creations. She knew he questioned
whether Olivia had kept their mutual promise to make family a priority, but was that
the only reason?

"I need to make a decision about Miriam
in the next few weeks," Simon told her after
their appointment the second Monday. "Is
there any chance you can make some calls
to find out what your contacts in the fashion world have to say about her? I'd like as
much information as possible before taking action."

"I'll see what I can do," Rachel promised.

When he was gone she placed several
calls, but it wasn't until the next day that
anyone could get back to her. Unfortunately,
her contacts had few observations to make
about Miriam Timmons.

Adequate.

A fair organizer.

Keeps a low profile.

The "low profile" remark was probably a

compliment since designers preferred being in the spotlight. She finally took her own advice and searched for both Miriam Timmons and Janine Jenkins on social media. The things she learned were interesting and after additional research, she called Simon to share her conclusions since they didn't have an appointment scheduled.

"How about discussing it over dinner tonight?" he suggested. "Livvie is having a sleepover with a friend from school and I'm at loose ends."

"Mr. Overprotective Daddy is letting his daughter go to a sleepover?" Rachel teased.

"Do overprotective fathers let their children have a kitten with very sharp claws and teeth?"

"That depends. What else has happened with Jelly Bean?" So far she'd been regaled with tales of Jelly Bean climbing the curtains, getting on top of the kitchen cabinets and breaking Livvie's laptop.

"She should be renamed Tornado. Last night she destroyed my CD player and sank every single claw into me when I rescued her from the fishbowl, which, by the way, now belongs to the barista at the Java Train Shop. Rocky mostly sleeps on his back with his paws in the air, or watches Jelly Bean's antics with bored disdain. He's a relaxed personality. Practically catatonic."

Rachel bit her lip to stop a laugh. "Somebody should have warned you that kittens have an excess of energy. They don't even stand flat on their feet, they just dance around on the tips of their toes, wreaking havoc."

"So I've discovered. How is Binx? Any damage to report?" Simon sounded hopeful.

"Nope. We're slowly making friends. I'm letting everything go at his pace. Meanwhile, I'm doing my best to keep Binx entertained with a feather-filled cancan show... meaning I've put out a bird feeder. It isn't against the condo association bylaws, so I'm assuming no one will complain. Birds are great eye candy. You should see Binx quiver as they flit in and out. On the other side of the glass, of course."

"Of course."

Rachel spun in her chair to look out the window and saw dark clouds were gathering. A brisk wind sent a flurry of leaves across the parking area and the water on the lake was choppy. Rain was practically a daily occurrence in Washington, but she'd rather be close to home that evening if a major storm was coming in.

"Shall we meet at the Just Like Home Café near the Carthage?" she asked. "I don't eat out often, but that's usually where I go."

SIMON WASN'T SURE about the suggestion.

A café just like home?

His mother had relied on dishes such as mac and cheese, chili and spaghetti because they were inexpensive and filling. Karen had employed a cook who'd informed him that she didn't prepare special food for children; he could eat what she made or go hungry. As an adult he could appreciate the meals had been gourmet. As a kid he'd hated them, which was why he didn't ask Livvie to do more than taste a new dish.

"Sure," he agreed, in spite of his doubts. "How about five o'clock? That way we'll miss the evening rush."

"I don't think our neighborhood *has* an evening rush, but five is fine. By going early, we might get home ahead of the weather."

Simon got off the phone and stared at the message his assistant had given him earlier. His so-called father had called. *For the fourth time.* Apparently he was in Seattle and wanted to talk, but Simon didn't have anything to say, and wasn't interested in anything Richard had to say, either.

He crumpled the paper and tossed it in the trash can, the same as he'd done with the other messages.

Rachel was already at a table when Simon arrived at the café. She was talking with the server. "Hi, Simon. Meet Ginny. She's a theater arts major at the U-Dub."

He nodded a greeting, vaguely irritated to discover Rachel was recruiting a new client while waiting for him. When they were alone, he lifted an eyebrow. "Do you find new clients wherever you go?"

"Ginny isn't a prospective client. When it comes to actors, Moonlight Ventures wants to see a performance before talking with someone. I'm too busy to search out new talent right now, but maybe once our last partner, Logan, arrives, I'll work more actively to increase my client list."

Simon felt churlish for his initial reaction. Besides, he didn't have any reason to object, even if Rachel *had* been using their meeting time to recruit another client. Liv'ing Creations was consuming a huge chunk of her time and she had a living to make. "Logan is the photographer, right?"

"Right."

They opened their menus and he saw chili and spaghetti listed. Maybe this place *was* just like home. Then another item caught his attention. "Meat loaf sandwich?"

"Don't knock something until you've tried it. My mom makes a killer lemon-barbecue loaf that we love on sourdough rolls with horseradish. This one is different, but I like it, too."

Ginny returned with glasses of water and a breadbasket. "Have you decided what you want?"

Rachel tapped a spot on the menu. "I'll take a Caesar salad with the seared chicken breast. Light on the dressing."

"Meat loaf sandwich," Simon decided. There were more ways than one to be adventurous. "With horseradish."

"Gotcha."

Rachel smiled when Ginny left to give their order to the kitchen. "If you don't care for the meat loaf, they have sushi at the little grocery store up the street. You could grab some on the way home."

He doubted that plastic-wrapped sushi on

a disposable tray could compete with a sushi bar in downtown Seattle, but didn't say so. By unspoken accord they chatted about various subjects until the food arrived. His sandwich was generous and quite tasty.

"I don't know why people turn up their noses at this stuff," he commented after he'd munched down a few bites. "It's good. So, you have something to tell me about Miriam Timmons?"

"I made a number of calls, but my contacts don't know her well. That can be a good thing, meaning she's simply focused on her job. A few mentioned she had okay organizational skills."

"Not exactly a resounding vote of approval."

Simon ate a crisp french fry. "How about Janine Jenkins?"

"Actually, that's where my research got more interesting. It seems she has other connections to Miriam. They graduated from the same university, a year apart, with similar majors. They're also sorority sisters."

"Really?"

RACHEL NOTICED SIMON was wearing his poker face expression, suggesting something was bubbling beneath the surface.

She hesitated. "You should know that a few sororities are sworn to support each other, no matter what."

"Meaning Miriam didn't necessarily think Janine was a good designer, but recommended her because of something she'd promised to do back in school."

"It's possible."

His face was grim. "So much for her loyalty to my wife."

"It's just a possibility," Rachel said quietly. "It could simply explain where they met. I know people who are supportive of their sorority sisters but don't make decisions based on the relationship."

Simon grimaced. "Except Miriam told me she'd met Janine at a Paris fashion show. She even implied that Liv had admired her work. Given the differences in style, I find that hard to believe. She took advantage of how chaotic things were after Liv's death to get me to hire Janine, hoping it would work out okay."

Rachel pulled a slice of crusty bread from the basket. Simon was justifiably upset, but she was more convinced than ever it went beyond a sense of betrayal that Miriam Timmons had fudged the truth.

"Don't make any snap judgments," she said. "Ms. Timmons could have heard Olivia say something about Ms. Jenkins's designs and didn't realize she was just being polite."

"You don't seriously believe that."

"I believe it's wise to question whether Miriam Timmons is still the right fit for Liv'ing Creations, but think it should be done with a clear head. I also think most of your anger is at yourself, because you didn't keep a closer watch on the design house after promising your wife you'd preserve it for Livvie."

He glared at her.

"Sometimes it sounds as if you hold a grudge against the place," Rachel added impulsively, "maybe because Olivia loved it so much." It was rash to raise such a touchy subject. Still, she'd said to him that friends told each other things they needed to hear. "So just be sure you aren't taking those feelings out on someone who doesn't deserve it."

"I'm not—" Simon stopped and seemed to be fighting an internal battle. "Fine. Whatever. I'll take everything into consideration when I make a decision. Anything else?"

He bit off a huge chunk of his sandwich,

and Rachel suspected it was to keep his frustration in check.

"Just that if you decide to dispense with Ms. Timmons's services, you might consider promoting from within. You could conduct interviews with each of the employees and try to get their views, find out how well they understand the overall operation and that sort of thing."

He wiped his mouth with a napkin. "Sure. It's a good thought."

Little else was said the remainder of the meal. Rachel had an expense account with Moonlight Ventures and intended to pay the check since agents commonly treated their clients, but Simon refused the offer.

"You're a consultant, not an agent," he said. "And I still don't have your first bill for services. So *send* it."

He sounded worse than a bear with a thorn in its paw.

If they hadn't been business associates, she might be tempted to just confront him and yank the thorn out, so to speak. But it would be a mistake. She couldn't deny that she was beginning to have feelings for Simon. She also couldn't deny that getting involved with him would be the same as begging for heartbreak.

The shock had been when he'd talked about them becoming friends. Her consulting services for Liv'ing Designs would eventually end, but true friends should be forever. Maybe it was the small-town girl in her. Her hometown was near Seattle, yet in some ways it could be anywhere people brought chicken soup to sick neighbors, the volunteer fire department turned out to help paint the community center and everyone showed up for parades.

How did Simon see friendship? He'd mentioned not having many friends, which could mean he saw friendship as transitory.

It turned out they'd both parked in the Carthage garage and walked to the café, so they returned together, mostly in silence.

They had finished devising a plan for Liv'ing Creations, but where they went from here was unknown.

In the Carthage lobby, Rachel resolutely went to the elevator.

"You don't have to take it because of me," Simon told her.

"I'm not." That wasn't true, but she hadn't wanted to remind him of her minor phobia.

His disbelief when she'd said the past was over had made her do some soul-searching. Perhaps she *hadn't* got over the accident and the failure of her marriage as well as she'd thought.

Inside the elevator she pressed the button for the second floor. When the door opened she hurried out without a backward glance, which wasn't easy. She might have chosen friendship over romance, but this was also the first time since her divorce that she'd been seriously drawn to a man. Not that it was an issue—Simon would have to be available, and he'd made it patently clear that he wasn't.

The scary part was knowing her heart was already teetering on the edge of falling in love with him.

CHAPTER FOURTEEN

ONCE SHE'D GOT HOME, Rachel tried to let go of her tension. Binx could sense when she was stressed and got skittish. She didn't want to lose the progress she'd made with him. After all, this was one male it seemed safe to love wholeheartedly.

"Have fun today?" she asked.

He blinked and yawned, making her grin. It could take weeks or months for him to warm up, but she wasn't going to lose patience. She didn't doubt he was hungry for affection. He always managed to be in the same room with her and now faithfully slept on a corner of the bed.

Rachel checked his food and gave him fresh water, then looked at the phone to see she had voice mail. She entered her code to play the message.

"Oh, hi. It's Gemma. I thought you'd be home. I'll talk to you another time. Bye."

Hmm. Rachel rang her cell number back.

"Rachel?" Gemma answered. "You didn't need to call me. I shouldn't have bothered you."

"It's no bother. Is your dad okay?"

"Yeah, he's fine. I'm in Victoria. I didn't know it was so beautiful here. I mean, I heard it was, but until you're here, it's hard to imagine it could be so amazing."

Binx jumped on the couch and settled down a couple of feet away. "I love it there, too. Be sure to visit the Royal British Columbia Museum near the harbor. It's terrific."

"I'll put it on the list. Have you seen Livvie and Mr. Kessler lately? I feel bad about being away."

Rachel dangled a feather on a stick and Binx lazily batted at it. "There's no reason to feel bad. You deserve your vacation."

A sigh came over the line. "That doesn't stop me from worrying. Livvie has been having more nightmares than usual lately and doesn't like going to her father because she thinks it upsets him."

Now Rachel was worried. "Does Simon know?"

"She made me promise not to tell him. Um, by the way, what is your opinion of Matt Tupper? I'm still making up my mind."

Intriguing. A fishing expedition for information. Rachel kicked off her shoes and tucked her legs beneath her. "He seems to be a good guy. I also know what Kevin McClaskey told me about him. Kevin used to own the Moonlight Ventures building, and a long time ago he was my agent. Mostly I've heard Matt is extremely independent."

"No kidding." The tone in Gemma's voice spoke volumes. "He practically snarled when he thought I was avoiding words like *look* and *see*. But I wasn't. The thing is, one minute he's nice, and the next he's…"

"Impossible?"

"Exactly."

"I know the feeling. Pure frustration, right?"

Gemma giggled. "Are you having relationship troubles, too?"

The question made Rachel bolt upright, startling Binx. "No more than usual."

Gemma laughed again. "I thought guys were hard to understand when I was in high school and now it's worse. What else do you know about Matt?"

"Let's see, Kevin mentioned that he grew up over in Kirkland. He's hugely talented, a whiz at all that electronic recording stuff.

Some of the big recording companies would love to hire him, but he prefers being his own boss. Oh, and the driver who hit him was both under the influence and texting on his cell phone, which may be the reason Matt actively supports a teen education program for safe and sober driving. That's the extent of my knowledge."

Under the influence?

A cold sensation went through Gemma. Was that why Matt had made such a sharp comment about her mother enabling her father to drink? It wasn't anything she hadn't thought herself a thousand times, but it was different for Matt. He'd been blinded by a drunk driver.

"Gemma, are you there?" Rachel asked. "Is something wrong?"

"I just… Well, my father is a heavy drinker. I was frustrated after an argument with my mom a few weeks ago and mentioned it to Matt. As far as I know, Dad doesn't drink and drive, but…"

"Matt can't hold what happened to him against everyone he meets. He'll be lonely, if nothing else."

"I suppose," Gemma returned, trying to

sound unconcerned. She'd gone from being worried about getting involved with a man who might become an alcoholic, to worried that the man she liked would resent her father's history of alcohol abuse. But if Matt had a hang-up about it, why had he suggested they get a beer and a pizza together?

To test her?

"Matt also believes a lot of women couldn't handle him being blind," she admitted.

"He brought the subject up?"

"I wouldn't have had the nerve to do it myself," Gemma admitted. "But I made a joke about him being a man after my heart and he felt compelled to explain why I was wrong."

Rachel tsk-tsked. "It's disappointing that he doesn't have a sense of humor. Just remember, it's his loss."

"Yeah. Well, I'd better let you go."

"Enjoy Victoria. I hope you can find a place to have an old-fashioned high tea. We used to go to a farm in the country where they served clotted cream with the scones, but I have no idea how to get there now, or if they're open this time of year."

"I'll ask around. Good night."

"'Night."

Rachel turned off the phone and tried to relax, but she couldn't stop thinking that Matt had warned Gemma away just as Simon had warned her away. *What was wrong with them?* She knew Gemma well enough to know she hadn't been talking to Matt about wanting to get married. As for Simon's warnings? He might have backed off on the subject, but it was still annoying to think about. The only reason she'd told Simon about her own decision to avoid romance was because he'd brought it up first.

Binx had retreated to the other end of the couch, and his watchful posture suggested he wasn't coming closer in the immediate future. Casually ignoring him seemed best, so she got up to take a shower.

The long, stone walk-in shower stall was one of the features that had sold her on the condo in the first place, but as she stood under the spray of water, she pictured the guest bathroom in her grandmother's house. The last update had been over thirty years ago, but it had a warm, homey feel that this one, however nice, couldn't replicate.

You're also living in the Carthage, instead

of a country house, which is what you'd prefer.

"Get out of my head, Simon," she grumbled.

She hadn't expected him to guess so accurately how she felt about certain things.

"Meerroow."

Rachel looked around and saw Binx at the shower opening. Cats never respected privacy. Rather than being upset about the fine droplets spattering in his direction, he appeared to be trying to catch them in his mouth.

She turned off the water and walked out slowly so he'd have time to retreat if he wanted. Sure enough, he spun and raced away, though he seemed more playful than spooked. The wet paw prints he left behind suggested he'd ventured farther into the shower stall than she'd realized.

The stone tile floor of the bathroom was heated, a feature she loved, even if it wasn't the same as the one in her grandmother's house. As a kid her toes had frozen in the winter when visiting Grandma. A brief midnight trip to the bathroom had meant shivering under the blankets for an hour after getting back into bed.

She wrapped a towel around herself and yawned.

It was barely 7:00 p.m., but she was tired, probably because Simon had been so annoying. She went to the bed and pulled the comforter down. Going to sleep early was a good idea since she wanted to get to the agency early to catch up on work. Consulting for Liv'ing Creations was eating into time for her other commitments.

As for sending him a bill?

Fine.

She'd tracked her hours spent on the design firm, not counting the time with Livvie. Moonlight Venture's contract with Simon had specified the consulting fee, so she'd have Chelsea create an invoice.

Rachel dropped a silk nightshirt over her head and crawled between the sheets. Binx leaped up a minute later and stretched out within an arm's length. Carefully she slid her hand over to rub the base of his ear. A low purr started.

"You're just a big softy at heart, aren't you?" she whispered.

He pressed his head against her fingers.

"Do you think there's going to be a storm

tonight? That would be okay. Pitter-patter, pitter-patter, with us snug inside."

Binx purred louder and Rachel smiled sleepily. They could have turned the corner on trust.

The Carthage walls and floors were too well insulated to hear much from outside or from neighbors…but it was easy to envision Simon on the floor above her. Was he watching television, pacing, working in his home office or just sitting out in the garden, missing Olivia? He might even be contemplating how to finally end his association with Moonlight Ventures.

It was his choice.

She'd done her best and *he* was the one who'd moved them into personal territory on more than one occasion. It was on his head if he had regrets.

With that uneasy thought, she closed her eyes and let Binx's purr lull her into sleep.

EVER SINCE THE last recording session with Gemma, Matt had felt like slime for what he'd said. Throwing her father's drinking in her face had been a lousy thing to do. She'd trusted him enough to reveal something that troubled her, then he'd used it as a verbal weapon.

And why?

Because she'd said the kind of innocent, teasing thing that men and women said to each other.

It would serve him right if she didn't return to finish the novel they were recording. Foolishly he'd let the editor at the publishing house listen to a portion of Gemma's recording. She'd got excited and said it would be fabulous to sell audio copies as well as the print version, provided terms could be agreed upon.

It was an interesting proposition, but Matt's first concern was to finish the recording for its original purpose.

And apologize to Gemma.

He didn't know what had come over him. In the months after losing his sight, one of the hardest things had been thinking what would happen with women. It hadn't been easy for a seventeen-year-old testosterone-driven kid to accept he'd never see a pretty girl again, or watch the mysterious, wonderful movements of their bodies. Now a woman could be drop-dead gorgeous and he'd have no way of knowing, aside from someone telling him.

But the hardest adjustment had come when he realized people often felt sorry for him, or believed he needed help. It had galled him more than usual to think Gemma might feel that way.

Saturday morning, he waited at the studio, tense, until a knock came at precisely 9:00 a.m.

"Gemma?" he said, opening the door.

"Were you expecting someone else?" Her tone was distinctly cool.

"Not at all. But first, let me apologize for my behavior two weeks ago."

"I don't know what you mean."

Irritation instantly swamped his good intentions. "Don't treat me like that, Gemma. I'm blind, not stupid."

GEMMA STARED.

"Does everything come back to that for you?" she asked incredulously. "I was trying to get past the awkwardness of what happened by ignoring it, but you automatically attribute the courtesy to your being blind. I swear, you put people to the test and feel superior when they don't respond the way you think they should."

Matt straightened. The truth had hit home. "That isn't true."

"It sounds like it to me," she said hotly. "I don't deny that I'm not a very confident person. I'm working on it, but it's hard to overcome a lifetime of being that way."

A funny smile played on his face. "You aren't avoiding conflict now."

"Maybe I'm tired of not standing up for myself. For your information, it doesn't matter to me that you can't see. But it requires a different way of communicating and you aren't making it any easier for me to figure things out. Maybe you should try seeing how it feels from someone else's point of view, not just your own."

"I don't know what you mean. Just talk to me."

"Well, *you* still use nonverbal communications such as smiling and gesturing with your hands while talking, but I forget you can't see when I do that and it flusters me. Then you make assumptions that aren't true and get huffy."

He didn't say anything for a long minute. "I didn't intend to make you uncomfortable.

Maybe I react poorly, but I *don't* get huffy. I just—"

"I'm sorry you feel threatened by being called huffy," Gemma shot back, amazed at her own daring. "If anything, huffy is the way a cat behaves when its dignity is ruffled. You remind me of a stalking cat that got startled."

Matt began to laugh, a full no-holds-barred laugh. "Okay, you win. I blew it up. How do I make amends?"

Gemma wrinkled her nose, only to remember he couldn't see the expression. "You could let me ask questions, without assuming I have a hang-up about your eyesight. Because I don't. The hang-up is in your head, not mine."

"That seems fair. What do you want to know?"

"For one, does it bother you that my father has a drinking problem? Rachel mentioned the driver who hit you was under the influence."

MATT FROWNED. "*Under the influence* doesn't necessarily mean alcohol. The man who ran into me and my friends was on strong prescription drugs and shouldn't have been behind the wheel. Then he started texting someone."

"But you're involved in a program to keep kids from drinking and driving."

"Because it's a worthy cause," he explained. "The thing with your father bothers me, though not for personal reasons. Your mother put pressure on you to keep him from drinking because she couldn't do it herself. I don't think that's fair."

"Spinning my wheels about fairness isn't going to get me anywhere. I used to wonder why I couldn't have a father like my friends', who didn't drown his disappointment with whiskey. Now it sounds minor compared to what you've gone through. You must still be angry."

Matt was stunned. He didn't know how many hours he'd chewed the accident over in his head, his brain racing through scenarios where he didn't end up blind. The therapist had urged him to stop being angry and accept what had happened, but no one had just said, *It's awful. You got a raw deal. It's okay to be mad for a while.*

Now Gemma was saying what he'd felt for years.

Pepper nudged his hand with her nose.

He'd left her in the control room, but as usual, she'd followed and was worried about him. He didn't know if the training facility would approve of her behavior, but he found it reassuring.

"I'm trying to let go of being angry," he admitted. "It's easier than it used to be. Do you have other questions?"

"Well, I know I should pretend Pepper isn't there when she's working, but is it ever acceptable to give her attention? I adore dogs. They don't care if I'm shy, they give love, anyway."

A laugh rolled out of Matt's chest and he removed Pepper's harness. "It's okay when she's off duty, which means when the harness is off. Pepper, give Gemma some love," he ordered, giving her a gesture with his hand.

A moment later Gemma laughed and he heard her patting Pepper. "You're such a sweet girl," she murmured. "Beautiful, too. I'm sorry I don't have any treats for you."

"I probably feed her more treats than she should get," Matt admitted. "But we walk it off. Do you have anything else to ask?"

"Not right now. It just… It would help if

you didn't get so touchy. Are you that way
with everyone, or just me?"

Ouch. Generally Matt had a good relationship with people at the studio or in social situations, but something about Gemma
had got to him from the beginning. With her
shyness, it must have been doubly difficult
to be honest with him.

"Mostly with you," he admitted. "I liked
you so much, I got my nose out of joint when
I shouldn't have. Can we start over?"

"Does starting over mean you're going
to repeat that bit about how some women
can't handle your being blind? Because I'm
tired of men deciding they know what we
can handle."

Matt was starting to think Gemma could
handle anything. It scared him in several
ways, but he'd be a fool not to find out where
this could go between them.

"I wouldn't be stupid enough to say that
again."

Gemma chuckled. "Good, you're learning. Now, let's finish recording that book."

Matt made another gesture and Pepper
returned, standing patiently as he put the
harness back on. He could tell that she was
thrilled to see Gemma.

Which reminded him...

"How is your arm, Gemma? And the rest of your bruises?"

"They turned into a revolting yellow-and-green patchwork with purple undertones, then faded away. I've stopped wrapping my wrist, even though it still aches."

She was good at painting visual pictures. And not just with words, but tone. No surprise. It was one of the reasons she was a great reader.

"I'm glad you're recovering. I have an interesting proposition from the publisher," he explained as they walked toward the studio.

"What kind of proposition?"

"If you let me take you to lunch, I'll tell you all about it."

"Pizza and a beer?"

"Nah. First dates should be somewhere nicer."

For a moment all he heard was a quick intake of breath. "Sure. That sounds good."

ON WEDNESDAY MORNING Rachel checked on several photo shoots for her clients, then stopped at Pike Place Market to search for a dream catcher to give Livvie. She'd already looked for one at the Crystal Connection and other shops near the agency and was beginning to think she'd never find what she wanted.

She hadn't heard from Simon since the evening they'd had dinner at the café, but on Monday she'd made sure an invoice went out for her "consulting" services. In a way it made her uncomfortable, yet it wasn't fair to her partners at Moonlight Ventures to be less than professional.

Rachel went from store to store at the market before locating a dream catcher she thought was relatively authentic. At the very least it was on a willow hoop and the feathers weren't dyed. Before talking with Gemma she hadn't known Livvie was having nightmares, and she hoped the symbolism of the dream catcher would help.

Her next dilemma was figuring out how to give it to Livvie without upsetting her father. She couldn't exactly hang out at the parking garage, hoping to see them when Simon took her to school. But when she arrived back at the agency she found both Simon and Livvie waiting in the lobby.

"There's Rachel," Livvie shrieked and ran to give her a hug. "It's been days and days. I missed you," she declared fervently.

"I missed you, too. Here, this is a gift." Rachel gave her the bag she carried. "It's a Native American tradition. They say it helps stop bad dreams."

Livvie's eyes widened as she took out the dream catcher. "How does it work?"

"You put it above your bed. The bad dreams are supposed to get caught in the netting, but the good ones are smart enough to slip through, sliding down the feathers to reach you."

"Ooh, it's pretty. What are these?" She touched the beads woven into the pattern.

"They're turquoise. It's a beautiful stone and there's a legend that it can protect you. That doesn't mean you don't have to be careful, but we all need help sometimes."

Livvie's expression was awed. "Thank you, thank you, *thank you*. It's splendid."

"You're very welcome." Rachel glanced at Simon. "I didn't know we had an appointment today."

"We didn't." He looked embarrassed. "But Gemma isn't back until a week from next Monday and Livvie's school had an early day. We're hoping you'll have lunch with us."

"Rachel, you don't have any commitments this afternoon," Chelsea interjected, "so you're free."

Rachel stared at her and received an innocent smile in return. The last time she'd talked to Chelsea about Simon, the office manager's opinion of him had been decidedly negative. She went over to the reception desk. "Chelsea, are you *sure* I don't have anything on my schedule?"

"Positive. Isn't this nice? Nicole and Adam were just saying you work through too many lunches and need more breaks."

"They're fine ones to talk," Rachel muttered. It was only after Adam had fallen in love with Cassie and Nicole with Jordan that they'd stopped spending insane hours at the agency. She threw her shoulders back and returned to where Simon and Livvie were waiting. "Since it appears I'm free, it would be lovely to have lunch together."

"Excellent." Simon gestured to the door. "Shall we?" Livvie ran to the car and he leaned close to whisper, "Didn't some Native American warriors believe turquoise helped them in battle? Livvie isn't going into battle."

Rachel shrugged. "I'm not sure. It's just something I heard as a kid. The important

thing is to help Livvie feel safe and protected and this might help. But don't worry,
I'm not getting ideas about becoming her
mother," she teased, a small smile playing
on her lips.

LATELY SIMON'S ASSUMPTIONS had been taking a beating, especially the ones about Rachel. He was even starting to understand
why his wife had often claimed he was be-
having foolishly.

"Who's worried? You'd be a fabulous
mother," he declared and meant it. "Is something wrong?" he asked when Rachel remained silent.

"No, just remembering lost dreams. The
other day I was thinking I could become an
official-type cat lady like Hannah. In spite
of one or two setbacks, I've finally won Binx
over. He's become the most amazing cuddle
bug."

"I'm convinced you could do anything,
but what about your clients?"

"I'd just do official cat lady as a sideline."

Simon chuckled.

He'd worried that he had messed things
up with Rachel, but she seemed to have a
generous capacity for forgiveness. She'd be-

come far more than a business consultant. Sometimes she seemed able to peer into his soul…the dark parts he didn't want to acknowledge. More important, she was willing to shine a light into those dark places and make him look at himself and do better.

Rachel had said he held a grudge against the design house, and after days of soul-searching, he'd realized it was true.

He was a workaholic, but his wife had been consumed heart and soul by her career. Even when they'd agreed to put family first, he'd changed more than she had, which was why the picture books bothered him. But Rachel had made a valid point when she'd said creative people couldn't just turn that part of themselves off. And no matter what else they represented, the books had probably been the best way for Liv to share herself with their daughter.

And how could he begrudge Livvie something that made her feel connected to her mother's memory? He'd avoided talking about Olivia after her death, thinking it would be hard on his daughter to be reminded her mother was gone. Instead, he'd probably just made the loss worse for them both.

CHAPTER FIFTEEN

SOMEHOW LUNCH WITH Livvie and Simon ended up as a trip to Bainbridge Island on the ferry. They ate at a restaurant overlooking the Puget Sound while Rachel told them about different sights on the island, including Bloedel Reserve, a public garden that spanned a hundred and fifty acres. Livvie was so excited, Rachel agreed to explore it with them.

"This place is amazing," Simon said as they visited different sections of the reserve. "I had no idea there was so much to see on Bainbridge Island."

"I haven't been here since I was eleven, though I wrote a paper about Mr. Bloedel in high school," Rachel explained. "How did you end up in Washington, anyway? I've got the impression you grew up on the East Coast."

"I lived in Maryland until I was eleven, then it was Chicago."

"Daddy met Mommy on a business trip," Livvie chirped. "He says it was love at first sight. They got married after just a week. Isn't that splendid?"

"Yes, it was." Rachel cast a sideways glance at Simon.

He'd mentioned his marriage had been fast, but a week? She wouldn't have thought he believed in love at first sight, so the attraction must have been extraordinarily powerful to knock his cynical distrust for a loop.

Livvie skipped ahead on the trail and they lengthened their stride to keep her in view.

"This is quite a place," Simon commented, obviously trying to direct the subject away from personal matters. "We should have got a picnic and eaten here."

"Picnics aren't allowed. I think the idea is for visitors to simply connect with nature. Mr. Bloedel was a lumberman and this became his legacy."

Simon didn't say anything for a long minute. "Well, thanks to you, *Liv's* legacy may survive for our daughter."

A rush of conflicting emotions caught Rachel by surprise, anger, sorrow...regret. It wouldn't be easy to continue being friends with Simon, knowing there would never be anything more between them. He'd called Olivia the love of his life and was devoted to her memory.

Another woman couldn't compete with that.

"I just did what you asked," Rachel said lightly, resisting the urge to add that she'd done what he was *paying* her to do. It could come off as confrontational and she didn't want to get into a disagreement on such a nice day.

"You did more than I thought was possible. By the way, I hired the two designers we talked about last Friday. They're going to work on storyboards and technical flats for the next collection at a temporary location. I didn't want to expose them to Janine and Miriam while they're still here to finish the current line."

"I see. You know, the funding you gave to medical research is another legacy."

Simon appeared to tense, then relax. "Thankfully Livvie doesn't have a genetic predisposition for what took her mother, but I still thought it was important for her future."

"It's important for a lot of children's futures.

I suspect you're a softy at heart and don't want to admit it, just like Rocky and Binx."

"Hardly. They're neutered and I'm not."

Rachel smiled at his joke.

Just then they reached a wilder section of the reserve and it was as beautiful and raw as she remembered. In his own way, Prentice Bloedel had been an artist, with the northwest landscape as his canvas.

"Eeyoooh," Livvie exclaimed. "Look, Daddy." She pointed to a huge olive green slug creeping along a decaying log.

"That's a banana slug," Rachel told her softly. "They're an important part of the forest."

"It's icky."

Simon crouched next to his daughter. "Not to another banana slug. He's probably a very handsome fellow to a lady slug."

Rachel remembered that banana slugs weren't strictly male or female, but it wasn't important. "Livvie, did you know banana slugs can be bright yellow? Sometimes they have spots on the yellow."

"Like a banana."

"That's right. Like a ripe banana."

It was a while before Livvie lost interest in the slug. Her fascination with the great outdoors seemed boundless and Rachel wondered if she'd ever visited a place where nature ruled.

"This is nice," Simon whispered, his voice almost reverential.

"It is. It truly is." Rachel undid the top buttons of her coat, feeling warm despite the chilly breeze. "I've noticed how much Livvie loves the lake and nature in general. If she becomes a designer, she may want a studio out in the woods. She might even end up in sportswear, rather than high fashion."

Simon grinned and Rachel was glad he knew she was teasing.

"Could be. Who knows?"

Simon looked at his daughter, thinking she was rarely interested in the balcony garden attached to the condo, but he had to admit, it seemed more like an imitation than the real thing.

"We need to visit spots like this more often," he said.

"I know what you mean. In Los Angeles you can't go anywhere without being surrounded by crowds. Even the beach is covered with people. Here there are places so quiet, you could believe you're the only person for miles."

"Luckily a coffee shop isn't that far away."

Rachel chuckled. "That's because you're addicted to having a barista on every street corner. Did you love coffee this much before moving to the Northwest?"

"I had my moments."

After another hour Simon suggested they call it a day. Livvie was getting tired and he didn't want Rachel to overtax her leg. She was so proud and stubborn she probably wouldn't tell him if it was hurting more than usual.

"How about dinner at the Just Like Home Café?" he asked as they rode the ferry back to Seattle.

"That isn't necessary."

"I didn't say it was necessary, I asked if you wanted to eat with us. We had an active afternoon in cold, fresh air, and I keep thinking about the mulligan stew I saw on the café's menu."

Rachel made a scoffing noise. "Have you ever eaten stew?"

"No, but the meat loaf sandwich was good and I'm open to new experiences. We can go straight to the Carthage and walk to the café. In the morning I'll give you a ride to Moonlight Ventures when I take Livvie to school."

"Please come, Rachel," Livvie pleaded.

"You aren't playing fair, asking in front of her," Rachel said sotto voce.

He grinned. "I didn't know she was listening."

Though Rachel questioned the wisdom of spending even more time with Simon and Livvie, she enjoyed the meal. But it was too much like being a family, and she didn't want to start hoping for more.

When they were walking back toward the Carthage, she noticed a long limousine parked in the loading zone in front of the building.

"We don't see many limos in this neighborhood. I wonder who it is," she mused.

A moment later the driver opened the back door. Simon growled something under his breath as the passenger emerged.

"Somebody you know?" Rachel asked.

"You could say that. What are you doing here?" he called to the other man. "And how did you get this address?"

"I have my ways. You wouldn't return my calls. What else was I supposed to do?"

Simon turned to her. "Rachel, would you take Livvie up to your condo?" The urgency in his voice was unmistakable.

"Of course." She held out her hand to Livvie. "Let's go upstairs, hon."

"Just a minute. We haven't been introduced," the newcomer declared, stepping into their path and staring at Rachel. "I'm Richard Kessler, and you're positively delicious."

Richard Kessler, as in Simon's father?

Rachel narrowed her eyes. Richard might think he was being charming, but the fact he didn't even glance at his granddaughter appalled her.

"You're in my way," she said coolly.

"Come now, I know I've seen you before. I heard Simon call you Rachel. Don't I get more than that?"

"It's Rachel Clarion. Good night."

"Ah, yes. Clarion. You used to be a model." His quick gaze seemed to flick all over her body, but most especially her face. "A lifetime of great nights would never be enough with you, gorgeous. How would you like to fly to Paris for breakfast?"

Ugh. Simon's mother must have been very young and impressionable to fall for him. While Richard was a handsome man who wore his age well, he positively oozed snake oil.

"I wouldn't cross the street with you," Rachel said crisply. "Come along, sweetie."

Livvie seemed confused, but she obediently walked into the Carthage lobby. "Who is that, Rachel?"

"Somebody your daddy knows." Rachel punched the elevator button and it immediately opened.

"But his name is Kessler, too."

"It's, uh, really complicated. Ask your daddy when he gets here." She pressed the button for the second floor and was grateful when the elevator closed and the car moved upward. For once the small space didn't bother her. She was just grateful to get away from the slimy jerk downstairs.

Once they were inside the condo, she locked the door and wished she could take a shower. No wonder Simon disliked his father so much. They didn't share a single shred of common ground as far she was concerned.

Binx regarded Livvie warily, but he didn't move...probably because he felt safe on the floor-to-ceiling cat tree Rachel had got installed over the weekend.

"Livvie, do you want to watch *Finding Nemo* again?" she asked. She'd purchased a handful of child-friendly movies when Livvie stayed with her the first time.

"Okay."

Soon she was settled on the couch, her eyelids drooping as the animated film began to play.

Rachel got out a patchwork quilt her grandmother had made and tucked it around Livvie before sitting down herself...all the while wondering what was happening on the street below.

Simon sent a hard look at Richard. He hadn't seen his father since shortly after his marriage, and had never expected to see him again. "As I said, why are you here?"

Richard spread his hands. "Is it a crime to miss my son? I wanted to see you."

"I find that hard to believe."

"Surely you don't think I'm holding a grudge because you took over my company? I made money on the deal. I told you that when I met your wife."

"And then promptly insulted her."

Richard snorted. "It's no insult to tell a woman she's attractive. But Olivia had nothing on that sweet little number you were just with. I never forget a beautiful woman. She's the model who got her face messed up a few years ago, right? Wouldn't know it to look at her."

"Leave Rachel out of this."

"Hey, it's no skin off my nose if you want a trophy wife. Your mother divorced me a few months ago, so I'm looking for one myself."

Simon shook his head. He'd heard enough. "Karen isn't my mother, but she's a decent woman, and I'm glad she's free of you."

"I loved Karen. I gave her everything she wanted," Richard spit, suddenly looking enraged. "How dare she leave me?"

"Seriously? She wanted a philandering husband who forced her to adopt the child he'd fathered with another woman? Oh, yeah, that's every woman's dream of a loving spouse."

If possible, Richard looked angrier. "You're forgetting that I took you out of a crappy three-bedroom ranch house and gave you a mansion to live in. I could have left you where I found you."

"I wish you had," Simon returned with quiet intensity. "My foster parents were good people who cared about me. The only reason you dragged me out of there was from a deluded idea of dynasty, to get a son to carry on your name. Except maybe now with Karen gone and old age creeping up your neck, you're hoping to find someone who cares, so you won't die alone with only strangers to take care of you."

Richard seemed to shrink, to instantly become an old man.

"There...there's nothing wrong with wanting my son in my life," he mumbled.

"Go home," Simon told him. "It takes more than genetics or a legal document to make someone a father."

"What about my granddaughter?"

Richard sounded almost desperate, but Simon hardened his resolve.

"It's Livvie I'm thinking about. She's loving and innocent and I can't take the chance you'd hurt her, the way you hurt my mother and the rest of us."

He turned and walked into the Carthage.

On the second floor Simon tapped on Rachel's door. She opened it after a moment and put a finger to her lips.

"Come in. Livvie's asleep. She dropped off, practically the minute she sat in front of the television. I know you try to limit how much TV she watches, but—"

"It's fine. I've started easing up on it, anyway. Now that she's going to school, she keeps hearing about television programs the other kids are watching. It obviously made her feel left out and different."

"I suppose child rearing is a constant balancing act."

Simon wanted to pull Rachel close and let her warmth drive away the chill inside. Seeing Richard had been completely unexpected, and was all the worse because Livvie and Rachel were there to witness it.

"I'm sorry." Simon kept his voice low as they went into the kitchen, close enough to keep an eye on Livvie, and far enough away to talk quietly. "There's no excuse for Richard. He thought we were involved, and he still hit on you. Can you believe that?"

Rachel put a kettle onto the stove and turned on the burner. "You have nothing to apologize for, though if I'd kicked him the way he deserved, you might have enjoyed seeing him writhe on the ground. Believe me, I was tempted."

A chuckle escaped Simon's tight chest. "That would have been something to watch. As it turns out, Karen finally divorced him. He's in his midseventies now and I figure he's starting to wonder who will be there when age catches up. He should have paid more attention to that bumper sticker—'Be nice to your kids, they pick your nursing home.'"

"Don't worry about him. He'll have lawyers, accountants and household staff," Rachel said promptly. "Probably a revolving set, since I can't see anyone putting up with his garbage for long. Would you like a cup of tea?"

"Sure."

He watched her supple movements as she took a tin of loose-leaf tea from the cupboard. Soon they were sitting at the breakfast bar. Simon tapped the handle of his steaming cup, still brooding.

"I don't know why I let Richard get to me, but I told him to leave and not come back. Things might be different if it was just me, but I can't take the chance he'd hurt Livvie."

"He gets to you because of the what-ifs," Rachel said softly. "What if he'd supported your mother after getting her pregnant?

What if he'd become a better person, and *that's* why he brought you home? What if he didn't see people as commodities, to be bought and sold and leered at? But the sad truth is, there's something vital, something good, missing inside him."

"What if I'm missing the same thing?" Simon asked.

Rachel put her hand over his. "You aren't," she whispered. "You really aren't."

Simon just hoped it was true.

MATT HAD LOVED it when Gemma started regularly stopping by the studio to say hi or so they could have lunch together. She was still on vacation from her job as a nanny and he'd miss seeing her as often when she returned to work.

But even if they eventually ended up getting married, she couldn't spend her days popping in on him. She'd get her degree and do other things, like teaching or becoming a voice-over star.

Her frequents visits had led Sherrie and Tara to tease him about his "new girlfriend." He didn't mind. "Pride goes before a fall" was a proverb his grandfather often quoted, but it was just as true now as when it had been first coined. Gemma was too special to let his pride get in the way of something amazing.

He kept thinking about Gemma's assertion that he judged people unfairly by the way they acted around him. It was uncomfortably close to the truth. He *had* put people at a distance, including his own family.

Was it because he'd felt sorry for himself, thinking they couldn't understand what it was like to be blind?

Possibly.

What he'd forgotten was that nobody could fully grasp how someone else felt. It was a simple, universal truth.

Gemma had reminded him that perspective was important. It might take a while to let go of his expectations, but there would be freedom in it, too.

"Hey, it's me," said Gemma's voice, breaking him out of his reverie. "Tara told me you didn't have anyone in the live studio."

"Yeah, my last recording session is done for the day." Matt put his hand up and she caught it. "Want to go get dinner?"

"Maybe I could fix something for us at your place."

An automatic refusal sprang to his mouth, but he choked it down. There was nothing unusual about a woman wanting to prepare a meal for her boyfriend, and since Gemma lived in the Kesslers' condo, it was only logical to offer to do it at his apartment.

"Sure, unless you'd rather eat out."

"You may wish we'd eaten out," she said, half laughing. "I'm not much in the kitchen, but I can make scrambled eggs and Mickey Mouse pancakes like no other nanny in Seattle. I hope you like basic breakfast food. That's my specialty."

Matt got up, a grin growing on his face. "I'm a fair cook, but my fridge is bare. Let's go to the grocery store, and I'll fix dinner for *you*."

"That sounds good."

"Great. Pepper, come." Pepper promptly scrambled out from under the table.

Underlying the offer to prepare dinner was the knowledge Gemma would be driving. Until now they'd eaten at restaurants or the deli near the studio. Insisting on a taxi or taking the access van would be absurd, so he took hold of the golden retriever's harness and turned to Gemma.

"How large is the back seat of your car? Pepper is a pretty big girl."

"It's a four-door, so she should fit. With your long legs, you may be more uncomfortable than she is. Mr. Kessler bought it for me when we came back to Seattle so I could drive Livvie to school and back. He offered to get me a car in New York, but the traffic is so frenetic, I couldn't imagine driving there."

"He sounds like a decent employer."

"Some people don't like him, but he's been nice to me. I didn't want to leave Washington, but he was devastated when his wife died and I couldn't say no, mostly because I couldn't abandon Livvie."

Matt wondered if it was too soon in their relationship to ask whether Gemma wanted a family. He hadn't thought much about children. Now he felt the time might be right. Still, the biggest question might be how she'd feel about having kids with a man who couldn't even drive them to school or the doctor's office.

GEMMA SAW MATT'S mouth flatten and knew something was churning inside his head.

"What's bothering you?" she asked. "If

you don't want to eat at home, we can grab a sandwich or something."

"It isn't that. I was just thinking what a big responsibility it is to have children."

"Oh. Sure. But somebody has to do it or the human race will die out."

"Does that mean you want a family?"

She bit the inside of her lip. It was still difficult for her to speak her mind. "If I say yes, will that scare you away?"

"I'm more worried about scaring *you* away."

A warm confidence filled her. "Don't you think if that could happen, it would have already? I'm like the cowardly lion who found its courage. You aren't getting rid of me easily."

Matt chuckled and pulled her close for a kiss. "I'm glad. Okay, I'll say it first. I'd love to have kids. But I'm also aware that it wouldn't be easy."

"Nothing worthwhile is easy. So we're on the same page when it comes to having a family. Can we get on the same page for dinner? 'Cause I'm hungry." She kept her tone light. Neither one of them was ready for a commitment, though her heart was screaming for more than just a casual relationship with Matt.

"Sure. How about steak and salad? That's fast and simple."

"It sounds perfect. Let's go."

CHAPTER SIXTEEN

SIMON DIDN'T EXPECT to hear from Richard again, but after some reflection, he asked his executive assistant to try locating Karen's contact information. If anyone could find a way to get the info he wanted, it was Fiona.

He and Rachel had talked for hours after the ugly scene in front of the Carthage, and it had been her suggestion that he check on Karen. Simon wanted to believe he would have done it without being prompted, but he couldn't be certain.

"I found the number," Fiona said the next day, bringing in a sheet of paper. "She's going by her maiden name, Truit, and lives in Tucson."

"Thanks, Fiona."

He debated for an hour before picking up his cell phone. He wouldn't blame Karen if she ducked his call, but to his surprise, she answered on the second ring.

"Is that really you, Simon?" She sounded incredulous.

"Yeah, I just learned about the divorce a couple of days ago. Good for you. It couldn't have been easy."

"I simply… I simply couldn't stay with him any longer. How are you and Livvie? I wanted to get in touch when you lost Olivia, but I didn't know what to say. I didn't even know if you'd take a call from me."

The warmth and regret in Karen's voice sent shock waves through Simon. He'd always seen her as cool and remote, but maybe that was the only way she'd been able to survive.

"We're doing well. We moved to New York for a couple of years, then returned to the Seattle area."

"Please don't think I was prying, but I used to visit the Liv'ing Creations website, just to feel in touch with your life. When Livvie was born, your wife posted the most beautiful picture of her…the one where she's sleeping and has all that coppery hair. I printed a copy to keep. She's so beautiful."

Simon's throat ached with emotions he hadn't realized he was holding back. "Thanks. I'll send more pictures if you'd like."

"I'd love that. I'll frame them and… Well, if you don't mind, I'd like to tell people she's my granddaughter. I realize I don't have any right, but…"

An echo of his own words rang in his ears as her voice trailed off. *Karen isn't my mother.* Maybe not, despite the legalities involved, but with time they might become friends or even something closer. And he was touched that she considered herself Livvie's grandmother.

"That would be nice," he said. "Have you taken up golfing down there in Arizona?"

"Mostly I'm soaking up the sun and peace. I finally feel free. I should have left Richard years ago."

"Be careful," Simon warned. "He showed up here this week and he's still angry about the divorce."

"He can't do anything to me now, he's already done it all." Karen's laugh was tinged with bitterness. "And if he violates the restraining order I got, he'll be in big trouble. Please don't let him have anything to do with you or Livvie. I wasted my life hoping he'd change and it isn't going to happen."

"Not a chance," Simon promised. "How about giving me your address?" He wrote it down and then made sure she had his cell and home number.

"Thanks. If you're ever near Tucson..." Karen said hesitantly, "I'm easy to find."

"The same goes for you and Seattle. Let's keep in touch."

"That would mean so much. Take care."

"You, too. Bye, Karen."

He disconnected and pinched the bridge of his nose. A few weeks ago he wouldn't have believed he could have a heartfelt conversation with Karen, much less one that ended with promises to stay in contact. While he'd never disliked her, she was a part of his life that he'd rather forget.

Except now he'd met Rachel, and she'd made him a better man than he'd ever thought he could be.

Rachel.

Simon closed his eyes and inhaled, imagining the faint, sweet scent of gardenias surrounding him...then waited for the guilt to follow.

It didn't.

Liv would have liked Rachel and she would have been exasperated he wasn't following his heart. He'd loved Liv and nothing would diminish that, but Rachel was his soul and the air he breathed. He loved her beyond anything he could have imagined possible. The question was whether she could ever feel the same about him.

At least he didn't have to worry how Livvie would react. She adored Rachel. Simon pulled out the plastic ring his daughter had given him, a keepsake she kept in her treasure box. He didn't know where the ring had come from originally, but she'd given him explicit instructions about what to do with it and now was the time to follow those directions.

But first he needed to do a little shopping.

"You're glowing," Rachel said to Gemma when she came by Moonlight Ventures on Friday afternoon.

"I don't know about glowing, but, uh, well, Matt and I are dating and it's starting to get serious. The other day he even brought up the question of how I feel about having kids."

A pang went through Rachel. She was happy for the other woman, but wished things were going as well for her.

The morning after Simon's father had shown up, Simon had driven her to Moonlight Ventures, where she had left her car. When he'd asked if she had plans for the weekend, she had told him that her family was expecting her on Saturday and Sunday.

He had simply nodded without offering the reason he'd asked, or what his own plans might be.

Inviting Simon and Livvie to the Clarion family Sunday meal had been on the tip of Rachel's tongue, but she'd resisted. The state of their relationship defied definition. They weren't romantically involved. They had a business connection, but it seemed inadequate to define the balance of their relationship as "friendship." Maybe it seemed inadequate because her feelings went far beyond the platonic bond she shared with Logan and Adam.

She focused on Gemma. "Then Matt no longer resists the idea of a girlfriend." Rachel kept her voice light.

"Not after we hashed it out. Anyhow, it's been great. We still have rough moments, but I guess that's to be expected in any relationship."

"I'm glad you both can talk about it."

The acknowledgment was ironic. Rachel had thought she was past the angst of her accident, yet she'd been intensely self-conscious when Richard Kessler had stared at her face. In his case she was *certain* he'd been looking for scars. After all, it wouldn't do to leer at a woman he didn't think was good enough for him.

Richard's behavior had been a reminder that she'd let the accident and her ex-husband influence her perspective on love and marriage. Simon had made her see the truth, whether she'd wanted to or not. And she was still giving her injuries too much power over what she did, including where she lived. The Carthage was nice and had the view of the lake, but what she really wanted was a true country home. There were gardening services even out in Kilterton, where she'd grown up, so it wouldn't be impossible.

Rachel shook herself and looked at Gemma. "Have you decided to search for voice work?" she asked, wondering if that was part of the reason for her visit to the agency.

"I'm curious about it," Gemma admitted. "I finished reading the novel and Matt told me the publisher now wants to sell the audio version, too. They also want me to record other books for them. I don't want to hold anyone up for big money, but I also want to be sure the legalities are covered."

"I understand. Let me give you a copy of the standard contract with Moonlight Ventures. You can read it and decide if you want the agency to be your representative."

An uncertain expression crossed Gemma's face.

Rachel leaned forward. "If you'd prefer one of the other partners to represent you since we're friends, I wouldn't be offend—"

"Not at all," Gemma declared hastily. "You're the agent I'd want, but doing recordings for the blind is my top priority and they aren't for profit."

"I'm fine with that. The agreement has a clause about work for nonprofit purposes." Rachel printed the basic voice artist representation agreement and gave it to her. "See if you're comfortable with this and let me know."

Gemma gave her a hug. "Thanks. Matt and I have a date tonight and I'll talk it over with him." If possible her face glowed brighter.

When she was gone, Rachel shut her computer off and drove home. She'd thought about spending both Friday and Saturday night with her grandmother, but hadn't been sure about leaving Binx alone for that long. She hadn't been kidding when she'd called him a cuddle bug. These days she couldn't sit down without him bounding onto her lap.

Tonight was the same. The minute he saw her, he leaped from the cat tree to the couch and into her arms, purring madly.

"Such a good, big boy. So pretty," she sweet-talked him. "I'm going to be away tomorrow night. I hope you won't mind. It's only for—"

The abrupt ring of the doorbell made him jump down and race out of the room. Someday she hoped he'd be comfortable with strangers, but for now he was still skittish.

Rachel looked through the peephole and was astonished to see Simon.

"Hi, is something up?" she asked, opening the door.

"I called earlier and left a message. You didn't get it?"

"Oh, sorry. Binx demands my attention when I first come home. It's become a ritual. I can't even change out of my work clothes until he gets his share of loving."

"I see." Simon appeared restless. "Livvie is at a birthday slumber party. They're all the rage at the school she's attending. Do you mind if I come in?"

Embarrassed, Rachel stepped backward. "Sorry, I wasn't thinking. Have you heard from Gemma?"

"Just a text that she'll be back full-time a week from Monday, as scheduled."

"You must be missing her help."

"Actually, I'm enjoying the extra time with Livvie. Taking her to school and picking her up also means I've met more of the parents. And the teachers immediately recognize me now, instead of looking suspicious until I introduce myself and Livvie throws her arms around me."

Rachel laughed. "Just be glad they're careful. What about your work?"

"I'm doing half of it at home. It'll be nice when Gemma gets back, but it's reassuring to know I can manage without her. Of course, I can't make the Mickey Mouse pancakes that Livvie loves so much, but you can't have everything. I might have been able to do something with a mix, but Gemma does them from scratch."

"If she didn't, I wouldn't have had the ingredients to bake cookies with Livvie," Rachel said, trying not to feel depressed. It was good for Simon to know he could manage without Gemma, because chances were, he'd be losing a nanny in the next few months. She'd recognized the look in Gemma's eyes, the excitement of being in love.

"I should just buy a baking mix and give pancakes a shot," Simon said. "I've also been exploring the deli cases and ready-to-eat meals at different markets instead of ordering out so much. Some of the stuff isn't bad."

Rachel sat down and motioned for him to do the same, wondering why he'd come in the first place. "What was the message you left earlier?" she prompted.

"That Livvie was gone overnight and would you have dinner with me. I know you're leaving town tomorrow."

"I'm not going to the moon. Kilterton is just a half hour away if you don't run into traffic. But Livvie isn't the only one having a sleepover. My grandmother misses having us at her house the way we did as children, so I suggested to my brothers and sister that we all stay there on Saturday. She's ecstatic."

"Sounds special."

Rachel was looking forward to it. She'd offered to pick up ingredients for s'mores and other treats, but Grandma had said she'd already gone shopping and was making her deluxe lasagna for dinner.

"I was going to make a meal here," Rachel said finally. "Something simple. Since you're at loose ends again, you're welcome to join me."

"I'm not at loose ends, exactly, but I'd enjoy that."

She hurried into the kitchen and put chicken breasts into the oven, glazed with a quick Dijon mustard and honey sauce, then made a salad, minus the spring greens he didn't like.

"I want you to look at something," Simon said when they were waiting for the chicken to bake.

He'd settled at the breakfast bar and spread a number of papers across the surface. Rachel frowned when she saw they were real estate flyers.

"Are you looking for a house?" she asked. "You just moved into the Carthage a few months ago."

"So did you. Take a look."

They were for homes in rural settings, some newer construction, some older. They all had long, wide porches and big yards. And they all had Kilterton addresses.

Rachel's nerves twisted.

"I see," she said finally. "Getting me to move would ensure you don't have to be uncomfortable about us being in the same building. After all, I know way too much about you now. How awkward to encounter one another in the garage or at the Java Train Stop."

SIMON GROANED.

He'd thought he was being clever showing Rachel the flyers, but she'd taken it the wrong way.

"That isn't what I meant."

"Of course it isn't. This is just your well-meaning attempt to push me into getting the house I would have bought if my leg hadn't got hurt."

Rachel stalked to the stove and checked the contents of the oven.

With a sigh, Simon got up, caught her shoulders and looked intently into her eyes. "Listen to me very carefully, Rachel Clarion. I'm crazy about you. Totally, insanely crazy. I want us to choose a new house together."

"What? But…Olivia was the love of your life."

They were his own words, coming back to haunt him. "As you pointed out to me, not so long ago, I'm a different man now. I'll always cherish Liv's memory, but I've never experienced what I feel with you. That doesn't diminish what I felt for her, just that I've learned and grown and changed. If she could talk to me, she'd tell me to get on with things. To stop wallowing in my memories and make new ones."

"How can you be so sure of that?"

"Because Liv attacked life and expected me to do the same. I used to wonder why we didn't talk about what would happen when she was gone. Now I've realized she didn't believe it was necessary. If anything, she'd be disappointed that it took me weeks to recognize what was right in front of my eyes. *The future*."

Rachel closed her amazing eyes and he waited, praying she was understanding what he was trying to say.

"It's one thing if you don't love me," he said urgently. "But please don't turn away from what we could have because you don't believe I love you more than my life."

RACHEL WANTED TO believe Simon; she wanted it more than she'd ever wanted anything.

Real love didn't have boundaries. It grew and multiplied. The more you loved, the greater your ability to love. She knew that in her head, but the part of her that had been hurt was having trouble. Was it possible that in a few weeks Simon had gone from being devoted to Olivia's memory to loving someone else with a devotion that was no less intense? Because she couldn't accept anything less.

She looked at Simon...difficult, proud, handsome. He was brilliant, decent and honest, and adored his daughter. Sometimes he was exasperating but he was also the man she loved.

"What about your contention that two career people might not be the best mix for marriage and parenting?" she asked, knowing there wasn't a future for them unless she was certain in her heart that she wasn't just a pale substitute for Olivia. "I know you were concerned about what the picture books represented, but was there more to it?"

"In a way. From the beginning a part of me was trying to resist the way you made me feel. I never felt guilty about the other women I'd dated because we hadn't really connected. But it was different with you. Getting uptight about the career thing was another reason to put up barriers between us."

"We weren't dating," Rachel pointed out wryly. "We're just business associates, remember?"

Simon took her hand. "Rachel, I've never confided in anyone the way I have with you. I thought it was because we were becoming friends, but it was so much more. You've become my conscience and my best friend, but you're also the woman I trust wholly and completely with my heart. I need you more than I need the air I breathe."

The raw honesty in his eyes was impossible to doubt and happiness began welling in Rachel.

SIMON FELT RACHEL'S fingers curl around his and was certain she'd started to believe him.

"Will you marry me?" he whispered. "And be Livvie's mother? We'll get a great big house in Kilterton and make it warm and happy. The commute will be a little longer to our respective companies, but well worth it. After all, your family is there."

"Livvie may not be ready for a new mother."

He grinned. "Livvie is unusually wise for her age. She gave me a ring and said I should propose to you before someone else did. She's turning into a little worrywart. We should teach her to play more. Maybe get a dog to go with that great big yard we want."

Simon held up his free hand. The plastic ring his daughter had presented to him was on his forefinger, along with a sapphire engagement band.

"Come on, Rachel. It's only the rest of our lives. I dare you to take a chance on me."

"Dare me? What, are we fourteen?"

He tugged her close. "Now you're procrastinating."

Rachel grinned and kissed him, a lingering caress that left them both breathless. "I'll have you know I don't procrastinate, I make measured decisions and then throw caution to the wind. It's one of my most charming personality quirks."

"You have a number of charming personality quirks," Simon said hoarsely. "Ones that drive me out of my mind. Including not answering that question I asked you."

"To be clear, you had more than one question."

He tried to think, but it wasn't easy with Rachel's sweet warmth pressed close to his heart. "I asked you to marry me."

"And to be Livvie's mother. Yes to all of it. Oh…and that other thing you didn't actually come out and ask? I love you, too. Heart and soul."

Happiness flooded Simon. He understood why Rachel had hesitated. She'd wanted to be sure, the way he was sure.

He kissed her again, wondering how he could have wasted so much time worrying about the risk of loving again.

Love might be a risk, but he knew with Rachel it was worth everything.

EPILOGUE

RACHEL PUT HER feet up on the white wicker hassock, enjoying being outside in the lingering warmth of summer. She yawned lazily. The big, wide porch looked out across a broad lawn dotted with clusters of trees. Across the road was a protected wooded area, so they wouldn't have to be concerned about developers transforming their lovely view.

The house was on the edge of Kilterton, just down the road from her grandmother's place. An aunt and uncle weren't far away. The same with her parents.

Their new dog lay on the porch next to her. They'd adopted Rufus a couple of weeks earlier. Contrary to her parents' expectations, Livvie had chosen an adult English bulldog, rather than one of the wriggling puppies filling the kennels. Rufus was so ugly that he was absolutely adorable. And he'd quickly become devoted to the entire family.

The side screen door opened and closed and she looked over to see Livvie shaking a finger at the door. "I told you, Jelly Bean, you can't come out. Be good." She came over, gave Rufus a hug, then happily plopped onto the outdoor love seat.

"Do you have your homework from Friday done?" Rachel asked, smoothing Livvie's hair.

"Uh-huh. When are we going to Grandma and Grandpa's? Grandpa is making my favorite cake and homemade ice cream for dinner."

Now that they were living in Kilterton, the monthly family dinner had become a weekly event.

"We'll go in a couple of hours."

Livvie was enjoying her status as the only grandchild and great-grandchild. A kick from the baby reminded Rachel that in around ten weeks, Livvie's status would change to being the *eldest* grandchild and great-grandchild.

Rachel patted her swollen tummy. She'd got pregnant soon after the wedding and was contemplating when to take time off for maternity leave. As her own boss, the schedule was up to her and the doctor.

"Is my little sister kicking? Daddy says she's going to be a soccer player," Livvie said excitedly.

"I'm getting a kick or two."

"Can I feel?"

"Of course." Rachel lifted the little girl's hand and put it over the small flutters of movement. They'd kept the baby's sex a secret for a while, then it had finally slipped out. But her grandmother had still decided to make a crib quilt with green and yellow instead of using pink. The patchwork quilt Grandma had made for Livvie's eighth birthday was in rich shades of green, purple and turquoise, the colors that Livvie had selected.

"Are you going to enjoy having a baby sister?" Rachel asked Livvie.

"Oh, *yes*! My friend Belinda has two little brothers. A sister is much better."

Rachel gently tugged a lock of Livvie's hair. "You never know, you might have a brother someday."

"That's okay." Livvie straightened. "I'm going to play fetch with Rufus."

"Remember, don't throw the ball too far. He's still getting used to playing outside."

Rufus had resided at the animal shelter for over a year and needed to build his stamina.

"I'll be careful. Come on, Rufus."

Rufus got to his feet and walked down the front steps. Livvie threw the ball a short distance. He didn't actually run to the ball—it was more a slow, lumbering trot—but he seemed excited.

Rachel pulled a note from her pocket that she'd got from Karen and read it again. It was sweet. Her parents had invited Karen to the baby shower they were hosting and she wanted to know if Simon would be all right with her coming. He'd immediately phoned to say she was welcome. Simon had thoroughly embraced extended family life and happily included his adoptive mother.

The screen door opened and shut again. This time it was Simon. "It's too cold out here for you," he fussed, shaking out a blanket.

"I'm perfectly all right," Rachel said sleepily. He ignored the protest and tucked the blanket around her. "Hey, you've been through this once already. You should be the calm one."

"How can I be calm?" he demanded. "You won't take it easy. You even insisted on making yeast rolls and pasta salad this morning. It's the weekend. You're supposed to be relaxing."

"I wanted to contribute something for tonight."

"We're bringing a bushel of corn on the cob, fresh from the field, and a case of sparkling apple juice."

Rachel just smiled.

Life was good.

They no longer had a nanny. Gemma had married Matt Tupper that summer and they didn't plan to hire anyone else. Simon had created a playroom adjacent to his office for Livvie, while Rachel's parents, grandmother and aunts had eagerly jumped in to help with babysitting. He often joked that he didn't have enough daughter to go around the Clarion family.

After the baby was old enough, Rachel would bring her into the agency. It was one of the perks of being self-employed. Her office might be a little crowded with both a crib and playpen, but that was okay.

Simon sat on the wicker hassock, moved her feet to his lap and began massaging them. It was a delicious luxury and she closed her eyes.

"Have you seen the latest sales figures for Liv'ing Creations?" she asked him. "The ones for the new designs are through the roof. Almost back to where they used to be."

"Yeah, it's going well. Have you looked at the latest storyboards from the designers? They seem to be the sort of thing that Liv used to do. Colorful, definitely."

"Yup," she agreed. "They're good. The owner of the company likes them, too."

SIMON CHUCKLED. Rachel still enjoyed teasing him about Livvie being the real owner of Liv'ing Creations. With Rachel's help, it looked as if the company would be alive and well by the time their daughter was old enough to take over. At the same time, he was becoming more and more aware that Livvie *might* make other choices.

That was all right. Olivia wouldn't have wanted Livvie to feel forced into becoming a clothes designer.

Simon eased his wife's feet back onto the hassock and shifted to sit next to her. By marrying Rachel, he'd got more than the woman he loved desperately. He'd got an entire family and a sense of peace he'd never before experienced. Once he would have believed it impossible, but life was really good. As for the problems every family faced, he knew the secret was not having to go it alone.

Rachel put her head on his shoulder. "Happy?" she whispered.

"The happiest," he promised.

* * * * *

*Coming next in the Emerald City Stories miniseries is a romance for the agency's fourth and final partner,
Logan Kensington...*

And if you need to catch up on the miniseries, check out these previous titles from Callie Endicott:

Moonlight Over Seattle
A Father for the Twins

Available at www.Harlequin.com!

Get 4 FREE REWARDS!

We'll send you 2 FREE Books plus 2 FREE Mystery Gifts.

Love Inspired® books feature contemporary inspirational romances with Christian characters facing the challenges of life and love.

FREE Value Over $20

Get 4 FREE REWARDS!

We'll send you 2 FREE Books plus 2 FREE Mystery Gifts.

Love Inspired® Suspense books feature Christian characters facing challenges to their faith... and lives.

FREE Value Over $20

2018 CHRISTMAS ROMANCE COLLECTION!

You'll get TWO FREE GIFTS & TWO FREE BOOKS in your first shipment, plus a trade paperback by *New York Times* bestselling author RaeAnne Thayne!

This collection is packed with holiday romances by internationally famous *USA TODAY* and *New York Times* bestselling authors!

Get 4 FREE REWARDS!

We'll send you 2 FREE Books <u>plus</u> 2 FREE Mystery Gifts.

FREE
Value Over
$20

Both the **Romance** and **Suspense** collections feature compelling novels written by many of today's best-selling authors.

Get 4 FREE REWARDS!

We'll send you 2 FREE Books plus 2 FREE Mystery Gifts.

Harlequin® Special Edition books feature heroines finding the balance between their work life and personal life on the way to finding true love.

FREE Value Over $20

YES! Please send me 2 FREE Harlequin® Special Edition novels and my 2 FREE gifts (gifts are worth about $10 retail). After receiving them, if I don't wish to receive any more books, I can return the shipping statement marked "cancel." If I don't cancel, I will receive 6 brand-new novels every month and be billed just $4.99 per book in the U.S. or $5.74 per book in Canada. That's a savings of at least 12% off the cover price! It's quite a bargain! Shipping and handling is just 50¢ per book in the U.S. and 75¢ per book in Canada.* I understand that accepting the 2 free books and gifts places me under no obligation to buy anything. I can always return a shipment and cancel at any time. The free books and gifts are mine to keep no matter what I decide.

235/335 HDN GMY2

Name (please print)

Address   Apt. #

City   State/Province   Zip/Postal Code

Mail to the Reader Service:
IN U.S.A.: P.O. Box 1341, Buffalo, NY 14240-8531
IN CANADA: P.O. Box 603, Fort Erie, Ontario L2A 5X3

Want to try 2 free books from another series! Call 1-800-873-8635 or visit www.ReaderService.com.

---

*Terms and prices subject to change without notice. Prices do not include sales taxes, which will be charged (if applicable) based on your state or country of residence. Canadian residents will be charged applicable taxes. Offer not valid in Quebec. This offer is limited to one order per household. Books received may not be as shown. Not valid for current subscribers to Harlequin® Special Edition books. All orders subject to approval. Credit or debit balances in a customer's account(s) may be offset by any other outstanding balance owed by or to the customer. Please allow 4 to 6 weeks for delivery. Offer available while quantities last.

Your Privacy—The Reader Service is committed to protecting your privacy. Our Privacy Policy is available online at www.ReaderService.com or upon request from the Reader Service. We make a portion of our mailing list available to reputable third parties that offer products we believe may interest you. If you prefer that we not exchange your name with third parties, or if you wish to clarify or modify your communication preferences, please visit us at www.ReaderService.com/consumerschoice or write to us at Reader Service Preference Service, P.O. Box 9062, Buffalo, NY 14240-9062. Include your complete name and address.

HSE19R